Four Dates and a Forever: A Witty and Heartfelt Second-Chance Romantic Comedy

Heroes of St. Helena series
Need You for Keeps
Need You for Always
Need You for Mine

St. Helena Vineyard series
Kissing Under the Mistletoe
Summer in Napa
Autumn in the Vineyard
Be Mine Forever
From the Moment We Met

Sugar, Georgia series
Sugar's Twice as Sweet
Sugar on Top
A Taste of Sugar

FOUR DATES AND A FOREVER: A WITTY AND HEARTFELT SECOND-CHANCE ROMANTIC COMEDY

The Eastons

MARINA ADAIR

*To Jessica Poore,
my personal Chicago Manual of Style,
and dear friend. Here's to umbrella
drinks on a sandy beach somewhere.*

TABLE OF CONTENTS

Chapter One 1
Chapter Two 16
Chapter Three 29
Chapter Four 41
Chapter Five 53
Chapter Six 72
Chapter Seven 83
Chapter Eight 98
Chapter Nine 109
Chapter Ten 123
Chapter Eleven 134
Chapter Twelve 149
Chapter Thirteen 159
Chapter Fourteen 173
Chapter Fifteen 190
Chapter Sixteen 199
Chapter Seventeen 211
Chapter Eighteen 218
Chapter Nineteen 235
Chapter Twenty 244
Chapter Twenty-one 267
Chapter Twenty-two 276
Chapter Twenty-three 281

Epilogue 287
About the Author 315

CHAPTER ONE

Dating Tips from Elsie Dodd
Never bring your ex into things.

"I vow, from this day forward, in honesty and love, to take you, Elsie Dodd, to be the hero of your own destiny and to give to you all that I have and love, for better or for worse, for richer or for poorer, in sickness and in health, to love and to cherish, till death do us part," Elsie said to herself, then popped the cork on an expensive bottle of champagne.

It had taken six lawyers, four depositions, a single dotted line—and nearly all of Elsie's life savings—but she was finally a free woman. Free to sleep in the middle of the bed, to eat ice cream straight from the carton—free to focus on herself and her own dreams. And it all began with her divorce party, which was supposed to start—she looked at the clock on the wall and grinned—in just under two hours.

The house was decorated with condom balloons, penis-shaped candies, and a Pin the Junk on the Hunk wall game. Not to forget the alcohol, lots of alcohol in every color and variety, which came with Marcus, a twenty-something bartender with the ass of a Chippendale, whom her best friend, Carla, had hired.

Then there was the dress. The insanely expensive couture LBD that she'd charged on her ex's business account before the divorce papers were finalized. He'd lost his mind, but it was worth every second of Axel's bitching, because it was more than just a dress. It was a statement for everyone everywhere that the former Miss Portland and current award-winning interior architect was back—and ready to kick some ass.

Today was her day to embrace her strength, channel the inner goddess, and rally. Tomorrow she'd deal with the fallout.

Elsie poured herself a flute of champagne and headed through the modern masterpiece she'd designed from the ground up. It was the sole property she and Axel had owned together. Since she couldn't afford to buy Axel out, in a few months it would belong to someone else. Her heart ached more over that than from the disillusion she felt over her marriage.

She took a sip of her drink, the bubbles tickling her tongue. She went in for a second sip when the doorbell rang.

Praying it wasn't her mom, who had a habit of showing up uninvited, she readied herself and opened the door to discover a trunk of a man standing on her front doorstep. He smoothed down his T-shirt, which read CARL on the chest pocket. Perched above his name the logo of a cat wielding a chainsaw.

"You Ms. Elsie Ross?" the man asked, his eyes working extra hard to stay laser focused north of the equator. That's when Elsie remembered she was in nothing but a cami and short set, with a matching robe that hung indecently high and showed off all one-thousand-and-one of Victoria's secrets.

"Elsie Dodd," she corrected, tightening the belt of her robe. She'd changed back to her maiden name the day she discovered Axel hiding his drumstick up a backup singer's skirt.

Man, what a fool she'd been. She'd ignored the whispers, turned a blind eye to the big red flags waving in the wind, and naively believed him when he said he'd loved her. In the end, her marriage was a complete sham. Had been from the beginning. Sadly, she was the last one in on the joke.

"How can I help you?" she asked.

"I'm Carl, from Don't Blame the Messenger." He reached into his back pocket and presented a badge, flashing it like he was the feds, when in actuality it was nothing more than a laminated ID card. "We also do chain saw rentals and cat sitting. I just need you to sign here. Here and here." He pointed to the three official-looking Xs on the form.

Something deep inside Elsie's gut told her to back the hell up, slam the door, and call the real feds. Five years of marriage taught Elsie that her ex had the unique ability to put the "dick" in unpredictable. And this had dick-move written all over it.

"And if I refuse to sign?"

Carl looked baffled. He took off his flat tweed cap and wiped his brow before replacing it low on his bald head. "No one's ever not signed."

She steeled her eyes and Carl swallowed hard. "Ever?"

"Not a once." She could tell it was a lie. A big, fat, man lie.

"Can you at least explain to me what I'm signing for?"

"Don't know, ma'am. I just deliver what they tell me to."

"And who are *they*?"

He didn't seem to have an answer.

A good dose of anxiety mixed with curiosity coursed through her system but in the end curiosity won out. Elsie used the pen tied to the clipboard and signed for the certified letter. Carl had barely handed it to her when Elsie flipped the envelope over and glanced at the return address.

Panic bubbled in her throat.

"I change my mind. I don't want it," she said, but Carl was already on the run.

"Sorry, no take backs," he hollered over his shoulder, then climbed into the cab of his truck, quickly locking the doors.

Elsie sprinted down the steps in her bare feet, the hot pavement burning her soles. Once she reached the car, she pressed the envelope to the window. With a panicked expression on his face, Carl revved the engine.

"Oh no you don't. Not today, Carl. Not today!" She raced around the front of the truck, arms wide over the hood, blocking his exit. "You have to take it back. Just say I wasn't home. In fact, say the place was boarded up and it didn't look as if anyone had lived here in months."

Which, until last night, had been true. Axel loved the glam of Los Angeles. The night life, the fast pace, the slight notoriety around town—drummers weren't all that famous outside of the music scene. Elsie preferred it here, in the quiet of her peaceful neighborhood nestled in the hills above Portland. She also preferred monogamy—and being close to family.

Well, at the moment, family just extended to her grandmother. Her mother was another story.

"Don't blame the messenger." He threw it into reverse. "If you're satisfied with my service, be sure you leave a review. And you have a good day, Ms. Ross."

"Dodd. It's Ms. Dodd!" she hollered to the taillights disappearing around the corner. "D-O-D-D. Dodd."

"You're back and as disruptive as ever," a lemon-puckered voice called from the side yard one house over. It was Ms. Gilford, self-appointed neighborhood president and busybody. "Is everything okay over there?"

"Yes, Ms. Gilford. Just seeing off an old friend," she lied. It was bad enough that she'd come home broke and divorced, she wasn't about to give her nosy neighbors food for fodder.

"What is this about you being a Dodd?" Garden-gloved hands and a mauve sunhat with big black glasses appeared over the fence. "Does that mean you're no longer a Ross?"

"Born a Dodd, will die a Dodd," was all she had to say on that matter.

"Well, Ms. *Dodd*, you might want to take yourself inside. Mr. Ashkenazi's got his binoculars out and you know how bad his heart is," the older woman said. "Wouldn't want him to file an indecent exposure complaint with the community board."

Elsie looked across the street at Mr. Ashkenazi and gave her shoulders a little shimmy. "Hi, Mr. Ashkenazi." The man was half blind and old enough to have picked apples with George Washington, but he dropped the binoculars and excitedly waved back. "I don't think he'll be filing any complaints today."

Ms. Gilford harumphed. She'd been itching to cite Elsie ever since Elsie's house was named Greenhill's brightest star on the community Facebook group.

"Well, you just be sure to keep it down over there. Ten o'clock is the mandated neighborhood noise ordinance. So please, let Mr. Ross know that we won't stand for his late night 'jam' sessions." Ms. Gilford tossed up some seriously aggressive air quotes.

Shoulders back and chin up, she reminded herself.

"I don't think that will be a problem." *See, that wasn't so hard.* "And a good afternoon to you, Ms. Gilford."

With a Queen Elizabeth wave, Elsie went back inside the house, that letter turning to lead in her hand. By the time she got to the kitchen, where she poured herself a screwdriver, vodka minus the OJ, she was certain she'd be sick.

"Tomorrow," she said and stuffed the envelope into the junk drawer and out of sight. She took three steps and her feet stuck to the floor. There was no way she could enjoy tonight with the weight of that letter looming overhead.

She pulled out the envelope and stared at it, then finally tore it open. The paper was heavy weight, meticulously folded in thirds, and the top line read, *Harry, Waxer, and Bush LLP,* with the address of Axel's law firm. It went on to say:

Dear Ms. Ross,

This letter is to inform you that you have thirty days to vacate the property. The residence has been sold and is in escrow. Upon the sale, the profits will be divided in half as specified by the prearranged divorce decree.

Sincerely,
Benjamin Harry, Esq.

"No, no, no, no, no," she whispered, clutching her chest. She needed more than thirty days. She needed the whole summer. She'd promised herself the summer in the house that held so many memories. Some bad, but most of them good. Plus, the small bungalow she'd purchased across town, which would double as her residence and office, wouldn't be available until end of August.

She should call her lawyer and fight this. She picked up the phone, then remembered she'd fired her lawyer. Not only was he completely inept—classic case of "you get what you pay for"—she also didn't have the money. Between the prenup and Axel moving all their assets overseas, every penny she had was either tied up in this house or earmarked for her new boutique interior architect firm, *Space Reimagined*. Firm might be stretching it, since it was a business of one, but over this past year Elsie had learned that all she needed was belief in herself. And money—which was tied up in the sale of the Greenhill property. A property she just couldn't sell until the end of the summer. Axel knew this.

Elsie punched in her ex's number. It went straight to voice mail.

"You son of a bitch! I don't know what you're trying to pull, but you can't evict me from my own house, you two-timing rat fink! This is my home, and you can't sell it without my permission." At least that's what her lawyer had told her. "If you try, you will find yourself back in court." She started to hit end, but pulled out her lucky coin and kissed it before adding, "I hope you get a disease and your dick falls off!"

She set the phone on the counter and took a deep breath. Her hands were shaking.

You will not cry, Elsie Marie Dobbs. Today was about her dress and her friends and her fresh-start party—not a pity party. She gave herself permission to shed a single tear, then she'd finish her hair and makeup. Except both eyes teared up and she knew it was going to be a doozy of a breakdown.

Elsie thought of her house, which she'd purchased before the marriage, with money her grandpa had willed her. After the wedding, she'd stupidly put Axel on the title, which led to his entitled attitude.

To her this wasn't just a house, it was a showcase for her clients to see her skills and talent. It was also her last marital asset, which would sever every last tie to Axel. But as she looked around, nostalgia took over. It wasn't a big space, but it was a stunner. With its stone and redwood frame, vaulted ceilings, and wall-to-wall windows that connected the inside to the outside, the space was an award winner and had been featured in the local paper.

It offered a warm contemporary lifestyle, showcasing comfort and beauty with timeless materials, and it wasn't quite finished. She still had a few renovations to tie up— renovations that she *needed* to finish. It was as if something inside her had been broken and through the process of transforming the house she'd transform herself and be able to fully walk away and start anew.

God, she didn't want to sell her dream. She'd put her heart into every corner of that house, and Axel had sold it right out from under her. Yes, she was flat broke, but the thought of someone coming in with their own furniture, their own little touches, and their own style was like a punch to the gut.

Would they expect her to finish? God, she hoped so. Or what if they decided to go with a different designer? What if they didn't like her idea to blow out the wall between the office and the guest room or reframe the music room? What if they hired someone else to finish what was supposed to be her mark on the world?

Her heart sank and her eyes began to fill again when she heard a noise coming from upstairs. It sounded like water draining. Knowing her luck, it was probably a cracked pipe in her walls.

Elsie wiped her eyes and headed for the staircase. She reached the landing when the water abruptly stopped and the sound of wet feet hitting tile whispered past.

She froze. A tiny trill of terror tiptoed down her spine. She heard the footsteps again, coming from the master bathroom, and panic wove its way up her throat and wrapped itself around tightly. She hit 9-1-1 on her cell, her finger hovering over the green call button as she crept down the hallway and into the bathroom to peek around the corner. Steam filled every corner of the room like a scene from some horror flick.

Her first thought was that it was an ax murderer. Her second thought, and this was what had rage boiling up, was that Axel had flown all the way from LA to Portland to see the look on Elsie's face when she opened that letter. Only when she entered the bathroom, it wasn't Axel's ass staring back at her. It was the most spectacular ax-murderer ass she'd ever seen.

She grabbed the first thing she found—a hair dryer—then stuck it to the intruder's very muscular back. "Put your hands up and don't move."

There was a long, terrifying pause. "Which one is it? Hands up or don't move."

Elsie heard the amusement in his tone and knew exactly whose unwanted and uninvited ass was on display in her bathroom.

It was Rhett Easton, her ex's buddy, and the guy who hadn't even bothered to check in on her after an incredibly horrible year. In fact, Rhett, former playboy and total pain in her ass, was the one person she had hoped to hear from but never did.

Not that she should be surprised. He'd ghosted her before.

Long before Elsie had met her ex, she and Rhett had a one-night stand. Rhett was a nobody solo artist who played dive bars and college parties. It was at one of these parties that they met, flirted, and eventually wound up in bed together—spending the entire weekend making love and sharing dreams. The connection was unlike anything she'd ever felt, which was why when the sun came up, Elsie wasn't so sure that she wanted things to end. Rhett assured her that he felt the same, which was why she'd given him her number. But he'd never called.

It wasn't until a year later, when her then boyfriend, Axel, introduced her to the band's new singer, that their paths crossed again. There was an awkward and sexually charged moment, then they'd both laughed it off as a long-ago weekend and agreed to be friends. And they had been. At least she thought they had.

She'd never been naive to the fact that Rhett was Axel's friend and that she was the third wheel in their bromance, but she'd thought that Rhett had considered her a good enough friend to at least see how she was handling everything—which, for a period, was terribly.

She was mad at her mom for practically siding with Axel, her LA friends had told her to look past the infidelities—plural—while *their* friends had stuck with the more famous of the two, and her lawyer was a joke, leaving Elsie with just Grandma Harriet. Who was enough, but that didn't mean Elsie hadn't been alone and terrified throughout the whole ordeal.

Rhett started to turn and Elsie slammed her eyes shut. "*Ohmygod!* What are you doing? I said don't move."

"I was reaching for a towel."

"Okay, fine, turn around and cover yourself." She shielded her eyes because closing them wasn't enough when he was the full monty. "You said you were grabbing a towel."

"You didn't specify the order. Shall I grab the towel?" When she didn't answer—because her tongue was stuck to the roof of her mouth, he chuckled. A moment later he said, "You can open your eyes. I'm decent."

She split her fingers and peeked through the crack and then snapped it back together. "*That* is not decent."

He was in faded blue jeans, which hung low on his hips, no shirt, no shoes, glistening abs. The man was built like Thor—and that was just his upper portion. The accidental glimpse of his other portion, and the memory of that long ago weekend, reminded her that his top and bottom matched.

"Is that a blow dryer or are you just happy to see me?"

Telling herself that she was an adult and she'd seen it all before—she opened her eyes. "I could say the same."

They both look down at the bulge behind the zipper and without an ounce of embarrassment he said, "Hey, it's morning."

It had been a while since they'd seen each other—even longer since they'd seen each other naked—and he stilled look great. Big and built, with the sexiest, stare-into-them-too-long-and-you'll-be-mesmerized blue eyes.

She, on the other hand, came from good, solid peasant stock and her metabolism was saving itself for the zombie apocalypse. No matter how hard she sucked in her belly, it was impossible to fit into her pre-divorce jeans, while this guy effortlessly looked like a magazine cover. Then again, he'd graced the cover of about every magazine in the world. Not that she'd paid attention. Much.

"It's two in the afternoon," she pointed out.

"Since I got in at six a.m., it's my morning."

She gasped. "You slept here? Where?"

He pointed to the unmade master bed, which looked as if there'd been a wrestling match on it. *She* hadn't even slept there. *She'd* slept in the guest room since she wasn't quite ready to face her marital bed.

His eyes softened and he took a step toward her. "You look great, Els."

She didn't know why, maybe it was the use of her long-ago nickname or the simple compliment, but she choked up a tiny bit. Steeling herself from his infamous charm, she crossed her arms. His gaze dropped to her cleavage, so she tugged the silky robe tightly around her.

"Why are you here?" she asked.

"Right back at you." He brushed past her to the bed, where he picked up a shirt and slid it over his impressive pecs. "You're supposed to be at Harriet's."

"Yeah, that isn't going to happen." Last spring, her mom had moved in with her grandmother, and Elsie had more interest in having a mammogram than she did seeing her mom. She loved her mom, she really did, but right then she was so mad at her she could cry. Most people usually cried on their mom's shoulder. Elsie and Faye had never had that kind of relationship.

"You're supposed to be in your own shower across town," she pointed out.

"Yeah, that isn't going to happen either."

Something in his eyes told her that she wasn't the only one who got screwed in the love department. While her divorce had been nasty, it had been private. Rhett's divorce had been plastered all over the news. So had his every conquest since.

"Well, this reunion was super fun." She turned and walked toward the door. "After you dry off, you can pack your things and leave."

"I was going to say the same to you."

"This is my house," she said primly over her shoulder.

"Actually, according to the agreement, in thirty days it's my house."

She came to a full stop, nearly tripping over her feet. She spun around. "What do you mean?"

"I bought the house." He looked at her as if she should be privy to this information. "And Axel and I have an agreement that I get to stay here until escrow closes."

"Axel and I have an agreement, approved by a judge, that I own half the house until it sells. And I haven't agreed to sell my half yet."

Rhett pondered this for such a long moment Elsie knew that this was all news to him. "Axel implied it was all worked out."

"Axel is a lying piece of shit. And he promised me that I had until the end of the summer to list the house."

"It looks like we have ourselves a problem. Two binding contracts."

"We could always ask the judge what he thinks." But even as she said it she knew that with Rhett's lawyers she'd once again find herself on the losing end of a stressful battle.

His eyes went soft, and so did his voice. And this time when he stepped toward her, she didn't back away. "Do you really want to go back to court? I know that it's the last place I want to revisit. Plus, I'd never do that to you."

She swallowed hard. Not only did he know she was bluffing, he knew his lawyers would pick apart every line and dot of her divorce papers and destroy her in court. "You wouldn't?"

Something flashed across his face, something she couldn't quite decipher but she could have sworn it was unpleasant surprise. "Did you really believe I would?"

"I don't know what I believe anymore."

His eyes never left hers. "You can believe me."

"Thank you," she whispered, even though her trust well was in the negative. "The truth is—" And this was where it got embarrassing. Unable to hold his gaze, she studied her freshly painted pink toes. "My place isn't ready for another few months and I don't have anywhere else to go."

"What about Harriet's?"

She shrugged. "It's complicated. What about your place in LA?"

"It's complicated," he said.

She let out a frustrated breath. They were both in an Axel-derived situation with no way out.

"We can always cut it right down the middle," he said, his eyes twinkling with amusement.

Elsie felt the first smile come on since the knock on the door. "I have painters' tape."

They both laughed because back in college Rhett had crashed with Elsie and Axel for a blink of time. Being typical guys, they were loud, messy, and, sometimes, invasive. Needing a man-free zone, Elsie had used painters' tape to block off her own she-shed in the corner of the family room.

"Why does this feel like old times?" he teased.

She was about to say something very olive branchy when the doorbell rang. Seconds later she heard the front door flung open.

"Rhett?" a sultry voice called out, and in walked a stunning twenty-something who was rocking a pair of ass-hugging yoga pants and a Namaste tank which showed off half her midriff.

Elsie looked at Rhett. "You're right, this feels just like old times," she deadpanned. "Oh, and by the way, I have a party tonight. So you and Namaste will have to find other accommodations for your 'yoga' class."

His gaze traveled the length of her, from her cleavage to her bare legs and back—ever so slowly. "Is it a pajama party? Count me in. Although I have to warn you, I like to cuddle."

CHAPTER TWO

Dating Tips from Elsie Dodd
*When people show you who they are,
listen.*

Elsie Dodd.

Man oh man. Talk about an unexpected blast from his long ago past. She was still stubborn, smart, and the sexiest woman to walk the planet. Back in college, they'd shared a weekend—a single, blow-your-mind, hold-on-for-dear-life kind of weekend that scared the shit out of him. He'd wanted it to be more, so had she, but finding out that his dad was terminal had wrecked him. Then came the news that he'd landed his first big sponsor, giving his career much needed traction, which had further cemented what his gut had been telling him—to walk away.

Biggest mistake of his life.

Rhett had always chalked it up to right girl, wrong time, but that was a decade ago. Once she'd hooked up with Axel she was—according to bro-code—off-limits. Not that he'd minded watching her squirm in that oh-so inspiring robe of hers earlier. If she hadn't seemed so close to tears, he would have looked his fill just to raise her hackles. But he wasn't willing to play with fire—not even for her. She'd rammed him in the nuts once—duly deserved—and he wasn't open for a replay.

Lately, his life had been one gigantic knee to the nuts. Starting with his separation, then his very public divorce, and even more public dating life. Not that there had been a ton of dating, but he'd gone out with a few women, including "Namaste,"—whose date he'd gently canceled. He'd told himself it was because he had to work, but that'd been a lie. He hadn't been able to write worth a damn since the divorce. It was the pressure, he decided. Not that anyone knew.

He handled his problems like he handled everything else, with a big-ass grin. It started out as his trademark, then morphed into something automatic. He'd become a pro at faking it. Playing it up for the press, his ex, even his family—for whom he didn't want to cause any more undo stress. They were already treating him with kid gloves. Which was part of the reason he needed his own space.

According to his brothers, he had four houses he could crash at. All of which had their own guest suite. Then there were the seventy-three-hundred hotel rooms to choose from in the greater Portland area. Not to mention all the Airbnbs around. Unfortunately, none of these allowed him the two things he'd come back home for: peace and quiet. Not to mention a music room and a private recording studio, which was in the basement. The Greenhill house had all four—if he could get his squatter to move out.

Rhett had made the decision last year after his divorce that he needed a change and decided to go solo for one album. Getting his label on board had been step one. Then it was breaking it to the band. At first the other members of Subtle Warfare felt blindsided, but quickly got on board.

Most of his bandmates were husbands and dads, desperate for some downtime to spend watching their kids grow up.

Now that Rhett had what he wanted, a chance at a solo career, he seemed to be floundering. Not only with the music, but the creative direction he wanted to the album to take. He had songs, he just wasn't sure they were the right songs, which was why he'd come home to the one place he felt like he could be himself without all the pressure of being a commodity.

"You going to drink that or is this your idea of foreplay?" Owen, the second eldest brother, asked, pointing his chin toward the beer Rhett had been nursing for the past thirty minutes.

It was Friday night at Stout, which meant Four-Dollar Drafts—and all four brothers had dragged him to the family bar. The big screens were tuned into different ball games, including the Dodgers versus the Giants, so the place was packed like Madison Square Garden during a Beyoncé concert. The bar was overflowing with beautiful single women, including a pretty redhead sitting across the way giving him the green light, and he needed a little go-time in his life right about now. Except, another pesky red head kept popping into his mind, which was all kinds of ridiculous.

He didn't know much about Elsie anymore, except that she'd walked out on Axel—a play from Steph's book—then made his life a living hell. According to his friend, Elsie had nearly cleaned him out, which was why Axel had started doing studio work between tours. Rhett also knew that she'd owned her own award-winning design company, and still looked as beautiful as ever. Not that he was looking. He'd had his fill of complicated women and wasn't about to get involved with another—even as friends. He liked the idea of love and devotion for other people, it just hadn't worked out in his favor. Which was why he needed to come up with a solution that pleased both parties.

Rhett looked back over his shoulder at the table of beauties smiling his way and winked. The bolder of the group winked back, then gave a little *come hither* wiggle of the finger. He saluted her with his mug, then turned back to the guys.

"My technique seems to still work magic."

Owen snorted. "Says the guy who looks like he hasn't had any as of late."

"Leave him alone," Abi said from behind the counter, gifting Owen a smack to the butt.

Abi was a teacher who ran a summer program for local under-privileged kids. She was also Owen's fiancée. They were the least likely couple of anyone in the family. And not because Owen was built like the Sears Tower and Abi barely came up to his chest. In addition to running a bar, his brother also rented space as a tattoo artist across town and had enough muscle and ink to double as a biker gang member. Abi was sweet and cute in that kindergarten teacher kind of way, and she could smell BS a mile away. Hilarious since Owen was the biggest BSer on the planet.

They met last fall when Abi came to Portland looking for a do-over and sweet-talked her way into working at the bar. It didn't take long before she sweet-talked her way into Owen's heart. Things had worked out; Rhett hadn't seen his brother this happy since before their dad passed. It was intimidating.

"Or what?" Owen said, and Abi lifted a single brow and, just like that, Owen caved. "Sorry, bro. I was joking."

With a content smile, Abi turned to Rhett. "Can I tempt you with something else? Maybe a slice of my Mee-maw's triple berry cobbler?"

"That's my slice," Owen whined.

Abi went up on her toes and whispered something that spread Owen's grin from ear to ear. "You can have the slice, bro." Then he gave Abi a sound smack on the lips and watched her walk away.

Rhett couldn't watch any of it. It was bad enough his love life had crumbled around him, but every time he was around the family, it was a constant reminder of what he'd lost.

"He's right. You look like shit," Gage, his agent and least favorite brother at the moment, said.

"Why did I agree to come tonight?" he asked. "Oh, I didn't."

Today was supposed to be some much-needed down-time, an afternoon on the water in his boat where he'd have the chance to regroup, figure out his Elsie problem, maybe even put a few chords together into something that resembled a melody. Somehow it ended up being a bro-trip. After, they dragged him to the bar, and the entire day had passed without him getting a moment's peace. His brothers were on him like white on rice ever since he'd come home.

They were worried, he got it.

He was worried as well.

Divorce was hard, but his had been particularly brutal. Oh, the separation of assets had been a breeze—except for his music rights, he'd given his ex whatever she wanted. But the truth was that he'd blown his chance at love. He'd sacrificed a lot to make things work with his wife, even cancel-ing his press tour, moving around his schedule, anything so that he could spend more time with her, to show her how much he loved her and wanted to make things work. But her actions and unwillingness to meet him halfway—hell, he'd have even taken a quarter of the way—made it crystal clear that he hadn't been worth fighting for, and that's what was tripping him up.

That's what kept him up at night and kept him from putting himself out there again. He didn't want to find himself in a vulnerable situation ever again. It hurt too much.

His ex had already moved on. Where his career was stagnant, hers was thriving. He'd had a few one-night stands here and there while Steph had found something serious. His tour bus might be top-of-the-line but it was still a moving bed, complete with a driver and bodyguard. Then there were the hotel rooms, where he was blessedly alone, but with all the people in his crew there was always something going on in the hallways.

"You need to get out," Gage said.

He needed to sleep. "I need to get this album written and I haven't slept in my own bed for any length of time in over six months."

Probably because he didn't have his own bed anymore. Steph received both houses in the divorce and he didn't have the time or energy to find another one. It wasn't as if he could buy any house, he needed the right location to ensure privacy, and the sort of neighborhood where people didn't give two shits that a celebrity lived next door.

The manicured property had a three-thousand-foot main house, an organic orchard and garden, stunning views of downtown Portland and Mount Hood in the distance and was equipped with a state-of-the-art studio in the basement. With its tall, lush foliage that disguised the house from the street and the positioning of the property, all three acres could easily be enclosed by security fences and privacy gates.

It wasn't the perfect property, but with a little work it could be. Which why he'd bought it sight unseen.

Correction, he'd been in the house a few years back, but it had been under renovation. It still was, but the house was nearly ready. That visit was also the last time he'd allowed himself to be alone with Elsie.

It had been an innocent run-in in the kitchen during a barbecue, where she'd given him a beer and invited him to sit at the counter while she showed him her latest sketches for the house. He'd sat right next to her, close enough that he could smell the summer air on her skin, and they'd talked—and talked—about everything. It was exactly like that weekend. Her eyes lighting bright as she shared her dreams, while he wondered what would happen if he kissed her—and he almost had. That's when he'd pulled himself up short. He wasn't the sort of guy to look at another man's wife. That's when he had gotten the hell out of dodge and never looked back.

That was four years ago. Before Steph, before his big break, and before he'd decided being around her was one hell of a temptation.

He'd cut the visit short, bowed out of future invitations, and found ways to avoid her after that. He knew his abrupt departure from her life had confused her, but it was about self-survival at that point. She might have been pissed, but it had been the right thing to do. Then he'd met Steph and he didn't have time to think about anything outside of making her happy and his music. Two conflicting priorities that led to heartbreak and disappointment.

"I thought you moved into the new place today," Clay said. He might be the baby of the family, but at six-four and two-hundred-twenty pounds he looked every bit the recipient of two Super Bowl rings.

"I did. Only when I got there, the previous owner was still in quarters."

"Why do you look so surprised?" Josh, the oldest, asked. He was dressed in a smart-looking suit and tie, which he'd loosened, and a goofy grin that spoke of a guy in love. Lucky bastard. "Axel was never the most reliable guy."

"What does that mean?"

"That when you and Axel were in the same band, he always struck me as a me-first sort of guy. His own best salesman. You know," Josh trailed off.

No, Rhett didn't know. It wasn't as if he and Axel had spent a ton of time together since that barbecue. In fact, he'd kept things casual, meeting for drinks a couple times, inviting him to the studio for a jam secession once, and talking a little business. But between the two men's schedules they'd barely seen each other in over a year.

Back in college they'd been close, inseparable, even started their own garage band. While they'd always kept in touch, once graduation happened, they'd gone their separate ways. Axel landed a gig as a drummer on a mid-sized tour and Rhett had followed his own path—which had more twists and turns than Axel's, and took a hell of a lot longer, but Rhett wouldn't switch landing spots for the world.

People change, and while Axel had always been a little self-serving, Rhett had never viewed him in the way Josh had described. Then again, Josh was an excellent judge of character, seeing things other people might overlook. It was what made him such a great district attorney.

Before he could ask his brother to clarify, Gage asked, "How long is Axel staying?"

Rhett ran a hand down his face. He almost lied and said Axel was leaving tomorrow just to keep them from giving him shit. But he knew in less than twenty-four hours the Easton wives would descend on his house, with casserole dishes, dating advice, and a list of phone numbers belonging to single their friends. The numbers would lead to dinners, which would lead to sex and eventually him sneaking out before dawn.

That's all he'd done since the divorce. The first few months, he was in stunned disbelief that he'd failed at the most important thing a man was supposed to do. After that, people started wondering where the infamous Rhett Easton had disappeared to. To get his label—and the women in his family—off his back he'd found appropriate dates to take to appropriate events, where both parties involved knew the deal.

Here he was a year later, and the deal was starting to get old.

"It isn't Axel," he admitted. "It's Elsie."

It was as if he'd admitted Elvis was in the building. The entire group went silent. Pin-drop, jaws-on-the-table, Elvis-is-really-alive kind of silent that told Rhett it was coming.

Owen was the first to crack a smile, which was followed by loads of laughter. "Elsie?" he asked, wiping at the humor in his eyes. "Way to bury the lede. You're living with Elsie Ross?"

"I think it's Dodd now, and that's not what I said."

"So, she's single now. On the market, so the speak," Owen said.

Clay was notorious for using silence to his benefit, so when he spoke, Rhett listened. "Recent divorce, I imagine she's still pretty tender and raw."

"What are you saying?"

"Tread lightly."

"I'm not looking to tread at all," he explained, but his brothers were already taking bets on just how big of an ass Rhett was about to make of himself. He didn't bother to tell them he'd already accomplished that. "My flight was late,

I'd barely gotten to the house, and Elsie interrupted my shower."

"So now you were showering with Elsie Ross?" Owen joked.

"Dodd." Why was he getting so defensive? "There was a mix-up and Axel told me I could have the house for the summer. Elsie claimed she didn't get the memo."

"And you believe *him*?" Josh asked.

"Why shouldn't I?" Although his brain was telling him something different than what his mouth was telling his brothers.

Clay sat back and folded his arms over his chest, studying Rhett for a long, uncomfortable moment. Even though he was the youngest, he was the most introspective. He was patient and precise, skills that made him one of the best running backs in the NFL. "What are you going to do?"

"Hotel rooms are out since I need quiet to write." And it wasn't as if he were some Regular Joe, who could check into a room and expect the privacy and anonymity that comes with a vacation. Not that this was a vacation.

Although today had felt like one. He might have given his brothers a hard time earlier for crashing his party of one, but being on the boat with them that afternoon—away from the prying eyes, fishing like they used to—felt good. Normal.

He needed some normal in his life. Another reason he'd come home. Take tonight for example. Even though his brothers were giving him shit, it felt like he was himself—at least more himself than he'd felt in months.

Man, his dad would've been happy to see his sons keeping up the Easton family tradition of spending summer days on the water. Which brought him to the thing that he didn't think his dad would have been happy to know, that his son couldn't make his marriage work.

Love. It was something every other Easton had managed to do and do spectacularly. Kids, wife, the whole package. That's what he wanted. Or had wanted, past tense. He didn't think he had it in him to give marriage another go-around.

Being gone for long stretches, new city every night, the invasiveness of the business. *Nah*, his life wasn't conducive to lasting relationships. That's why there was such a high rate of divorce in his world.

"So what's the plan?" Josh asked.

He didn't really know. Other than crashing in an actual bed for the next twelve hours, he had nothing. "The plan is I'm going to go back to the house I bought and sleep in my very expensive bed."

For all he knew, Elsie had found other accommodations. Then again, she was the most stubborn woman he'd ever met, and she'd never surrender that easily.

"What if she's still there?" Clay asked.

"Oh, she's there." Enjoying her little party. "We already talked about it. We'll divide up the house."

It wasn't as if he could kick her out—even if he was in the right. And it wasn't like he could pack up and move out. One of the reasons he'd bought that house, for an inflated price, was to help reestablish residency in Oregon for tax reasons and that started as soon as he closed escrow.

"You two gonna share the bathroom?" Owen asked.

"There's three bathrooms. Why are you trying to make a big deal out of this?" Again, his brothers exchanged the same look, like he was missing the punchline. "Since when do you guys hold back?"

"Since she nearly wrecked you," Gage said lowly, knowing how hard of a decision it had been for Rhett to walk away.

While his brothers knew about his fling with Elsie, Gage was the sole person who knew just how deep Rhett's time with Elsie had been. Gage had known something was up, so Rhett had confided in him about the weekend. Not about the sex, but about their insane connection. He'd also confided his reasoning for walking away.

"You have this amazing opportunity," Gage had told him. "An opportunity some of us will never have. Don't waste it."

But Rhett had brushed it off, citing his upcoming college tour as an excuse. Gage told him he'd regret the decision and Rhett had. Then he'd run into Axel and Elsie, and regret didn't even begin to describe how he'd felt.

"That was a long time ago." When he'd been young and naive and believed in things like love and commitment. "I'm looking for some peace and quiet." And wasn't that a damn shame. For a guy who couldn't wait to have kids and start a family, he'd sure become one cynical son of a bitch. Case in point, his unwillingness to get involved with a woman beyond one night.

After his divorce, he'd promised himself time to figure out who the hell he was minus a plus-one. He wasn't sure if it was a forever commitment, but he wasn't sure how to mingle his life with someone else and not lose sight of what was important—his music. He also wasn't sure if he trusted his gut anymore. He'd put everything into his marriage, praying it was enough, but he was left wondering what the hell went wrong.

"The offer still stands," Gage said. "Say the word and Darcy will make up the guest room."

"And your kids? Hard pass." Not that he didn't love his nieces, but the new twins were double the troublemakers, double the giggles, and double the sticky little hands that woke him up at five in the morning when they crawled into his bed. Then there were the diapers—a tour bus full of diapers.

Rhett had six weeks to pull his shit together, do whatever it took to get his sponsor behind the upcoming tour, then head back to LA to record the master tape of the new album. First though, he had to write the album and that wasn't going to happen if he didn't maintain focus.

"I need my own space right now." When Gage started to argue, Rhett held up a silencing finger. "A quiet space."

"You sure?" Gage asked, and the only one who seemed sure was Rhett. Which gave him pause.

"It was a long time ago."

Gage didn't look so convinced. He was the one person who knew just how messed up Rhett had been over Elsie and Axel back in the day. Even though the entire thing had felt like a bait and switch, Rhett had decided to be the bigger man.

"I'll take my luck with Elsie. At least I'll get some room to myself and some peace and quiet." As much as he could without wondering what she was doing or feeling—or wearing. Hell, he couldn't get that silky pink number out of his head.

"Be careful. She's getting out of a divorce and if she's anything like Jillian," Clay said, referring to his live-in girlfriend, "she'll be pretty vulnerable for some time."

"Vulnerable? She nearly electrocuted my nuts."

"He just means to tread lightly," Gage said. "For the both of you."

The only interest Rhett had in Elsie was helping her find another place to live. Preferably a place in a different zip code.

CHAPTER THREE

Dating Tips from Elsie Dodd
Meet someone the old-fashioned way.
Through alcohol and poor judgment.

The force of thumping bass and rowdy laughter nearly blasted Rhett back when he opened the front door. Women were everywhere, all dressed to impress, filling the main living space, which had been transformed into a night club with penis-inspired decorations strewn about.

Personally, Rhett did not see the point of a divorce party if the attendees were taking their drinks from penis-shaped shot glasses, but what did he know?

"Well, shit," he mumbled. He'd been sure that the party would have broken up by this hour. There was no way he was going to sleep through the noise. Then again, he'd said he wanted to go to his bed; he hadn't specified alone. And with at least thirty women at his fingertips—odds dictated that at least half were single—his night was looking up.

Rhett liked women. All kinds of women. He liked the way they smelled, the way they felt, the way they sounded calling out his name. He especially liked the last part.

He scanned the crowd looking for a new bed-buddy when he spotted the one woman he couldn't like—not in that way.

Elsie.

She was next to the bar in a short black dress—emphasis on short—with mile-high heels and a sash that read DICK-FREE DIET. Unlike earlier, her wavy red hair was twisted into some complicated knot at the base of her neck, with little wisps around her face that had escaped the confines. Her shoulders were bare, her breasts on glorious display, and her ass—that heart-shaped ass—was swaying back and forth to the music. Then there was her smile, big and bright and relaxed, yet somehow sad.

His little squatter had been drinking. And by the empty martini glass in her hand and the slight tilt to her posture, she'd been having her fair share of divorce party festivities.

Never one to show up to a shindig empty-handed, Rhett stopped by the store on the way home to pick up a present. But seeing the exhaustion in her eyes and the forced way she was talking, he decided he'd save it for tomorrow. He also decided that, instead of crashing her party, he'd quietly go to bed. Getting upstairs to the master was out, since it would bring him straight through the crowd and straight into a night of selfies and autographs. More importantly it would insert him right into the middle of Elsie's fun. And irritated or not, tonight he wanted her to have her fun. Because come tomorrow they'd discuss her new accommodations—across town.

Knowing he'd need his noise-canceling earphones to get even a wink of sleep, he snuck around the side hallway leading to the guest bedroom off the den. He was nearly out of sight when he spotted Elsie talking to some dude.

The bartender, who was putting another drink in Elsie's hand while putting his hand on her hip. Then there was the prick's expression, confident and zoned in on his target.

Rhett knew the look, wore it whenever he planned to hook up. And while Elsie was a grown woman who could handle herself, his brothers' words kept playing in his head.

"Walk away," he told himself. What happened was none of his damn business. Yet instead of walking into the den, he found his feet going in reverse until he was in direct line of sight with the guy. He stood there, waiting for the prick to look up, and when he did Rhett leveled him with a look and shook his head.

The bartender's hand jerked back, and he wisely focused his attention on doing his job. Mission accomplished, Rhett made his way to the back bedroom. He left his shoes at the door and threw his jacket over the arm of an office chair.

From what he could tell, the room was part guest room and part studio. Based on the sketches hanging from the wall and the blueprints on the desktop, this was where Elsie worked—and she'd been working hard. The desk was covered in loose textiles, paint swatches, and hand-drawn floorplans, complete with dimensions and layout.

In the middle of the table was a large pad of art paper. It was her current project, he could tell. The sketches were rougher and there was no furniture included, simply the structural design with textures and architectural details. Even in their earlier form, the concept was eye-catching.

It was a music room and not any music room, but the one here on the main level, with a piano placed in the middle. She'd rounded the edges, the acoustic paneling looked like a piece of art, and the two-by-two decorative ceiling tiles were reminiscent of Carnegie Hall. It was modern and unique and stunning.

Wanting to see the rest of her plans for the house, he flipped the page to the outline of a two-bedroom bungalow. The address put it down the street.

"What are you doing?"

Rhett looked over his shoulder to find a very pissed off roommate with her lips pursed and her hands on her hips.

"Getting ready for bed," he said casually. "Would you like to watch again or am I flying solo?"

She ignored this. "You're on my side of the house."

"I didn't know we'd established lines yet," he teased, but she was serious as hell.

"There was a hearing earlier. You missed it. It was thorough and detailed and, don't worry, I presented your case."

He rested a hip against the desk. "And what was the outcome?"

"I get the east side of the house, including the kitchen, guest rooms, family room, living room, garage, stairs, and," she waved a hand to include the entire room, "the study."

"Besides the master, what's left?"

She looked up at the ceiling as if counting all the other rooms in the house. She finally held up a single finger—the middle one. "The master en suite."

"And the music room?"

"That's mine too."

"Didn't know you played piano."

"I'm going to start taking lessons."

"So the master and adjoining bath." His lips quirked. "How will I get there if you possess the stairs?"

"There is a two-foot easement that allows you to walk through my property to get to yours," she said as though she'd put great thought into it.

"And if I get hungry?"

She shrugged. "I hear Uber Eats is good or you can try, I don't know, finding somewhere else to live."

"Not happening."

Her eyes went into two tipsy, pissed off slits. "I was here first."

"You had vacated the property when I arrived, then you joined me in the shower."

"I didn't join you! You were invading my house. You still are."

He wasn't sure where her mind had taken her, but her gaze wandered south, which he found interesting and unexpectedly arousing. "My eyes are up here, Red," he teased, and her cheeks flamed—so did her temper.

"I don't answer to that anymore."

"How about Hot Stuff?"

"Why are you even in here?"

Because he nearly unmanned some bartender for looking at her too long. "Because the party is out there, and I wanted to give you some privacy. It looked like a pretty big turnout."

There had to be thirty women out there, laughing and drinking and partying it up like it was New Year's Eve in Times Square. Elsie, on the other hand, looked as if she were counting down the seconds for the night to end.

"Embarrassingly enough, half of them came hoping to get the juicy details on what really went down between me and Axel. The parts of the story that Axel hasn't already shared with the world."

He thought back to his brothers' assessment of Axel's character, then took in the raw anguish and humiliation in Elsie's expression and wondered if maybe his brothers had a better read on the situation.

"The other half?" he asked, suddenly wanting to know more. Not the juicy details like the women in the other room, but the pieces of the story that made Elsie want to celebrate her divorce, when his had been one of the worst moments of his life.

"The other half made an appearance to ensure that if they ever needed a favor they could call me," she said, anger thick in her tone.

"A favor?" he asked, confused.

"You know, like concert tickets or backstage passes, meet and greets."

Ah, he did know. Had been there a thousand times. At first it felt good to have that kind of pull. After a while it got old, made people jaded. It was one of the reasons Rhett was so close with his brothers. He never had to question their motives. Which brought up another question. How could a woman who had a BS meter to rival Quantico suddenly turn a blind eye when there had clearly been red flags?

"Why invite them if they're not your real friends?"

She lifted a single, sad shoulder. "I guess I'm slow on the uptake. Plus, how pathetic would a divorce party of one be?" She gave a self-deprecating roll of the eye. "Let me take that back. It's not as tragic as I made it sound. In fact, I have some amazing friends. I just thought I had more of them than I actually do."

"Divorce can do that. Divide loyalties right down the middle. But not everyone takes a side or has secret motives," he said quietly. "I would have come to your party just for you."

She really did look beautiful. He knew she was going for sexy when she picked out that black dress, and she was sexy as hell, but right then, with the lamp casting a golden glow over her face, she looked like an angel.

There was a long, tense silence as she considered his comment. He could see the uncertainty in her gaze as if she wasn't sure she could believe him. He could also see the vulnerability and defeat shimmering in her eyes, as if her night had been a huge disappointment.

Rhett took a small step closer and tucked a strand of hair behind her ear. A jolt of sexual awareness shot up his arm and settled in his dick.

Well, shit. As if his life wasn't already complicated enough.

She must have felt it too because she jerked back, bumping into the wall. Her eyes were as wide as martini glasses, her lips parted in disbelief. And horror. Then her chin went up and her expression morphed into pissy woman with an ax to grind.

She looked down at her sketches, which were out of order. "That doesn't mean you get to look through my personal things." She held them tightly to her chest. "These are private."

"I didn't mean to snoop." She cocked a brow. "Okay, I didn't set out to snoop. I saw it lying there, glanced at the top page."

"The top page is page one not nine."

He held up his hands in surrender. "You're right."

She shuffled through them. "And you got them out of order." She meticulously righted the sketches—well as meticulous as one could be when they were three sheets to the wind.

"That wasn't my intention. Curiosity won out. I'm sorry."

She opened her mouth to argue, then she snapped it shut. "Thank you for the apology." She paused and he could tell she was weighing her next words. To his surprise, she worried her lower lip in that nervous way that used to get to him. "What did you think?" She held the portfolio closer to her chest. "Of my designs?"

The last thing he'd call Elsie was shy, but in that moment a quiet uncertainty washed over her. Clay was right, she wasn't as tough as she was letting on. And that got to him more than anything—even that sexy black number.

"Impressive."

He could see her discomfort and the fact that she didn't believe him. What had happened to that confident, fearless, and sure-as-shit woman?

"You can be honest," she said. "You won't hurt my feelings."

Maybe not, but someone had. He could tell. "I stand by my statement. If you let me have a longer peek, I can give you a more detailed list of the things I appreciate."

"Are we still talking about my sketches? Because you're looking at my boobs."

"There's a lot to appreciate." He watched as she considered this, then her face flushed and—well, would you look at that—her gaze dropped to his mouth. Again. "What do you want to talk about?"

"I think I've had too much to drink to answer that question."

He took a step closer. "Then I'll ask again tomorrow."

She shook her head, sending strands of auburn hair falling around her face. "That wouldn't be smart." He was convinced she was going to turn around and swish her song-inspiring ass right out of the room when she said," But maybe we can talk about my mock-ups. I mean, since you already peeked."

He was transported back to that day in her kitchen when he'd almost kissed her. He cleared his throat and took a step back—physically and emotionally. "I'd like that."

"The one on top isn't finished."

"And the rest?" He eyed the sketchbook she was clinging to so fiercely.

"The rest aren't ready yet either. Plus, they're on my side of the house."

Well, if that didn't make him feel like a bigger jerk. He knew how private she was, also knew what a perfectionist she was, tinkering with a single sketch until it was exactly what she wanted. "I'm really sorry, I know how private you are about your work. That would be like you looking at an unfinished song, then reshuffling the pages to screw with me."

Her voice went quiet. "Is that what this whole thing is about? Trying to screw with me?"

"No. Never." Again, she didn't believe him and that left him feeling uncertain. Sure, it had been a few years since they'd had a deep conversation—a conscious choice on his end—but she knew him well enough to know he wasn't a liar. "Why would you think that?"

She shrugged. "I don't know, recent experience, I guess." She went quiet for a moment, then looked down at her sketches. "Maybe I can show you one page, but only if you promise to be honest."

"Have you ever known me to be otherwise?" he asked. Her expression said she hadn't made up her mind—which hurt on a cellular level.

She didn't move to release her sketch pad, in fact she held it tighter and started this cute little sway. She was a little more than tipsy, she was on the fast track to drunk. "Will you regret this in the morning?"

"Probably." She took a step forward and set her pad on the desk, holding it closed with her hand. "I have a meeting with a new client on Wednesday. It's for a recording studio and I've been trying to find ways to make it feel more like a music hall, you know, aesthetically pleasing. Everyone in that room is a creative and I can't imagine how hard it would be as an artist to spend that much time in a foam-walled box." She took a tiny, tentative step toward him and flipped to the back of the pad.

Her eyes were big and luminescent and so damn nervous—they were also locked on his. Something passed between them, something charged and dangerous, but she didn't glance away.

Liquid courage, he thought. Earlier that afternoon she had a hard time meeting his gaze. Now, it was as though neither could look away. A slow sizzle started to build, and he found himself being pulled, once again, into her sexy vortex.

He cleared his throat. "May I?"

Spell broken, she blinked and stepped all the way back. "Yes, I mean sure. I mean, please do."

Biting back a grin, he stepped up to the desk and glanced down at a drawing of a recording studio. The vibe echoed the music room and recording studio she'd designed in this house, with clean lines and different textures. It turned a basic home studio into a sleek, top-of-the-line sound room like the ones he'd recorded at in LA.

The longer he studied it, the more anxious she became until he could feel the nerves rolling off her in waves. He knew a simple "like" or "dislike" wasn't what she was looking for. And a design this spectacular deserved more. "What are the walls made from?"

It was as if all the tension from earlier disappeared and she gifted him this bright, familiar smile that reminded him of their one mind-blowing weekend nearly a decade ago. This time he wasn't that lovesick college kid, he was a grown man who knew better than to mess around with a woman whose heart was clearly battered and bruised.

"Aren't they beautiful? They're made from hemlock wood and designed for acoustical performance. A sound engineer in Holland created it with his wife. He wanted a home studio, she's a designer, so they invented it together." She looked over at him and that's when he realized how close she'd moved—kissably close. "Isn't that romantic."

What was romantic was the simple desk light reflecting in her eyes.

"Each panel is a square with a smooth, unique grain that allows for a hundred different designs and applications. See." Her arm brushed his when she pointed to the drawing. "By rotating the panels it provides a custom look without sacrificing the diffusion quality. And if we alternate the tiles and complement them with some sleek lined furniture, comfortable of course—"

"Of course."

"—then it will feel more like an extension of the home rather than a dungy basement or padded cell."

"Dungy?" He couldn't help but smile—or notice that she'd swayed even closer.

"Like a dungeon. I used to joke with Axel that he was going down into the catacombs where bad songs go to die."

He laughed. While Axel was a world-class drummer, he wasn't the best songwriter. He was more of a "follow your lead" kind of musician. There was nothing wrong with that. Rhett and Axel were very different musicians and, now that he thought back to what his brothers said, very different men.

Axel loved the life whereas Rhett loved the music. And that's what he'd come home to get back to. The music.

Only right then all he could focus on was how amazing she smelled—like a dirty martini and sex rolled into one. Then there was the way she was looking at him, as if his opinion was all that mattered in her world. The problem was the way he was looking at her, as if tasting her was the one thing that mattered in his world.

"Rhett?" she whispered, her gaze dropping.

"Yeah," he whispered back, noting that she'd placed her hand on his bicep.

"I think..." Her voice faded.

He turned until they were facing each other, a scant inch apart. "You think, what?" *That this kiss is going to blow the roof off. Funny, I was thinking the same thing.*

"I think tonight was a bad idea." Then she puked all over his shoes.

CHAPTER FOUR

Dating Tips from Elsie Dodd
*Make sure your walk of shame is from your
television to the fridge.*

Elsie was naked.

All that separated her from utter humiliation was a set of sheets and a lace thong. She could hear a distant strumming thumping through her head. But the thumping was coming from beside her. Loud and rhythmic, and making her head feel as if it were about to burst like a grape.

She could feel the weight of a body beside her. She cracked an eye open to see a blurry, very male form—in her bed. Her heart leapt to life, and into her throat, while the rest of her went stock still beneath the soft cotton sheets.

She wasn't alone. This much she knew. Just like she knew who her unexpected and unwanted bedmate was. Her nipples recognized his scent. And her heart recognized his music. It wasn't a song she was familiar with, but the practiced strumming could only belong to one person.

Why, *oh why*, if she had to have a drunken one-night stand couldn't it have been with the bartender? Or anyone but *him*.

Maybe if she feigned sleep he'd get up and leave the room and they'd never have to talk about this.

Ever.

The strumming stopped and someone moved—closer. Elsie could feel the heat of his body tickle the back of her neck and goose bumps broke out over every inch of her flesh—even the inappropriate inches. Little traitors.

A sad side effect, she was sure, of acute sex deprivation.

Going completely still, roadkill style, she silently took stock. Okay, so she wasn't naked, just practically naked, and lying next to, she feared, her ex's best bro. She couldn't be *sure* sure, since she was still drunk.

She stealthily slid one leg out from under the covers and touched her toe to the floor to keep the earth from spinning. Not that it helped, her mind was spinning with possibilities when every detail from last night came rushing back.

There was fun and laughter and vodka, lots of vodka. And Marcus, the sexy bartender who was checking out her cleavage, which to be honest wasn't his fault since it was on full display. Then there was Rhett, the thoughtful and gentle Rhett from days past, who had once sweet-talked her out of her panties.

At least she had those firmly in place. She couldn't say the same for her self-respect or dignity.

She squeezed her eyes shut and even that hurt, enough that a groggy moan slipped out. The strumming stopped, for barely a millisecond but Elsie heard it.

"Rise and shine, Red."

She groaned, pushing a pillow over her face in hopes of suffocating herself to avoid this very awkward situation. "Can we just lay here and pretend nothing happened?"

"Depends on if you can tell me exactly 'what happened' refers to."

Well, there was conversation, a little flirting, then—*oh god* and then—she lost what little pride she had left all over his shoes. She didn't remember much past that, except—

"Did we dance the *Dirty Dancing* dance? The one where they crawl across the floor?"

"You danced, while I watched and clapped at the appropriate moments."

"And the inappropriate parts?"

"I closed my eyes."

She snapped them back closed. "Ouch."

"It's the hair," he said softly.

"Is this a 'redheads are fiery' comment?"

Reaching up, he took out the elastic band she was wearing. Her hair came loose and tumbled down and before she could ask him what he was doing, his fingers slid along her scalp, making massaging circles.

Her body started to tingle. And when he murmured, "I've always liked your fiery side," that annoying tingle became a full-blown hum.

No way in hell, she thought, batting his hands away.

She didn't have the time for men right now. And she didn't have the experience with men to tangle with a guy like Rhett Easton. She had zero faith in her instincts when it came to trust anymore. Little by little, her father had chiseled away at her ability to take people at their word. Every broken promise, every weekend she sat there waiting for him to show, only to be disappointed, left deep wounds. What little she'd managed to salvage after her childhood had been obliterated by Axel.

She didn't get to pick her parents, but she'd had a say in her choice of husband. Marrying a man whose career literally depended on his ability to pack up and head out at a moment's notice? To cancel plans and miss anniversaries and disappear when things got hard? That was all on her. She should have known from the start that their lifestyles were completely incompatible. Which was why she was done with people who didn't know how to stick.

Her immediate thought was to hide back under the covers. Then she remembered that this was her bed and that she was tired of running from men.

Sexy hum or not.

"Out." She sat up, making sure to tuck the sheets under her arms so that all her bits were hidden. When he didn't move, she shoved him. "Get out."

A growl was the only warning she got before she came face-to-face with two big, brown, wild-looking eyes. It was as if Fozzie the Bear and Cujo collided, creating a pocket-sized assassin, with sights locked on Elsie's jugular.

Grrr…

"What is *that?*" she asked as two dozen needle teeth flashed her way.

"Meet Littleshit, part of my divorce settlement." Rhett's divorce settlement moved to lunge right as Rhett picked him up. His little doggie legs didn't get the message and moved at the speed of light, paddling through the air as if trying to get to Elsie and eat her face off.

"With everything you had to divide, you asked for *that?*"

Arf. Arf! The teeth were back.

"More like a parting gift from my ex." Rhett kissed the little demon on the nose, who panted happily, then turned into putty at Rhett's touch. Had he been a cat he would have purred. "He gets a little jealous sometimes. Don't you, boy?"

Boy was dressed in a pink hoodie with a bedazzled FANCY sewn on the back and matching pink sneakers. Its owner was dressed in jeans, his guitar, no socks, and a vintage T-shirt that did little to conceal the hard body beneath.

Her heart skidded to a stop. Was there more to the night than she remembered?

"Why are you dressed like that?" she asked, holding the sheets tighter. "Where are your other clothes from last night?"

"I could ask you the same, except I know exactly where they are."

"Where's that?"

"Your dress is on the floor. Your bra is right here." He held it up and it dangled by his fingers. Elsie reached for it, but Littleshit snatched it and she found herself on the losing end of a game of tug-of-war with a travel-sized puffball.

"Let go!"

Arf! Arf! Grrr…

Jaw locked, eyes narrowed, the dog leaned into it, his little toothpick legs anchoring into the mattress for stability. The harder Elsie pulled, the deeper his teeth sank into the fabric until she heard a little rip and immediately let go.

"Will you help?' she asked.

"Only if you ask nicely."

"Will you retrieve my bra from your evil dog's clutches?"

"Since you asked so sweetly." Rhett snapped his fingers, and the dog dropped the bra.

With an irritated growl, Littleshit turned around, his tail standing up as if flipping her the bird. Then he jumped off the bed.

"As for your thong, it's—"

"Still firmly in place," she said primly, struggling to put her bra on under the covers. It took some talent and effort, but she managed to snap it closed.

"Not your red one. You swapped it out for pink, which looks great with your complexion by the way."

"I did not." She glanced under the sheets and squeaked. "What happened last night?"

"Don't worry. You sang your heart out to the porcelain god, then did a little dancing, which ended with you stripping off your clothes before collapsing into bed."

She swallowed past the embarrassment. "And *your* clothes?"

"In the wash. They got a little dirty while I was holding your hair back." His gaze softened. "Nothing happened, Red."

Sheets to chin, she collapsed back against the headboard. "Thank god!"

"You did try to kiss me but, for the record, I don't jump into bed with someone who's wasted."

"Good rule."

"To clarify, I sacked out here to make sure you were okay. Plus, I stayed on my side of the bed, on top of the sheets."

"How gentlemanly of you."

"As for jumping into things head on, I like to think I learned from my mistakes," he said softly, and it brought her right back to that night. How perfectly everything had gone. It was still the best sexual experience of her life. It was a lot of other things too, but then he'd ghosted her.

"I'm sure you have." She rolled her eyes, then groaned when her retinas nearly detached.

In her experience, people might learn from their mistakes, but they can't change their spots. And Rhett was a playboy through and through—exactly like Axel.

Back in the day, she'd found Rhett irresistible, so much so that she'd forgone her one rule: never sleep with musicians—AKA magicians, for their innate ability to magically disappear and reappear without warning. Then she'd gone ahead and married one and look where that landed her.

Searching the floor with her foot, she located her dress, snagged it with her toes, and dragged it under the covers. Then she disappeared to shimmy back into her skintight dress. "I never took you for a tiny dog sort of guy."

"Littleshit and I have been through a lot," he said, and there was something in his tone that spoke to her on some level. Disillusionment. "Steph and I share custody, which means she drops by every now and then to give him a few pets, then she's on a plane to Milan or Paris or New York. Thank god we didn't have kids."

"I know the feeling." She'd wanted kids so badly, but she didn't want to expose her babies to a world where their dad wasn't around enough to care. Being the daughter of a musician, she'd lived that life and wanted more for her kids. Axel had promised that once he settled in his career, the time would be right. Except he never showed any signs of slowing down, and she'd been the one to settle. Another red flag she should have taken to heart.

"So, you didn't want kids?"

He blinked at her like she was crazy, and she thought back to that weekend, lying naked in his arms, staring at the ceiling fan as they shared their common desire to have a family. "Steph wasn't on board. Plus, what kind of life would my kids have with two parents who are never home."

Elsie thought about that. Thought about how lonely it was to be on the road. Away from family and friends, away from everything that grounded a person, away from everything that really mattered. She'd lived on the other side of that equation for eight years, but she knew the toll it took on one's personal life. And on one's marriage.

It seemed Elsie's relationship wasn't the only one to fall victim to a rock and roll existence. It was challenging at best and devastating if both parties don't make a herculean effort. Then there were the sacrifices and the loneliness and the gaps of missing moments. Small ones, big ones, and especially the sweet, everyday moments that make a relationship.

She wondered, in Rhett's marriage, who was the one to sacrifice the most. In her marriage, it had been Elsie. She sacrificed her time, her dreams, and sometimes her happiness. Then there was her career. It was hard to be a business owner when your world was constantly in flux—last-minute trips to see Axel, unpredictable scheduling, surprise visits where she felt obligated to drop her life to make Axel's easier.

There was only room for one dreamer in her family, so Elsie put her own dreams of opening her firm on hold to be the kind of partner Axel needed to go the distance with his music. That was why Axel's betrayal hurt so deeply.

She pressed her fingers to the corners of her eyes. "What a nightmare this is. I really am sorry about Axel's duplicity. Now we're stuck in this mess together."

He laughed. "Not sure I can say the same. This is a pretty sexy mess to be stuck in."

She peeked out from under the covers and shot him a glare. "I'm not falling for your charm," she said, then shielded her eyes. "Stop giving that smile. It won't work on me." It was totally working on her. "And I'm serious about you finding another place to stay. After last night, it's nonnegotiable."

"And your big doe eyes won't work on me," he explained, then repositioned his guitar and began strumming. She ducked back under the covers and did a final shimmy into her dress.

Then there was more strumming. Beautiful strumming, as if it were the beginning of something with the level of depth that would stick.

The strumming stopped and she was met with silence before it restarted. It was the same melody, with a few more chords added—a real heartwarming, chest-swelling variety of song that was created to play on one's emotions. "Rhett?"

"Ah huh," he said distractedly.

She poked her head out and sucked in a breath. He had his guitar in his hands, his dog at his side, and his fingers slowly moving across the strings. But it was the from-the-heart, lost-in-a-moment humming that had her pausing.

His brow furrowed and his fingers stopped. Without a word he straightened, went to her desk, found a pad of paper, and scribbled down some notes, then smiled. It wasn't the playboy grin he'd used a moment ago, this was the kind of smile that was usually reserved for a private moment.

It was as if he'd forgotten Elsie was there. Then his gaze met hers and instead of the smile fading, it got brighter. She wasn't sure if it was that smile or the fact that he was so close, with all those muscles on display, but her body zinged.

Not sure what to do with *that*, Elsie cleared her throat. "Are you doodling on my sketch pad?"

"I'm not doodling. It's called *creating* and this is my journal."

She laughed. "Your journal? Do you scrapbook too?"

And the playboy was back. "Why, Red? You offering to give me some photos from last night?"

She ignored this. "Did you hear me? About the living arrangements?"

"Loud and clear." He sat back down on the edge of the bed. "But here's how it's going to go down. I've spent the past six months in a hotel room or on my bus. I need a real bed and a place where I can write. Plus, I have three months until I have to go out on the road again and I can't eat one more night of room service."

She threw the covers back. "Three months!" This was the worst possible situation that she could imagine. Stuck in this house for the remainder of her stay with a man who had the power to make her strip down to her thong.

"Why so scared? Afraid you might try to kiss me again?"

She eyeballed him. "I did not try to kiss you and I thought you'd be gone in a few days."

He casually went back to tinkering on his guitar. "Axel said I could live here from now until escrow closes."

"So you mentioned." She felt herself begin to sweat. "What you didn't mention was when that end-date was."

"I wanted a fast escrow, hopefully two weeks." She couldn't finish the house in two weeks' time. Plus, her new house wouldn't be ready until August.

"Can't you stay in your LA house? I mean, this house is still under renovation."

"Minor renovations. And the major rooms are finished." He shrugged. "And my real estate agent hired a crew to come in after I leave for my tour and finish off the renovations."

Panic had her tossing the covers back and standing. "You can't just hire *a crew* to finish up. You need the right crew, one that understands early modernist design and its origin. This isn't some DIY project, it's a showcase-worthy house."

"Then I'll have my agent find a showcase-worthy early modernist expert."

"That would be me!" Elsie was the best early modernist interior architect in the state. He needed her, but she could already tell he had his mind set. "With the right crew, I can have this all done in a month."

He set his guitar aside. "And try to write through construction?" He shook his head. "Hard pass. Look, I'm here because I have to establish residency here in Oregon for tax reasons. With Steph getting the house, I've already lived in LA for too long. That is the whole reason I agreed to pay above asking." He met her gaze. "I figured you already have your own place."

"This is my own place."

"I meant your new place."

"Yeah, I'll get right on that after I win the lottery. Not everyone can just go out and buy a house without selling their current house. Do you even know what a gallon of milk costs these days?"

He seemed to consider that, then grinned one of his cover-of-*Rolling-Stone* grins. "See, that right there is why I need to be around people who ground me. Remind me what's important."

"Milk is important?"

"Do you know the last time I bought my own milk?"

"No."

"Me either. And that's a problem. Which is why I'm not leaving. So how about a compromise. You move into a temporary place, and I'll pay the rent until escrow closes."

"So I give up my dream so you can accomplish yours? Not happening." She was going to finish this house, even if she laid the floor tile by tile. "And what do you do, throw money at everything?"

"I'm trying to be the nice guy. I even got you a present." He pointed to a small box sitting on her nightstand. It was pink with a white tie and looked suspiciously like it contained jewelry.

"What is it?"

"Think of it as a truce between friends."

She looked into his assessing blue eyes but could have sworn that she saw a flash of amusement. "Between friends, huh?"

When she didn't move to take it, he leaned across her, his shirt riding up enough to expose the two dimples on his very muscular lower back. Her stomach quivered.

He handed it over and she, ever so cautiously, untied the bow and set it aside. Watching his expression for any hint of his prankster side, she opened the box and braced herself for a glitter bomb—or worse.

When nothing happened, she moved aside the tissue paper and—

"You got me a keychain?"

"With a key attached." He flicked the key with his finger. "You can't overlook the key."

"I already have one. Remember the hearing, where everything in the house is mine for another few months?"

"Oh, this isn't for *my* house. This is for the Airbnb right down the street you're going to love. I found it online and with its sleek lines and modern feel, it's right up your alley. If you look inside the card, it lists the address."

She threw the box at him, and he ducked. "I'm not leaving. My workspace is here. My things are here. Sorry if that puts a wrench in your Sex-topia, but I am staying in *my* place until the end of the summer."

He seemed to hem and haw over her statement, then shrugged. "As long as I get to be the big spoon, I guess that works." He grabbed his guitar and headed for the door. Then over his shoulder, he said "Oh and Red, I sleep commando. But you already know that."

CHAPTER FIVE

Dating Tips from Elsie Dodd
*Try online dating. You can meet and
break up with someone without
leaving the house.*

"You missed half of your own party. In fact, you disappeared just when the fun stuff was going down," Carla accused. "We painted glowing penises on Ms. Gilford's car windows. And wrote FOR A GOOD TIME CALL, then left her number. Where did you go? Please tell me it was with the bartender."

"I was not with the bartender." Deciding that she was absolutely, positively not going to share the most humiliating moment of her life, Elsie pushed her Bluetooth deeper in her ear and said, "I was too busy arguing with the new owner of the house."

"Wait, new owner? Who?"

"Nobody." *Liar.* "Axel sold the house without even consulting me."

"Can he even do that?" Carla asked through the phone.

"According to my lawyer, either of us had the power to sell, Axel just beat me to it."

"Isn't this a good thing? You need the money from the sale, now you get it earlier."

"I wanted to finish this house first." No, for her mental health she *needed* to finish the house first. "After that I can think about closing escrow. But until it's done?" She shook her head. "I need more time."

"You can always countersue?"

"With what money? Axel leveraged this house to the eyeballs to pay off the LA house, which he got in the marriage." Because he had put it in his parents' name. He'd done a lot of sneaky shit like that. Like when he'd pitched Elsie the reason for taking out a second, stating that they had a better interest rate on the Greenhill house, it sounded so logical. But she should have dug deeper because her ex was so dynamic, he could sell a blind man a Picasso.

In fact, the only thing in this crappy situation that made her grin was that Rhett had paid well over market. Not that she'd walk away a millionaire, even though they'd fetched seven figures for the house.

"He sold me on the biggest financial mistake of my life and I happily signed. Lesson learned."

As it was, she'd walk away with just enough money to make the down payment on her bungalow and reboot her career. She might have had to walk away from her fledgling design business in LA, but she was going to give it another go. Even if that meant being a glorified interior decorator as a stepping stone toward her real dream of becoming an award-winning interior architect. Which was why she'd agreed to meet with a prospective client just that morning.

It didn't pay much, and it was more decorator than designer, but it would give her a reference, plus some photos for her portfolio.

"Look, I gotta go. I'm meeting Harriet for dinner."

"That should be fun," Carla said. "Tell your mom I say hi."

Elsie pulled into her grandma's driveway, relieved to see only her grandmother's 1969 VW Bug with Mother Earth painted on the hood. "No life coach Mercedes in sight, so I should be good."

"Love you," Carla said, and rung off. Elsie checked herself out in the rearview mirror and groaned. She looked stressed. Resigned.

Like she'd been mainlining martinis all night.

With a deep breath, she popped in a breath mint, slapped on some lip gloss, then flashed a bright smile. A smile that was one-hundred-percent bullshit.

Elsie's ability to BS was right up there with the best BSers. It was a talent she'd learned the first birthday her dad had missed. From there it had become habit. And tonight her BS needed to be on point.

She wasn't the only one who'd had a rough year. Harriet's boyfriend of five years had passed away. So when she'd asked Elsie to dinner, even though Elsie wanted to decline due to a hangover, she'd given a sunny yes. Now it was time to hone in on the brightness again and infuse it into her smile.

Harriet Whitmore lived in a two-bedroom cottage across the Columbia River on the outskirts of Vancouver, Washington, in a cozy, tree-lined neighborhood where the houses were made from brick, the fences picket, and the residents went three generations deep. It was a typical charming and cozy suburbia, and a place Elsie hoped never to return.

At least not for more than a visit because there was nothing typical or suburban in the house Elsie had grown up in. Behind that bright red door was a clash of the Titans.

After semi-retiring from her job as a doula and parent-whisperer—who believed in composting, going organic, and Willie Nelson—Elsie's grandmother started moonlighting as a wedding DJ. She'd traded in her scrubs for Skechers and put blue streaks in her silver hair. On the other hand, Elsie's mom, Faye, was a celebrity life coach who believed in poise, personal growth, and the power of positive thinking.

Elsie believed her family was nuts. Where most kids came home to warm cookies and milk, Elsie's afterschool snack was prune and pecan bars with a cold glass of hemp juice to wash it down. Her clothes were eco-friendly, her hair boardroom barracuda, and her home was a unique mix of self-help quotes and astrological insight.

Elsie trudged up the walkway, stepping over the overgrown tomato garden that had taken on a resemblance to the jungles of the Amazon. Even the hot July sun wasn't a match for Harriet's green thumb.

Before Elsie could knock, the door magically opened right as she hit the landing.

"Oh, my favorite girl in the world," Harriet said, yanking Elsie in for a warm and hearty hug. It felt like long ago memories and coming home.

Elsie held on, burying her nose in her grandma's hair and taking comfort in the familiar scent of burnt sage and mothballs. This was the first real I've-got-you hug since her divorce was finalized. That it was from her grandma made it all the more emotional.

"Now, now. None of that," Harriet whispered, then pulled back. "Come inside. I've got dinner in the oven."

"It smells... Tofurky-ish?"

"Eggplant parmesan with marinated tofu and sprinkled with baker's yeast. Served with a nine-bean salad. Your favorite."

Elsie held back a gag. "Yum."

One time Elsie had complimented how pretty her grandma's nine-bean salad looked, so Harriet would sometimes surprise Elsie with her infamous culinary masterpiece. Even Faye, who would eat anything that was plant-based, loathed Harriet's nine-bean salad.

"Does that mean Mom's not coming to dinner?"

Harriet waved a dismissive hand. "It's the season for dream boards and goal journals, so your mom's been working night and day. Between her clients and podcast, she hasn't had time to even breathe, let alone sit down for a meal, in weeks."

Part of Elsie screamed, *Thank God!* Maybe her luck would hold out and she wouldn't have to face her mom for another week—or three. Elsie knew she'd have to confront Faye eventually, but since she embraced confrontation with the same enthusiasm as she embraced nine-bean salad, she prayed for a little reprieve on the whole betrayal topic.

The other part was sad for her grandma. After losing her boyfriend, Buster, Harriet slipped into a deep depression, which was why Faye had moved back in. The whole goal was that Harriet wouldn't be alone for long stretches, but it sounded as if Harriet was still alone most of the time, even though her mom lived there.

Elsie sighed and looked up at the ceiling. Maybe this was the universe's way of saying it was time for her to come home and give up on the Greenhill house.

"Well, I'm here," she said quietly, not wanting her grandma to feel disappointed that the family dinner was for two.

Elsie stepped into the family room and smiled. Twenty-eight years and nothing had changed. A forest of plants had taken over the far corner by the fireplace and a collection of framed pictures from every era of Elsie's life were displayed on the entry table. The furniture was 1980's ratan chic, made from bamboo, with boldly patterned meditation floor pillows that gave it a Moroccan vibe.

The kitchen was straight through the gunshot-style house, allowing Elsie to get a glimpse of the table, which was already set... for three. Elsie narrowed her eyes in suspicion. "I thought you said Mom wasn't coming."

Harriet clapped her hands in delight right as the doorbell rang. Elsie's heart sank because she knew who was behind that door. Or at least what was behind the door. The one thing worse than being ambushed by her mom was one of her grandma's blind dates.

"Please, tell me you didn't."

She patted Elsie's cheek. "Swiping right will only end with you chopped to little pieces and tossed into the Puget Sound."

"Which is why I'm swiping left on life."

Before Elsie could run out the back, the door opened and a man peeked his head inside. For the second time that week a male she didn't want to see walked right into her life.

"Look how prompt you are." Harriet ushered him inside. "Elsie, don't you love a prompt man."

Elsie didn't love men period. Been there, done that, had an empty bank account to prove it.

"Elsie, this is Huey. Huey, this is my recently single granddaughter, Elsie." Harriet stepped back and gave a dramatic swoop of the arm, as if she were Vanna White and Elsie was the grand prize of the night. "She owns her own business, has an average golf score of ninety-three, and knows how to cook."

"It was mini golf," Elsie corrected. "Although I did make it through the windmill hole in three strokes. And I can make a mean grilled cheese." She deadpanned.

"And those teeth are all hers. Show him, dear." Harriet clapped her hands as if Elsie were a party trick. "No braces for this girl. She comes from good stock."

Huey looked appropriately scared. "Nice to meet you." He held out his hand and Elsie noticed how small they were. Somewhere between toddler sized and a Disney princess. He looked at Harriet. "You look stunning, Mrs. Whitmore." He turned to Elsie and paused. "You look... comfortable."

Elsie took in her dancing pug leggings and her plaster-speckled T-shirt, and she had to admit he was right. "Well. I'm dressed liked this because I didn't know I was on a date tonight." She eyeballed her grandmother.

"Surprise." Harriet made fireworks with her fingers. "You need some more surprises in your life, Moonbeam." She looked at Huey. "Why don't you go grab yourself a drink from the fridge." When Huey was gone, she turned to Elsie. "And why don't you go to the garage and get some pliers to pull the stick out of your ass."

"I don't have time for this tonight."

"Tonight, you're on the universe's time, so until the world chimes, you're all mine."

"Did you see how small his hands were?" Elsie whispered conspiratorially.

"Small hands don't necessarily equate to a bad lover. Buster had small hands and his doodle was divine."

Elsie put her hands over her ears. "La, la, la. I'm not listening."

"You're such a prude."

"Who's a prude?"

Elsie turned around and sighed when she saw Faye, dressed in navy palazzo pants with her hair down and flowing, held back with a polka-dotted colored scarf, looking ethereal and chic and sensuous, like Ingrid Bergman. Faye might dress as if she were from a 1960s movie set, but she didn't look a day over forty and had the effortless beauty that gave her a Mrs. Robinson factor.

"I didn't think you'd be here," Elsie said, glaring at Harriet. Harriet shrugged her innocence.

"I couldn't miss your first post-divorce date, could I?" Faye said. "I'm doing a video chat at seven, but until then I'm all yours."

Faye hadn't been all Elsie's since she, well, ever. Faye was a renowned speaker and author on overachieving and was beloved by all. Except Elsie—she was holding a grudge that she couldn't seem to let go of.

"How's work?" Faye asked Harriet as though there wasn't a giant elephant in the room that needed to personal-grow its ass right out the door.

"Last night I DJed a bachelor party, which is where I met Huey," Harriet said, as if that were the perfect place to pick up a date for her granddaughter.

"You invited some stranger to family dinner?" Elsie asked.

Harriet pulled them in for a group hug. "Look at us, one big happy family."

One big family. Happy? Elsie wasn't so sure. Her mom had made sure that happy wasn't an item on tonight's menu.

Huey stepped back into the room with three beers in his tiny hands. Harriet cleared her throat in reprimand and that's when Elsie realized she was staring.

"I am so excited about tonight," Faye said, then introduced herself.

Huey nearly tripped over his own tongue. "Had I known we had another visitor I would have brought another beer," he said, as if this were his house and he was greeting Blake Lively. "Let me go grab you a…?"

"Gin and tonic would be lovely."

"Gin and tonic it is." He set Elsie's beer, forgotten, on the coffee table and went to the small, well-stocked bar on the side of the room to make a gin and tonic like he was a bartender from the Ritz. "For you, beautiful."

Elsie rolled her eyes, but Faye ate up the attention.

"Huey, would you be a dear and take a photo. Family dinners can be so rewarding," Faye said.

His gaze snapped from Faye's body to her eyes. "Absolutely."

"Thank you." Faye took off her headscarf and tousled her effortlessly tousled hair, then turned to Elsie and ran a hand to smooth down her curls, which rebelled and sprang every which direction like a bouquet of Slinkies. Faye pinched Elsie's cheeks. "This is practice for when you're famous."

"The only thing I'm famous for is the most contentious divorce on this side of the continental divide."

"You just wait. Your time will come. If you can believe it, you can achieve it."

"Well, isn't this a moment," Elsie said, and Harriet pinched her thigh.

"None of that." Harriet smiled and handed Huey her camera, then pulled Elsie to one side and Faye to the other.

Huey looked at the screen. "Hang on. Let's shift a little. How about you sit on the arm of the couch," he said to Faye. "And Elsie, why don't you sit on the cushion with Harriet standing beside you both." They all shifted, bumping into each other and when Elsie was seated, she realized she was partially blocked by her mother's shoulder.

Faye struck a sultry pose and Huey snapped the photo. Harriet looked at the picture, beaming with pride. "My girls. Now, Huey, why don't you help me set another place at the table, so these two can catch up." Harriet leaned in. "You know the rules, no negative energy in my sanctuary."

When they disappeared into the kitchen, Elsie whispered, "Why are you really here?"

"I was just reading this book, *Letting That Shit Go.* It's about how self-doubt can hold one back from their greatest potential. I thought you could use it." Faye pulled the book from her purse and held it out.

Elsie jumped back like it was a lit flamethrower. "I don't need a book." What she needed was a mom. But she'd known better than to hope.

"With that defeatist look, you do. I can practically smell your bullshit filling the room." Faye held out her arms. "Can we at least agree that letting go is the healthiest way forward?"

"It's not some problem reading a book can fix," Elsie said. "You knew Axel wasn't happy and you didn't tell me. You allowed me to be blindsided."

"The divorce was hard on the both of you."

Elsie blinked—twice. "Hard on the both of us? Axel went behind my back, hid assets, and sold my house without telling me."

And sold it to not just anyone, but a sexy and annoying someone with whom she may or may not have shared a moment with last night. Not that it mattered, since it would never happen again.

Once upon a time she would have done anything for a shot at a relationship with Rhett, but she was no longer that naive girl. She could only hope that he'd lock himself in the basement studio for the duration of his time in Portland.

"I didn't want to be the one to crush your dreams."

Elsie took a step back. "So you let him lie to me?"

"There are always two heartaches to every divorce." She looked at her mom completely silent. Then Faye lifted her hands. "Switzerland."

"You're not supposed to be Switzerland, you're supposed to be Elsie-land."

"I still don't understand how he justified not telling you about the extra line of credit?" Fay asked. "Are you sure you weren't doing one of those things where you listen but forget to hear? You tend to do that when you're emotional."

"I'm allowed to be emotional and it's hard to hear something that was never said. And how did you justify not telling me that he wasn't happy?"

"I really believed that things would turn out how they were meant to."

"That's a cop-out. You didn't tell me because it would mean getting emotionally involved and you don't do emotions very well."

"I'm a life coach, I do emotions for a living."

"You dance conga line to 'Simply the Best' and do trust falls. They're clients, and growing up, you treated me like one. Warm but emotionally disconnected. When Dad left, you both left."

Faye went into her life-coach tone, which was chipper meets news broadcaster. "It isn't that simple. And as for Axel, he came to me seeking direction for a happier life. How could I say no?"

"Easy, you say, 'My daughter comes first, so kindly fuck off.'"

"Dwelling on failures merely opens up the portal for negative space."

"I didn't fail, he cheated."

"He made a mistake."

"Nine that I know of."

Faye took Elsie's hand. "I know this is hard, but he's been like a son to me for a long time. And your divorce doesn't make that go away."

She shouldn't be surprised by how much her mom's words hurt, but she was. "It still makes you *my* mom. And *you* should have told me the moment you knew he wasn't happy. You chose him over me."

"You weren't ready to hear the truth. I put the problem out there, really weighed the pros and cons, how it would affect your outlook on life, and I knew that the situation would resolve itself. And it did, just not in the way you expected it to."

"He cheated and yet he's the one who walked away the winner."

"He cheated?" Huey's voice came from the kitchen. "You might not want to add that to your dating bio. It might make you sound bitter."

"Well said," Faye agreed, and Elsie could practically hear Huey high-five himself. "That's why I didn't tell you that Axel wanted out of the marriage. That wasn't for me to intervene."

Elsie stopped dead in her tracks, like she'd been unknowingly entered into the ice bucket challenge. "You never told me that he wanted out. You said he wasn't happy."

Faye tilted her head. "Huh, I'm sure I did."

"No, Mom. You didn't. I had to find out from a mutual friend that he was cheating. And how could you keep something like that from me?" Even as she said the words, she already knew the answer. "Let me guess, intervening would stunt my personal growth?"

She was met with silence. Elsie put her palm to her eyes and pressed hard against the continuous pounding. She was too hungover for this.

"Nope. I can't do this." Elsie walked straight past her mom and into the kitchen. "I'm sorry, Grandma, I can't stay."

Harriet looked devastated and Elsie hated that, but she couldn't be around her mom for another second.

Like the middle child, always trying to make peace, Harriet took her hands. "There's no reason to let him get between you. Your mom is right about one thing, you landed where you were supposed to. You deserve better and you need to get yourself back out there."

Another man in her life was the last thing she needed. "Sorry, Huey, I'm not really dating right now."

Huey didn't seem to give two shits about Elsie leaving, he was mesmerized by Faye puckering her lips in a pout that could bring men to their knees.

"Don't leave, honey," Faye said. "Not on my account."

"I can't do this right now," she whispered.

"Before you go, can I at least tell you about my secret," Faye said, and Elsie practically groaned because Faye's most recent secret ended with her and Axel on a couples' retreat in Florida, which happened to be at a nudist colony.

Then there was the secret that broke Elsie's heart.

"Your last secret didn't work out so well for me."

"This one will, I promise. Just hear me out."

"I would have heard you out if you'd come to me about Axel as soon as you knew." She'd had no idea how miserable he was in the marriage. That things were wrong. That there were things he didn't love anymore—including Elsie. And her mom never said a word.

Elsie had found them a marriage counselor, was even going to counseling solo because Axel had convinced her that she was the problem. All the while he was having affairs with women he'd meet on the road. Then he'd come home and complain about every little thing Elsie did. That she was being clingy or needy, or that she was emotionally absent. Even worse, it seemed all her quirks and parts that he'd fallen in love with now irritated him.

No matter how hard she tried, she could never get it right. Her mom's secret gave Axel more time to crush Elsie's self-confidence and self-worth. Axel was already checked out of the marriage long before divorce was even mentioned.

"I don't think I can handle another one of your big reveals, Mom."

She knew her words hurt her mom, but that was okay because her mom's one decision had broken Elsie's heart.

"I got you your first decorating gig. A person I mentor is throwing a big party and needs an event planner."

"I'm an interior architect, which means I don't do event planning. I do space planning and aesthetic designs," she said for the hundredth time.

Well, she would as soon as she landed her big first client, which would be a little more challenging without a diverse portfolio or showcase house. She already had the house, but someone had bought it right out from under her.

"Look at you putting that book to good use. Really owning what you do," her mom said, but then in the next breath, "And I'm sure Claire would be willing to call you an interior architect if that makes you happy."

"It doesn't make me happy, it's my job title." Or at least it was her new title. Back in LA Elsie had spent so much time joining Axel on the road or making their time at home really count, she passed on bigger jobs. She dabbled with interior decorating, landed a few one-offs for friends, including her biggest project, a home studio for one of Axel's friends. They'd seen what she'd done with the Greenhill house and hired her on the spot. Axel always made it seem like she got the job because the guy wanted an in with Axel, and for a time she'd believed him. Then, toward the end of their marriage, she'd began to believe in her own talent and wanted to challenge herself, which was why she'd come back to Portland.

The Greenhill house was her grand opus. From the light fixtures to every bolt, that house was her proudest accomplishment. She'd eventually have to say goodbye; she just wasn't ready. Not yet. And she wasn't ready to give up the dream that she'd be able to finish Greenhill.

"Mom, I don't do parties."

"This is more than a party, it's an experience," her mom said. "It's a *Walking Dead* gender reveal party. Isn't that exciting."

"Fandom reveals are the latest craze," Huey said, and all eyes went to him. "My sister had one. Harry Potter. I dressed as Dobby."

"If anyone could pull off a Dobby costume it would be you," Harriet said, looking hopefully from Huey to Elsie, then mouthing, *What a catch.*

Huey's gaze quickly skittered to the nine-bean salad, which he was stirring. It seemed that Huey and Elsie could agree on one thing: this was the worst first date ever.

"This isn't working," she said.

"The date?" Harriet asked.

Elsie looked around. "All of it."

Harriet's face softened and she placed a hand on Elsie's shoulder. "I know this year has been hard on you."

"Which is why this is such a great opportunity," Faye said. "Claire's budget is more than your wedding was."

That wasn't a high bar, since Elsie's wedding had been a drive-through window with an Elvis impersonator as the officiate. She and Axel had been young, and it was before his career had taken off, but it wouldn't have mattered. Axel was cheap on things that didn't interest him. Like a wedding where his dad would show up with his twenty-something girlfriend. Funny how Axel's apple practically kissed the tree's trunk.

Talk about another red flag Elsie chose to ignore.

"Mom, I don't do parties anymore." That had been her first job, which she'd worked tirelessly at to save up for her own fledgling one-woman firm, which she'd lost right before Axel had filed for divorce. It was the first crack in what would become a broken marriage. The thought of going back to doing parties, starting over from scratch after she'd achieved her dream, tore at her. But if she was anything, she was relentless. If she did it once, she could do it again.

"What's the budget?" she asked, and her mom rattled off some insane number. "And your cut is ten percent."

It wasn't enough to refurbish the bungalow, but it would definitely help. But—

She looked at her grandma. "Why does it feel like a step back?"

"It's a step forward toward your new life. So you do a few parties or design a family room here and there. Use those experiences to build on! Use them to float you until you land your first big client. As ridiculous as the party sounds, that's a hundred people, who are at the first-house-buying age and will see what you can do. You might gain a new client," Harriet offered.

"Plus, one of the guests is from *Modern Masterpiece* and according to Claire, they're looking for houses in Portland for next year's Pacific Northwest edition."

Elsie's heart came to a hard stop. "Are you serious?"

"Can't you just see yourself on one of their shows?" Harriet asked.

"It's a magazine." And yes, yes she could. It had been her dream since college. She had taken a class on Frank Lloyd Wright and early modern architecture and fallen in love.

"Which is why I told Claire you'd take the job."

Her mouth fell open, then snapped shut. "You did what! You haven't even talked to me. What if I don't have time?" Not only was her house in mid-renovation, thanks to Axel it technically was only her house for another few weeks. And that wasn't enough time to finish what needed finishing.

She couldn't fix what went wrong in her marriage, but she could fix every crack and scratch in her house. She was two rooms from perfection, and she'd be damned if another man stole her chance.

"I looked into it and the chosen house is featured on the cover and there's an interview about the designer's original point of view. Think of all the people who will see your work. It's better than some sketches and drawings."

A piece in *Modern Masterpiece* magazine had catapulted careers. A trampoline would be awesome, but a catapult? That could change her life. She had every edition going back a decade. Had studied them. Even followed the careers of the designers who'd been featured. Being in *Modern Masterpiece* wasn't just a dream of hers, it was at the top of her list.

Except there was the embarrassing snafu. "I won't have a house to showcase."

According to her lawyer, she didn't have a house at all. Not that she was going to worry her grandmother with that fun fact. Harriet would force Elsie to move in, and, not wanting to upset her grandmother, Elsie would agree. Then she'd be a big fat failure who slept on her grandmother's couch.

"I'm sure Axel would be supportive," Faye said.

"Are we talking about the same Axel?" Elsie asked.

"He might have gone through a mid-life crisis—"

"He's thirty-one."

"Age is but a number," Huey said, staring at Faye with lovesick eyes. "Wouldn't you say, Ms. Dodd?"

"Indeed," Faye said with a wink, and Huey practically fell out of the chair.

"He sold the house without telling me," she accidently blurted out, then regrated it when her grandma's eyes flickered with fire.

"He what!" Harriet said.

"Axel sold the Greenhill house. It's already in escrow."

Harriet pulled Elsie in for a hug and whispered, "That dickless wonder. Did you use the blessed coin I gave you?"

"Sure did. His dongle should be falling off any minute now."

Harriet patted Elsie's cheek. "Always such a smart girl, my little artist."

"Maybe the new owner will lend you the house for the day?" Faye said.

Elsie snorted. The new owner was barely giving her a chance to pack her bags before he kicked her broke ass out the door. There was no way he'd agree to someone invading his privacy. He'd purchased the Greenhill property for anonymity; she doubted he'd want to advertise where he lived to millions of subscribers. If she were selected, there would be a solid week of shooting. Meaning, Rhett would either have to disappear for the duration or run the risk of the magazine discovering who the new owner was and adding it to the article.

Not that it mattered. "Do you know how many entries they get? Hundreds, and there are a select few chosen."

"And who's to say you can't be one," Faye said. Elsie looked at her mom, the person who'd hurt her more than Axel, and wanted to cry. Here she had a shot at something real, but she was too scared to go for it. "Don't let your anger at me cost you your dream. Come meet Claire, see what she has in mind for her party, and go from there. What do you have to lose?"

CHAPTER SIX

Dating Tips from Elsie Dodd
Make sure you're the crazy one.

Rhett woke with a start, heart pounding out of his chest, sweat beading on his forehead, and a familiar feeling of displacement clogging his throat. He had absolutely zero idea where he was, so disoriented he couldn't tell if he was on the bus or in a hotel room. The blinds were drawn so it was too dark to tell, but then he heard the distant sounds of power tools.

Loud power tools that woke him from a dead sleep.

Running a hand down his face, he rolled over and closed his eyes. And that's when the pounding started. It sounded as if a herd of rhinos were stampeding through his house. Usually, when he was sleep deprived, nothing woke him. But lately, between his schedule and insomnia, he was lucky to get even a few hours. Today it had been—he looked at his phone and swore—two hours.

At the next bang, he tossed back the covers. Littleshit, who was curled up like Rhett's little spoon, didn't move, except to squeeze his eyes shut tightly.

"I know you're awake."

Littleshit let out a snore.

"Asshole." Rhett stood and padded into the hallway. That's when he knew he was screwed. And not in the way he'd imagined when Elsie had come up on him in that black dress and mile-high heels the other night. She'd been all fire and sass, and concealing an inspiring pair of red panties, not that he looked. The minute she started losing lace, he'd kept his eyes due north. Which was a testament to just how much a gentleman his mom raised him to be. That's not to say he didn't take a peek or two when she'd ditched the dress, but once things got real, he'd taken his role as her wingman seriously.

But today the rules had changed. She wasn't vulnerable or still reeling from the news that he was her new landlord. Nope, his little squatter was playing dirty. And he meant dirty.

The further down the steps he walked, and the closer to the kitchen he got, the stronger his admiration—and irritation—for Elsie grew. Admiration because the woman was as stubborn as she was sexy. There were a half-dozen construction lights set up, a table saw where the kitchen table should be, and enough corrugated foamcore to design an identical replica of the Taj Mahal.

She was at the island, dressed in a pair of well-worn jeans and fitted tank, which read I ENJOY ROMANTIC WALKS THROUGH THE HARDWARE STORE, and her hair pulled through the back of a ball cap—all of which were covered in a light coat of dust. It also sounded like she was running the nail gun, electric drill, and sander all at the same time—like she didn't know he'd been up writing music until sunup.

Okay, writing seemed a strong word for what had transpired. But at least he'd been inspired enough to pick up his guitar. Something that hadn't happened organically in months. There was something about this house that calmed him, grounded him in a way he hadn't felt since his divorce.

Then there was the dancing. Rhett couldn't hear what song she was listening to through her earbuds, but based on the way she was shimmying, it was some upbeat pop song. So instead of calling out her name, he decided to watch the show for a moment.

That moment turned into a minute and before he knew it, Rhett had gone from an observer to a peeper. He should have made his presence known, but then she bent over—all the way over—her head disappearing into a toolbox, her ass sticking straight up in the air, swaying back and forth.

With Elsie, there were a lot of should'ves and would'ves he'd chosen to ignore over the years. Which was why, after a long night locked in the studio, he chose to stand on the open walkway above the kitchen, spying on the enemy.

And damn, what a formidable opponent she was. She'd managed to leave traces of herself everywhere without being seen. Her perfume lingered in the air, her designs had multiplied and taken over the office and kitchen counters. And then there was her army of fuck-me pumps, which lined the front door every night.

He needed to get her out of the house before another *almost* moment presented itself. Because if she hadn't been three martinis in, that almost moment might have turned into a would-be kiss. And that would further complicate an already complicated situation.

Elsie straightened with a tiny razor and a circular ruler in hand. Using the ruler, she made some complicated calculations, compared them to a sheet of paper that had all kinds of numbers and equations on it, then painstakingly sliced off a miniscule piece of white foamboard. It was a single stair, he realized as she glued it to a larger foam structure that looked like a dead ringer for the sketches of the recording studio he'd seen the other night.

He didn't know how long he stood there watching her—didn't care. All he knew was that she had a world-class ass. Now, Rhett had been all over the world, and he considered himself an ass-connoisseur, and he could say with great authority that when it came to Elsie, there was no competition.

There was a time when Rhett felt like, no matter now ridiculous, that he was in a non-stop competition with Axel for her attention. He'd never crossed the line and he'd never inserted himself between their relationship, but it was hard not to compare himself to the guy who'd won her heart. Comparing himself to a physically available man didn't do anyone any favors. Rhett had made his decision, hard as it was, then moved on. And Elsie had done the same.

Yet now they were sharing three-thousand square feet and she was no longer Axel's. Didn't mean she could be his. Rhett didn't do regrets and he didn't live in the past. The proven way to achieve in his industry was to maintain a steady relationship with the future. The days were flying by, and he wasn't any closer to buttoning up the album. He had nine solid tracks but was still down three. Not to mention, he was missing a song strong enough to be his first single. It had to appeal to the Subtle Warfare's existing audience while attracting a new fanbase—and that took the perfect song. And writing the perfect song was proving to be impossible.

So then why was he standing there, in nothing but his pajama bottoms and bedhead, smiling like an idiot while she was making enough noise to wake the neighborhood?

Not wanting to give her the satisfaction of knowing her plan worked, Rhett decided to leave, except it was too late.

Elsie happened to look up at the exact moment he'd turned, and their gazes locked.

She didn't look shocked or surprised or any of the expected expressions one would give when waking in on one's roomie. In fact, she looked rather smug. With an innocent smile, she went back to centering a blueprint on the foamboard.

"I'm guessing you're in violation of one of the local noise ordinances," he hollered over the sound of the wood sander, which was going for no reason.

Elsie pointed to the earbuds in her ears. "What was that? I can't hear you."

To prove it, she revved the sander a few times before shutting it off and smiling up at him.

"What's with the noise?"

"Progress," was all she said, but he could barely hear her over some drilling coming from the back of the house.

"Aren't you afraid you're going to wake the neighborhood? The sun's not even up."

She looked over her right shoulder, then her left, and shrugged—all innocence. "You're up. I'm up. We're all up. So I don't see the problem. Do you see a problem?"

Yeah, there was a big problem. Starting with the amused glimmer in her mesmerizing green eyes and ending with the way his body was reacting to her.

"No problems from where I stand, Ms. D," a bulldozer of a man, with barbells for arms, said as he walked through the kitchen. He was also staring at Elsie's hypnotic ass.

Oh, there was a problem all right. First, there was the fact that his house, which had been in a state of dormant refurbishing, was now in full-on remodel. Then there was the way that every time he looked at her all he could think about was what color thong she had on today. And finally, the way she was looking at him as if waiting for him to react had a little stubborn streak rearing its competitive head.

"What's that?" he pointed to the human forklift.

"That's Big Pete."

"Who's Big Pete?"

"Hey, man. Big fan." Big Pete gave a thumbs up as he walked by, balancing a set of four-by-fours over a single shoulder. Behind him a team holding sheetrock walked by, accidently banging the wall hard enough to leave a dent.

"My bad," the smaller of the two said, giving Elsie a shy smile.

Elsie, he noticed, didn't even look up from her work. Which was odd. Elsie was a hands-on enforcer of clean and quality work when it came to her crews. She'd been renovating the kitchen a few years back during that barbecue, and he'd seen her in action. She was meticulous and laser focused when it came to her work. The world could be under siege, and she would work straight through it.

"Why aren't you losing your shit? Normally you'd be all over someone for this." Normally she'd also be at the helm, driving the ship. As for this ship, it was hitting icebergs right and left. It was as if they'd been sent in with a location but no map.

"Oh, this isn't my problem," she said. "First, the room is on your side of the easement, so technically *this* is your problem. Second, it isn't my crew."

"I thought the music room was yours?"

She shrugged. "No time for lessons since I have such a narrow window. So why be selfish." She looked up with a smart-ass grin. "So it's all yours. You're welcome."

He snatched her mug of coffee and followed Tweedle Dee and Tweedle Dumber to the back of the house where they'd torn down the back wall of the music room. There were tarps everywhere, dust in the air, and nail guns sounding off like a twenty-one-gun salute.

The destruction was out of control.

He felt Elsie at his back, could smell her shampoo. Then she put a hand on his shoulder, steadying herself as she peeked over him, putting her front directly against his back, and his body manned up.

Completely oblivious to how close they were, she said, "Looking good, Big Pete. I really like the color choice."

Pete took off his hat to wipe his forehead. "Thanks, Ms. D. They were out of Modern Eggshell, so I called Ms. Margo and she approved Igloo Frost."

"Bold choice," she said, and Rhett glowered at her over his shoulder. He could tell by her tone that she hated it. Just like he could tell by her sunny smile that she wasn't as on board with the situation as she was letting on.

"Bold choice?" he whispered. "You hate it."

She took her mug back and took a sip. "Not my house, remember? You're the official owner of an Igloo Frost music room."

"A room I have to be able to work in and Igloo Frost sounds, well, frosty."

"Well, then you might want to tell the crew."

He looked from Pete to Elsie. "Whose crew it is?"

She took another sip of coffee. "Somebody named Margo?"

Rhett sighed. He should have known his mother would be involved somehow.

"They knocked on the door around seven thirty," she continued, "had fresh doughnuts in hand, and said they were here to start on the exterior fences, but since it's drizzly I suggested they start inside today and save the security fence for a sunnier day."

Rhett looked out the window to find clear skies. He ran a hand down his face, noticing he had three days' growth. "You just let them in?"

"They seemed legitimate. Why don't we ask," she said. "Hey, Big Pete, are you a legit contractor?"

"Even got a license to prove it. Can give you my number if you'd like to call the office." Big Pete stopped mid-lift, his arms bulging under the weight of the beam, then looked at Elsie with cow eyes. "Or I can give you my cell, in case you need anything."

Before Elsie could answer, Rhett heard himself say, "She's good."

Big Pete didn't back down, he stood there looking like some kind of tool-belted superhero, staring Rhett down. And he was willing to fight to the death. The man looked like the Hulk and Thor had a baby.

There was a moment of posturing, where Rhett moved closer to Elsie, and Big Pete took the temperature of the room. After a silent testosterone-fueled battle over the fair maiden's hand, Big Pete wisely went back to his job of making Rhett's world chaos.

"Whatever she's paying you, I'll give you double," he offered Big Pete.

Big Pete stopped to consider that, then laughed, big and booming. "No can do, the lady said that under no circumstances could we stop."

He jabbed a thumb at Elsie. "This lady?"

"Nope."

"See, told you," Elsie said, then disappeared back into the kitchen.

Shit. His mom had threatened to get his house ready for his arrival home. He'd assured her that he was a big boy and could handle things on his own just fine. But that wasn't how things in his family worked. Especially when it came to his mom, who was devoted to her sons and invading their privacy. She took love and micromanaging to new heights.

"Did Ms. Margo happen to mention that you weren't supposed to start on the inside of the house until the end of the summer?"

"That was the original start date," Big Pete informed him. "But she moved it up to today."

"Well, I'm moving it back to August."

Pete shrugged like he didn't give a shit what Rhett wanted. "I have to consult my client."

So Pete was doubling as contractor and spy. His mother would approve.

"I'm your client."

"You don't pay my salary."

Oh, Rhett would. His mom might have arranged the renovations, but every cent would come out of Rhett's pocket. "I own the house and I need you to pack up and move out for another few months. Or start on the fence outside."

"Actually, I own the house for now. Check the escrow terms," Elsie said. "I took the last few days to educate myself on the terms of the agreement. And while you get to live on the premises, it is still my house for another two weeks. Oh, and fun fact, you bought this as an 'as is' so any and all renovations made to the house from here forward is financially on you." She looked at the crew. "Carry on, fellas."

"Carry on?" Rhett said as he followed her into the kitchen. "You know how I need quiet to work."

"You know, I could have had this all handled for you. But I offered you my services and you declined."

His gaze ran the length of her, taking in every inch. "Can you define what service we're talkin'? That way I can form an appropriate answer."

She rolled her eyes and turned her back to walk into the kitchen. Rhett followed her, purposefully brushing past her on his way to grab a mug. Since she was in front of the cabinet, he reached over her head, boxing her in slightly, his bicep brushing her arm. She shivered and he grinned.

That's what I thought.

Not budging, he reached down and opened the drawer for his coffee grounds to find it empty. He checked the surrounding drawers. Empty.

She turned in his arms, bringing them breathably close. Her eyes went wide and her mouth formed the perfect circle of faux surprise.

"Whoops," she said. "I'm sorry–not sorry that I drank the last of the pot. And you might want to add coffee beans to the grocery list. You're out. Caffeinating a crew of eight can do that."

He didn't move, holding her hostage, or was she holding him hostage with those green eyes? Whichever, neither shifted—not even an inch. They stood there, steadily holding locked gazes.

He let his eyes roam down and back up, smiling when he noticed the pulse at the base of her neck hammering. Her face was flushed, and her mouth parted on a rush of air. "You okay, Red?"

She cleared her throat. "Fine."

"You sure, you're looking a little pink around the edges." She was also looking at his lips as if she was as curious about him as he was about her.

Chin up, she shifted a little closer, pressing all the way forward, her chest flush with his, and for one mind-blowing, heart-stopping, best-day-of-his-life moment, he thought she was actually going to kiss him. Then her eyes narrowed. "It's an allergic reaction to toxic dick syndrome."

He laughed out loud. "You might want to find a pill for that, because from now until you move out, I'm going to be right over your shoulder."

Smiling, he picked up her steaming mug, which was on the counter behind her. She reached for it, but he was quicker. Before she could snatch it back, he took a hearty sip.

With a prim huff, she turned back to her work and back to ignoring him. Which was why he sat next to her and bumped her hips with his. She bumped back. "Do you mind? I don't have time for distractions. I'm meeting my new client at two in the Pearl District, it's a second meeting, and this isn't anywhere close to done."

"Is this the recording studio?"

She glared up at him. "I thought you just looked at the first few pages."

"I may have glimpsed a few sketches on the wall while you were playing pink-thong roulette. Which, by the way, I think landed on the right choice for you." He looked down at her legs, the way her denim hugged every curve drove him crazy. "Any hint on today's choice? I hope it's bold, like peacock blue."

"What man says peacock-blue panties?"

He waggled a brow. "The kind of man who's seen peacock-blue panties?"

CHAPTER SEVEN

Dating Tips from Elsie Dodd
Forget the bad boy.
Go for the man.

Elsie wasn't a crier. If she allowed herself to give in whenever things didn't go her way, she'd be too busy wiping her tears to get anything accomplished. So worrying over her potential client's decision to meet with other more established designers, who would have extensive and impressive portfolios, would be pointless.

What she needed was a plan—a solid plan to showcase her skills. But since she was short on plans, solid or otherwise, she decided to consult Ben and Jerry for advice. She was two pity scoops in when she felt the energy in the air shift. It practically crackled.

"Is it safe to come out?" Rhett asked from the entry.

Not wanting to let him see how upset she was over something as silly as a maybe, she dialed up the smart-ass. "Depends on if you're clothed or not."

"You brave enough to find out?"

Oh, bravery didn't even factor into the equation. It was more raw, animalistic curiosity that had her turning around and, *lordy,* her mouth went dry—which was the opposite of what was happening down below.

He was insanely handsome, his hair just-from-the-shower finger-combed, his shirt sticking to his damp skin. And those eyes, those all-seeing eyes, had a hint of boyish mischief.

"You can put that," she jabbed the spoon at his smile, "away. It doesn't work on me anymore."

"So then you admit it once worked on you," he said with a flicker of amusement and something more concerning.

Interest.

Rhett, of the America's Sexiest Man Alive variety, was teasing her in a very playful and flirty way.

"You know, my grandma warned me about men whose wardrobe is bigger than mine."

He shrugged. "Easy fix. You watch as I try on every piece of clothing I own and decide what to get rid of. Then I watch as you try on your closet. I say we start with your underwear drawer."

Her laugh rang hollow and that's when his smile faded. He studied her for a long moment and she knew when *he* knew she was upset because his expression went from *How you doin'?* to *How are you doing?* in the span of a glance. Then there was this protective glimmer that made her heart skip a beat.

"You want to talk about it?" he asked. She held up the ice cream carton. "I see. You've already sought counsel."

Kicking off her heels, she hopped up on the island, her dress riding up her legs a tad. If he noticed, he didn't make a comment, just turned on that warm, lean-on-me smile he'd given her so many times before. Except this time it felt different.

"A crappy day at the office. You?"

"Crappy day at the office," he said, his words having edges like he was too tired to mask his emotions. Which was fair since hers were all over the place. A setup for disaster.

The smart thing to do would be to take Ben and Jerry on a nice date to a hot bubble bath. But she wasn't feeling all that smart. In fact, she stuck the spoon in the ice cream and held it out in invitation.

He lifted a questioning brow like, *You sure?* and she gave the carton a *Why not* wiggle. He padded toward her, leaning a hip against the counter and taking the spoon straight from the carton, then took a bite. She was mesmerized by the way his lips curled around the spoon—the same spoon she'd just had in her mouth. "So, your meeting?"

"Didn't go as planned. It started out great, then they asked to see the rest of my portfolio, which is lacking, so I picked up Ben and Jerry on the drive home."

"I saw your presentation and it was stellar," he assured her, passing back the ice cream.

"You have to say that. I'm in possession of the ice cream."

"There's another tub in the freezer."

"What flavor?" She held up a hand. "Wait, don't tell me that. My stomach can only handle one carton at a time."

He nudged her knee with his arm. "I meant what I said. And it isn't a matter of how many projects you've finished, all that matters is the quality. And your designs are unique and fresh, and they'd be idiots to go with someone else."

"That's what I said. Well, not to them, but to myself as part of my positive affirmation." She paused, horrified. "I sound like my mother." She turned to him. "You've met my mom. Did I just sound like my mom?"

His gaze tracked down to her bare legs, and back up, so that when he met her gaze his was heated. "I promise, nothing about you is remotely like your mother."

"Thank you," she whispered. Suddenly feeling shy and out of sorts, she took a big bite of ice cream and directed the conversation back to a safe topic. "It wasn't a no, just a not-sure-you're-the-girl-for-me kind of response." After licking the spoon, she set the carton between them on the counter. "What sucks is that you're right, I can rock that job. A life with a musician, the massive amounts of time I spent in recording studios to be supportive, it all prepared me for this specific project."

She knew that out of all the designers her experiences were unique to her, a life that few people not only get to live, but also get to look behind the scenes. So while she might be the new interior architect on the block, she was the most qualified.

"Sounds like you're a perfect match. But sometimes people have perfect right in front of them and somehow miss it."

She was quiet for a moment, touched and terrified by what he'd said. She could gloss over it, but she wanted to know, no needed to know, what his take on perfect was. "Was Stephanie your perfect?"

"I used to think so, but the further I get from my divorce, the more I realize how ill-suited we were for each other." He looked her in the eyes. "Even so, it hurts like a bitch that I failed at the one thing my brothers and parents got so right."

"Just because it didn't work the first-time around, doesn't mean it can't the next time," she said quietly.

"Do you believe that? Do you see a second chance after all this? Because I can't even contemplate going through that kind of pain again."

Elsie believed wholeheartedly in true love and marriage, she'd seen it work for her friends. She just didn't think it was possible for her. She was a third-generation divorcée from men suffering from slippery dick syndrome. She didn't even know what healthy love looked like.

"No. I'm a total enabler for my friends when it comes to love and relationships, but even the thought of going on another date makes my palms sweat."

"I didn't know you were dating," he said casually.

"I'm not, but my grandma didn't get the memo. She ambushed me at family dinner with a date, who ended the evening by asking my mom out for a movie."

A blink-and-you'll-miss-it flash of anger tinted his expression. "The guy's a dick."

She waved a dismissive hand, which she didn't feel. Sure, she and Huey were mismatched and had zero chemistry, but how many women could say that their first post-divorce date ended with her partner falling all over himself to impress his date's mom?

"Based on his tiny hands, calling him a dick is a big over-statement." As she'd hoped, he laughed. "Now that I've won the crappiest week crown, why don't you tell me about your day. How come you didn't write?"

"How do you know I didn't write?"

She glanced down at his very large, very manly hands. "When you're in creative mode your fingers are constantly in motion, even when you're not holding a guitar." She moved her fingers and, ever so slightly, strummed the air.

He lifted his hands as if they were no longer connected to his body. "I didn't even know I did that."

She shrugged. "That's how I knew you were a musician when we met that first night."

"The same night you told me you didn't date musicians."

She didn't. She'd had a strict off-limits rule where musi-cians were concerned. Growing up with an absent father, who put his music before his daughter, Elsie wanted some-thing more stable for her future. Someone who would be there for dinner, someone she'd wake up to every morning.

But she'd broken her rule for Rhett. One weekend, she'd promised herself. What was the harm?

Elsie discovered that no-strings relationships weren't in her genetic makeup. That weekend taught her that she was a to-her-core, no-exceptions, long-term kind of woman.

Suddenly her head began to throb. She told herself that it was brain freeze or the long and disappointing day, but that was a lie.

"Writing has always been your escape. What do you think changed?"

"I'm trying to escape too many things," he whispered, and her heart gave a tiny bump. "That's part of the reason I'm home, to figure out what's going on. In the beginning, I told myself it was the chaos surrounding my divorce, but it's far enough behind me that I can't use it as an excuse anymore. I mean, I spent six hours in the studio and didn't write a single useable note."

"What about the song you were tinkering with the other day?"

"I can't seem to get past the chorus."

"What do you normally do when you're stuck?"

"Hell if I know. I've never been stumped."

"Ever?" His expression was one of frustration and help-lessness. She handed him the overflowing spoon. "Okay, what do you love about being a musician?"

"Usually, it's the creative process. But it's hard to write about love when love didn't work out for me."

"You wrote about love before Steph, you can write about it now. Or maybe write about something different. Maybe heart-break," she said. "Or try a change in scenery. Find a stage."

She could see him pondering the idea, then he shook his head. "It's not like I can stand on a corner like I used to and play for passersby. I'd be mobbed."

"You're a smart guy, you'll figure it out." She patted his cheek and at the innocent contact, a warmth spread through her. He felt it too because his gaze jerked to hers. She immediately dropped her hand.

"Maybe a corner without all the drilling and pounding," he teased.

"The studio is soundproof. And I know this because when Axel would have the guys over for poker and I needed to work, I'd disappear down there for some quiet."

"Yeah, well the insulation wasn't thick enough to keep out Big Pete, who likes to sing when he works. Britney Spears is his top pick of tunes, in case you were wondering."

She snorted. "He did not."

"I came up for lunch and caught him doing the dance moves while using the nail gun in rhythm to the bass."

She bit back a smile. "Why not tell him to keep it down?"

"Because the guy is built like a tank, and he clearly doesn't like to be told what to do."

Panic made her forget the ice cream. "Please tell me that you didn't allow him to stray any more from the plans."

Rhett spooned off a bite and, around a mouthful of ice cream, he said, "He was more interested in making plans with you. In fact, he stayed an extra hour, waiting for you to walk through that door."

Elsie groaned. Her recent dating experience merely confirmed what she'd believed—the last thing she needed was to go on another date. No matter how good looking the guy.

She snatched the spoon back and took a heaping mouthful.

"Don't worry, Red, I told him you were on a dick-free diet."

She choked on the ice cream. "You did not." He looked so proud of himself. "How do you know I don't want to go out with him?"

"The look on your face right now." He moved closer until his thigh brushed hers and she wondered if he could tell what she was thinking right then. If so, she'd be in trouble. "We might not have seen a lot of each other recently, but a gym rat who bench presses pianos for a living isn't your cup of tea."

"What is my cup of tea?" *You,* her hormones said.

"I don't know, you tell me since you've been staring at my lips for the past few minutes."

What was wrong with her?

Her sex-free diet, that's what. Maybe her grandma was right, maybe she needed to put herself out there. Not with Rhett, or Big Pete, but with some good-looking nine-to-fiver searching for nothing more than a single night of fun. Then again, look at where the last one-night stand had ended.

Heartbroken and left to wonder if maybe she'd done something wrong, that's where. Rhett ghosting her had left its mark and, while she didn't like to think that she was still affected by it, being around him like this reminded her of the reason she'd taken him up on that offer all those years back. It also reminded her how easily someone can walk into and out of her life.

Good thing that she was no longer that naive, pie-in-the-sky, trusting girl looking for validation from men. She was a smart, worldly, grown-ass woman who knew better than to trust her hormones when it came to something as important as the opposite sex.

Didn't mean her heart didn't flutter when Rhett flashed that playboy grin her way. The double-barreled dimpled grin that somehow made her panties want to drop to the floor. She'd spent exactly three nights alone with Rhett and all three times they'd wound up in bed together. A fact that didn't bode well for their current living arrangements.

She picked up the carton and held it possessively to her chest. "You do know that you're on my side of the house."

"As long as my easement allows me to view the fashion show."

Before she could say another word, not that she knew what to say to that, her phone rang. She glanced at her screen and it was her grandma, who was supposed to be at bingo. Harriet never gave in to distraction when she was on a winning streak.

Her heart pounded as she answered. "Grandma, are you okay?"

"Just fleeced Clifford in double down bingo. Played ten cards, that's the trick. Increase the cards, increase the winnings. Play big to win big. Although watching that sourpuss spurt out cheating accusations, then being removed from the premises was the highlight. Although I was removed too."

Clifford was Harriet's neighbor and nemesis. After cutting down an apple tree, which split their property line, Harriet launched an all-out war. Reporting him to the community board, even calling the cops when he snatched one of Harriet's heirloom tomatoes. In turn, he reported her hand-painted Mother Earth mobile as visual vandalism and tried to have it towed away.

"Did you move around his chips again?" Harriet remained tightlipped on the subject. "I take that as a yes."

"He tried to get me arrested for indecent exposure for gardening in my own back yard. So I told the cops he was a voyeur. He wouldn't have seen the goods had he not been peeking over his fence."

Elsie didn't bother to remind her grandmother that her yard was in direct view of Clifford's porch. In the background, an auctioneer started calling off numbers. "I thought you were removed from the premises?"

"Changed my wig and snuck back in just like when you were little and I got busted for using phony cards. I used to put you in that stroller and wheel you to bingo." Nostalgia grew thick in her grandma's voice as if this were a normal grandmother/granddaughter memory. "People were so busy cooing you up, they missed important turning points in the game."

Some of Elsie's earliest memories were at the bingo house or casino with her grandma. She'd sit on Harriet's lap and Harriet would let her punch the stamp or pull the lever. It was a miracle Elsie didn't have a gambling habit. "Why are you calling?"

"Oh, I nearly forgot. A gift will be on your doorstep any minute," she said.

"Grandma, you don't have to get me anything."

"Think of it as a homecoming present of sorts."

"That's so sweet."

At that exact moment the doorbell rang. "Oh, he's already there."

Elsie froze. "What do you mean *he*? You said *it*." Elsie closed her eyes. "You got me a second *him*?"

"How many hims are there?" Rhett said, but she ignored him. He leaned back against the island watching the show like the latest rom-com.

"Of course I did. Clearly, Huey didn't get the job done and you need an orgasm in your life."

"If you need help with that, I know a guy," Rhett said, and she shushed him.

"Your shoulders are up to your ears all the time," Harriet went on. "And your mouth is pinched. So I'm sending in the B team. And he has massive hands, looks like a bricklayer with the mind of a scholar. Also, played football in college, so there aren't any doubts about how he ranks in that department."

"Grandma!"

"Ding dong, Red," Rhett said. "Twenty bucks says he's got a man bun."

"Says the guy dressed like a frat boy."

He looked down and frowned. "So I like vintage rock shirts. They're my trademark."

Funny, she thought his trademark was his ass.

"I don't need a man," she said to Harriet. "I have my own job, make my own money. Own my own house." She cupped her hand over the mouthpiece so Harriet couldn't hear, and whispered to Rhett, "And I can give myself an orgasm whenever I want."

"That sounds better than the fashion show. Let me know when and where and I'll bring the popcorn."

Elsie sent him a long glare. The doorbell rang a second time and she looked down at herself. She was still dressed for the success that she didn't achieve today. She sighed. "Grandma, this is a bad time."

"There's never a bad time for love."

While Elsie could argue a case against that ill-founded statement, she was more concerned with who was at the door, which rang for a third time. Before she could grab his arm, Rhett was on the move.

She heard a distant, "Who are you," then a returned, "I'm Elsie's date. Who are you?"

She could almost hear Rhett's chest puff out. "What are your plans and what time are you bringing her home?"

She was not in any mental or emotional state for this date. But she couldn't stomach the idea of standing that poor guy up. She knew what it felt like to be disappointed and would never do that to someone else. Plus, if she went out with Mr. B-team then maybe her grandma would let up on the dating thing.

"Fine, I'll go, but if the B-team can't bring it, I have zero interest in a C-team. Deal?"

"Why bring in another gentleman when this one fits you so well," Harriet said. "He works at the university, loves animals, and doesn't know how to play a single instrument."

"We're going to a music festival and I'm not sure," she heard B-team say to Rhett.

So much for a no-music date. "While that's all nice, you didn't answer the question," Elsie pointed out.

Harriet did not make her stance clear on the topic, but in the background Rhett was making his opinions crystal clear.

"I know that festival, know the kind of date that can take place there. Who's your designated driver?"

Feeling bad that B-team was being interrogated by the fun gestapo and knowing just how far Rhett would go, Elsie hopped off the counter. "Grandma, I gotta go. No more dates from this day forward. Understood?" Before Harriet could give her advice on how to relax her pelvic floor for better sex, Elsie disconnected.

"I'm only going to have a few," B-Team said.

"You mean none?"

"Hey aren't you—?"

"Nope." The door slammed loud enough to rattle the windows.

"What are you doing?' she whispered, reaching for the door handle, but he put his hand on the door above hers, keeping it shut.

"Saving you from another bad date." He moved closer, his body caging her in slightly. The air around them sizzled with awareness. He put his other hand above her head and suddenly he was closer. Except it hadn't been him who'd moved, it had been her.

Her gaze dropped to his lips and he grinned. "What if I don't want to be saved?" she whispered.

"Good thing, because I'm as far away from a prince as there is." His eyes slowly roamed down to her toes and back, making a few stops along the way. "You are so damn beautiful."

Her heart melted at the compliment and her determination to keep her distance diminished. Maybe it was their honest conversation or maybe it was the way he was looking at her, as if he wanted to kiss every inch of her body, but her insides sighed a big *oh my*.

"This is a bad idea. We're a bad idea. We can't even agree on whose house this is, how will we agree on what a kiss would mean?"

He didn't budge and neither did she. "I don't know."

There was a knock and she jumped, but he held his position.

"This is going to happen, Red. There's no way we can live together and keep our hands off each other. Not now."

"What changed?" she breathed.

"You could be mine."

It was as if a cold bucket of water had been thrown over the moment. "I don't want to be anyone's except my own. I came home to find myself, not find myself in another complicated relationship." There was another knock. "I have a date waiting on the other side of the door."

He paused, a shocked expression overtaking him. "Do you really want to go on this date? If so, I'll move."

"I don't know. While you've been traveling the world, I've been home, trying to balance my career and marriage and failing at both." And while she was mad at Axel, she was angrier at herself. She'd let him take the lead and then he left her in the dust. A hard lesson to learn. When there are two dreamers in a relationship, one had to become the realist.

So did she want to go on this date? Not really. But it was smarter than staying home with a fellow dreamer and sharing their secrets and deepest desires. "I'd at least like to meet B-team."

Without another word, he stepped back. But she could tell he didn't want to. She saw a flicker of disappointment before those walls slammed shut. "Then let's meet B-team."

"Does he really have a man bun?" she asked, teasing.

He smiled, a fun, easygoing, no harm–no foul smile. "You'll have to find out." With a playful wink, he opened the door and a knot of relief and confusion tightened in her chest.

She channeled Faye the Millionaire Whisperer and said, "Hi, I'm Elsie." Then took one glance at B-team, with his suave vibe, dark jeans, and well-fitted button-down.

"The name's Pierce. It's nice to meet you."

"Sorry about that. I forgot to let him out today," she said to B-team, who, in fact, did not have a man bun, but sleek black hair. She looked over at Rhett and stuck her hand out. With a groan he handed over a twenty.

He leaned in, "He probably has the IQ of a sloth."

"It is you," Pierce said excitedly to Rhett, sticking his hand out. When Rhett didn't move to shake, Elsie stepped on his toe.

"Ow," he said, then grinned. Then begrudgingly, he extended his hand. "Rhett," was all he said.

B-team beamed. "Wow, I mean, what are the odds. This is kismet." He looked at Elsie, who'd become the third wheel in an unrequited bromance.

"Kismet," Rhett said—to Elsie.

"I recently read a scientific study about how guitarist brains are different than others. They have the ability to sync their heart rate variability to the music while playing." When no one said a word, Pierce went a little red. "Sorry, I have a doctorate in music theory."

"Of course you do," Rhett mumbled.

Elsie quietly whispered to Rhett, "That will cost you another twenty."

"I'm short on cash."

"We have different definitions of being short on cash," she whispered.

"Well, I hope you two have a good time," he said, louder. And for a moment she wondered what would have happened if she'd taken Rhett up on that kiss.

CHAPTER EIGHT

Dating Tips from Elsie Dodd
A date is a two-person exchange.
Ignore the peanut gallery.

R hett had learned how to play the piano before he could walk. Was still in diapers when he got his first guitar. And was barely into elementary school when he discovered the ladies.

He still played piano, never left home without his guitar, and he still had ladies on the brain—tonight it was a specific lady. Which was how he found himself walking down the street with his guitar in hand and his focus firmly on business.

Elsie might be as tempting as a sexy summer fling in that flirty dress and strappy heels, with those mile-long legs and hand-cupping curves, but she was a temptation he couldn't give in to. Because behind that brave face was a raw vulnerability that had *handle with care* written all over it.

And while he could finesse the strings, Rhett didn't have the gentlest hands when it came to women. Just look at his marriage. His relationship with Steph had been hot from the word go and never slowed down. They went from dating to married in less than six months. But then the honeymoon period ended in a matter of weeks when their schedules came into play. Rhett tried to prioritize his marriage but between a national tour and other job-related obligations, not to mention Steph's commitments as a fashion influencer, going the distance wasn't a possibility. Getting them in the same time zone was hard enough, let alone in the same city.

If picking up the pieces after his divorce hadn't taught Rhett the downfalls of overcommitting, then his current situation did.

It took concentration, hard work, and laser focus to make an album and pull off a stadium tour. Unlike most of his brothers, his job wasn't a nine-to-five. His day started when most people were getting ready for bed. A stadium tour was exhausting, required his full concentration, and wreaked havoc on relationships.

It also didn't leave room for complicated cuties. Plus, this complicated cutie was his friend's ex. A clear reason to keep his distance, since Axel had been positioning himself to get his new band to open for Subtle Warfare. It wasn't going to happen. Rhett already had an opening act, but that didn't mean that every few months Axel wouldn't reach out—testing the waters.

In fact, he'd reached out today, which was why Rhett found himself at Stout looking for some advice. And maybe a stage to play on.

The sky was fading from pink to orange as the early-summer sun dipped behind the skyline, creating a silhouette over downtown Portland. When he reached his family's bar, he walked through the back entrance to the family-only section.

With enough recognizable faces and names in the Easton clan, Owen had the brilliant idea to create a roped off section so that the brothers could enjoy time together and throw back a cold one in the place their father had built from the ground up. For Rhett, it was also a place that reminded him of who he was—something that was getting harder and harder to keep in the forefront of his mind.

He wore so many hats, had so many people depending on him; he was being strangled by obligations and expectations. On the best of days, he felt like he was treading water, most days he felt like he was being pushed under.

Today, in that kitchen, with Elsie, he'd felt neither.

Ball cap pulled low, three days' growth on his face, Rhett slid onto a bar stool and did a quick glance around the room. The place was packed. Not surprising since the PGA Open Championship had started and people were looking to watch a game with family and friends. That's not why Rhett had come. He'd left the blessed privacy of his house to go to an overcrowded bar where, once recognized, people would hound him for everything from an autograph to a picture, because he needed to take his mind off what was transpiring on that date and get it back on his music.

He was also hungry for a little taste of home. And the one place, other than his mom's kitchen, that served meatloaf with smashed potatoes was Stout.

"Does Mom know that you're out past bedtime?" Owen asked, coming over. He leaned across the bar and gave Rhett a brotherly clap on the back.

"Does Mom know that you're bailing on family dinner this weekend to go on a trip to the family cabin without her?" he asked, knowing that Owen and his fiancée were taking a romantic weekend to Mount Hood.

Panicked, Owen glanced around the bar. "Lower your voice. That T-R-I-P is a surprise and no, I didn't tell Mom because she can't keep a secret to save her life. Work is already cockblocking me this week, I don't need to add Mom to the list."

Rhett thought about that for a moment, then heard himself ask, "How does it work?"

"Bro, if you're asking me how it works, then you have bigger problems than I thought. I mean, we all took health ed in high school."

"I'd already moved to practical application by then. Good to know that the class helped you so much," he said, and Owen gave him the finger. "But seriously, between your schedules and responsibilities, how do you two make it work?"

Owen looked at Rhett as if he were relationship inept. Hell, maybe he was.

"Showing up. And I don't mean popping your head in, but being present. Every night, no matter what my day has been, we meet on the patio and share a cup of tea and watch the sun set and share the best and worst parts of our day. Every morning I cook her breakfast in bed. My job is to make sure she knows that I'm there for her and that she's loved."

"And the mornings you can't be there?"

Owen shrugged. "Don't know. There hasn't been one."

Easy advice from someone who lived and worked in the same building and shared a bed with his fiancée. Try romancing someone when the days of the week blend together and every morning is a different city, different bed. A different life from anyone in his family. The guys on the road got it, but unless you lived it, it was hard to relate. The closest anyone in his family came to understanding the obstacles was Clay—and the guy, weeks after meeting the love of his life, had announced his retirement. Rhett wasn't anywhere near ready to retire. He was just getting started and, if things went his way, he'd have another few decades of living the dream.

Earlier, Elsie had been able to relate, but from the other person's perspective and it sounded rough. Lonely.

"Shouldn't you be at home working?" Owen asked. "Or do your overly insured hands need a little time out?"

"That was my thought," Gage said, taking a seat next to Rhett. "How's it going?"

Rhett sighed. "It's not. Tell me you have better news."

"I heard back from Brax Steven," Gage said, and Rhett's heart thumped loudly.

Brax Steven was one of the top producers in the world. He'd started out as a club DJ in Europe and transitioned over to music producer.

Last year, Brax had reached out to Rhett, asking if he wanted to do a collaboration. It was the first time Rhett had stepped out as a solo artist and the song had been a commercial sensation, launching him into the next stratosphere. It also helped Subtle Warfare gain a larger fanbase, but it was the catalyst for Rhett going solo for an album.

Working with Brax again would be incredible. It got Rhett thinking that maybe that's what he needed, to partner with a creative person on another collaboration. He already had the rough idea for their single and he knew that working with Brax would make it a hit. So he'd gone to his label with the idea. They'd loved it.

Now it was up to his agent, Gage, to make it happen. Rhett knew it took some finagling and negotiating, not to mention some scheduling conflicts and outstanding commitments, but Rhett had faith in his brother's ability.

If it could happen, Gage would make it happen. And based on his brother's giddy expression, he'd worked his magic and now Rhett needed to get his ass in gear.

"He's in?" Rhett asked, but he already knew the answer and, man, it took everything he had to stay seated. It was as if a surge of energy shot through him.

"Oh, he's in. Not only is he pumped about working with you again, he brought up producing the entire album."

Rhett felt a grin form. This was the best news he'd had in weeks. "The entire album?" Rhett had been hoping he'd produce a single song, two tops. But the whole album? "This shit is really going to happen, isn't it?"

Ten years ago, Rhett had lost his father to cancer. Disillusioned and angry at the world, he'd decided to channel all his energy into music. He'd said goodbye to the days of jamming with his buddies and got serious about making a go at having a professional career as a musician. He also made a go out of making his dad proud.

He'd known the next step was to start playing his own music and stop covering other people's. And that meant learning how to really write a hit song. His dad had given a lot of acts their start playing during open mic night at Stout, so Rhett called in some favors and started gigging and working with some of the older guys who'd been around the block a time or two. Then he went about hand-selecting a new band.

It took a few years, but Rhett finally wrote his first hit, earning the band an American Music Award and putting Subtle Warfare on the map. From there their popularity grew, and before long their band was a household name.

Now Rhett was looking to write an album that strayed from the band's solid mainstream sound and add a little rock and R&B vibes to the music. Subtle Warfare's next album would have to outshine their previous one, but Rhett's solo album would have to show growth and a level of mastery that proved he was there to stay. And all of that came down to the quality of the music—a task that, for once, fell squarely on Rhett's shoulders.

"His schedule is as crazy as yours, so he barely has a small slice of time."

A bad feeling settled in Rhett's chest. With only a handful of songs completed, and a guy like Brax on board, the pressure was bigger than ever. "What are we talking?"

"He has a two-week opening."

Rhett wasn't a guy who gave in to nerves, if he were he'd never step foot on the stage. But right then his nerves were beading on his forehead. "Jesus, that's a tight schedule."

"There's more," Gage said. "The hard start date is four weeks."

"Four weeks? I can't get enough material in four weeks."

"You already have two albums' worth of music," Gage pointed out. "And they're good."

"Not good enough." Rhett ran a hand down his face. He'd wanted this, but now that it was here he wasn't sure he could make the cut. "I also need a band." Since he was going solo, he'd need an entirely new band, who would be on salary as opposed to how it was with Subtle Warfare where they each split royalties and earnings. "I've barely started auditioning. I still need a bassist and a drummer."

"I have a lead on a great bassist and I got a call about a drummer."

"Great. Who?"

Gage rattled off the name of a world-renowned bassist and then a world-class drummer. Something in Rhett's gut tightened. "Axel Ross is looking for a gig? What happened to his band?"

"They broke up. Something about the guitarist sleeping with Axel's girlfriend."

Well, that was solid proof that karma was alive and well. It was also proof that Axel thought they were still tight. Something that a few weeks ago Rhett would have agreed with. But somehow talking about Axel possibly being a part of the new album felt like a betrayal.

"What do you want me to tell him?"

Rhett didn't have the time or energy to deal with Axel right then. "Hold off on telling him anything right now."

Gage's eyebrows disappeared into his hair line. "Are you sure this is how you want to play it?"

"No, but I need the best, and he's one of the best."

"Maybe, but he also comes with a world of complications. You might want to think through the ramifications."

He knew what Gage was saying, just like he knew that he needed a drummer and stat. He wasn't saying he was going to hire the guy, he needed to be sure he was giving himself options in case shit fell through. "We're talking studio musicians at this point. Putting the touring band together will take longer. So let's reach out to some other folks first, then go from there."

"Your call," Gage said, as if Rhett had made the worst call since proposing to Steph three weeks into their relationship.

Rhett ran a hand down his face. "I have a lot to do and not a lot of time to do it in."

Owen looked over the bar top, all business. "You've done it before, you can do it again."

"I didn't have this kind of pressure on me before." Or this many distractions. "Did you guys know about Mom hiring a crew to renovate the house?"

"Mom may have mentioned it," Owen said with a grin.

"How the hell am I supposed to write through all that noise? People are constantly coming and going. Then there's the drilling and nail guns. They start at eight. I don't even get to bed until five."

"I heard Mom's going to come over with breakfast tomorrow to make sure you're eating properly and that you're not working too hard."

"Well, she doesn't have to worry about the last. Although I did have a spark there for a moment." A brief moment before it disappeared.

His brothers shared a knowing look. "Have you talked to that pretty redhead about moving out?" Owen asked.

Irritation pricked Rhett's neck as he remembered the smile on B-team's face when Elsie came to the door wearing that flowy number that was sweet and sophisticated in a girl-next-door kind of way. It was blue with little white dots and this deep V neckline that disappeared beneath a fitted blazer, which was held together by tiny white buttons.

She'd smiled the same smile he'd witnessed a few times before—like if she were sunny enough people would believe it. And they did. Every time. But he knew better. Saw right through her pretense. It was clear that a date was the last thing she wanted to do but she didn't want to let anyone down. And she didn't want to be stuck with him in a house that was starting to feel too small for them both. Then there was the way the air caught fire when they were in the same room.

Shit, he was in trouble.

"I'll take that as a no," Gage said and burst out laughing.

"You're laughing like I have a choice."

"Oh, you have a ton of choices but you're choosing to share a house with the one who got away."

"She isn't the one who got a way. She's just someone I knew." She might not be the one who got away, but he'd known the minute they locked eyes at that college party that they'd have history.

He'd been tracking her movements all night and when she caught him staring, she stared right back. One moment they'd been on opposite sides of the party, the next she was kissing him. No "Hi" or "What's your name," she just planted one on him.

Later, she'd told him it was a dare. As far as he was concerned, it was the best dare in the history of the world. A dare that started out with a kiss and landed them into a weekend of tangled sheets.

What?" he asked.

"You tell us," Owen said.

"You can go anywhere, literally anywhere, so why stay?" Gage held up a silencing hand. "And before you give me that 'I need a studio' BS, let me remind you that there are over twenty recording studios at your disposal in Portland alone who would drop everything to have you hang out there."

"I need my own space. I've been around people non-stop for months. I need a place that I can *be*." Being around people wasn't working. In fact, it was giving him anxiety.

Gage studied him very carefully and Rhett knew what he saw, a burnt-out musician who couldn't write a song to save his life. "You aren't alone."

He knew Gage was talking about more than a house, but he didn't want to go there. Not after the day he'd had. "I offered to move her into an Airbnb."

"Did she bite?" Owen asked.

She damn near left marks. "No."

"Maybe it's because she's being kicked out of her house."

"I'm not kicking her out. Plus, I offered to pay for the rental and rent on her house. Generous on both parts if you ask me."

Rhett would move into the rental if it had a studio. But with the giant countdown clock ticking away, he'd need every minute in his own private studio so he could create.

"What did she say when you asked her?" Owen's voice told him he knew just how it went and that he found it hilarious.

About as well as asking to see what she'd been working on. She got defensive, secretive, and stubborn as hell.

"She pretty much told me to go screw myself." Then she'd asked him about his day after confiding about hers. She was giving mixed signals and it was driving him nuts.

"Do you blame her?" Gage asked. "You're kicking her out of her house after she was kicked out of her marriage."

"From what I understand she's the one who left Axel." As he said it his gut told him there was more to the story. Not that the who mattered. Divorce was divorce and both parties suffered. And there had been a moment there, when they'd been talking about her mom, that he'd seen a brief flash of someone who'd had a hard go of it lately, who'd suffered a heartache that went beyond her divorce and understood deep disappointment and loss, but was pushing through anyway.

She was rallying, putting on a brave face when she was really feeling exposed and raw. Two things he could relate to.

"I don't think she's going to go easily." Or at all. But a part of him, the lonely part, wasn't sure how he felt about that.

"What's the guitar for?" Owen jerked a chin at Rhett's bag.

"A friend reminded me that I'm the most creative when I'm on stage, so I was hoping it was free for the next hour."

CHAPTER NINE

Dating Tips from Elsie Dodd
*Never start with coffee. Start with dessert in case
you need to make a break for it.*

The morning of the gender reveal party, with her eyes scratchy from lack of sleep, Elsie walked down the front steps of the house with an armful of INFECTED ZONE posters, two gallons of fake blood, and a light coating of sawdust. She'd backed her car up against the bottom step after her last trip across town, but that still meant nine steps to navigate with a giant plastic meat cleaver strapped to her back like a samurai sword.

She made her way to her car and managed to locate her keys and pop the trunk, only to realize that with all the boxes, there was no way the signs were going to fit. The back and passenger seats were already taken up by decorations and three zombie mannequins, all belted in safely, so she couldn't drop the seats down to make more truck space. Which brought her to the trunk, already filled with a ream of commercial plastic slit curtain and several tubs of her oatmeal and mashed banana recipe to create enough brain matter for the butcher-room she had planned.

"You know it's against community ordinance to run one of those fishbowl parties out of your house. Attracts nothing but drug dealers and nefarious people."

Elsie turned to find Ms. Gilford standing at the base of the driveway, garden clippers in hand, teeth bared in what appeared to be a smile.

"No fishbowl, just loading up some decorations for a party."

Ms. Gilford craned her neck to look inside the car. "You using your inflatable friends to access the carpool lane illegally? Cuz I gotta tell you, Mr. Gilford bought one of them dolls as a plus one. Lola. I found her in the attic. A real beauty. Blonde hair, red lips, wearing a Marilyn Monroe dress. Filed the next day. No husband of mine is going to plus-one me."

"Sounds like a solid reason for a divorce." Elsie placed the jugs of fake blood into the trunk of her SUV.

"When that son of a bitch died, I buried him with Lola. Open casket so everyone could see him and his lover. Then I punctured her with the thorns of my rose and it sounded like she was squealing. The whole neighborhood was talking about it for months." Ms. Gilford strangled a rose by the neck and clipped it off with her sheers.

"Sorry I missed it," Elsie said, unsure how to respond.

"It was a beautiful ceremony," she said. "Patrice from the Food Hub & Grub sang 'You'll Never Walk Alone,' Patty from Sip Me donated the tea and coffee, and what was left of Mr. Gilford's little blue pills we tossed in the air. They flew like rice at a wedding." Ms. Gilford walked up the drive to get a better look inside the trunk, then pointed to the blonde mannequin. "She Mr. Ross's?"

"The doll?" she asked. "God no. I rented her." And didn't that sound creepy.

"You sure? That's quite a harem in there." Ms. Gilford's quiet, assessing eyes had Elsie squirming in her steel-toed boots which, when paired with her brown leather pants and matching corset, made for the perfect zombie-slayer costume. Or the perfect pervert.

"I'm sure. Mr. Ross didn't play with dolls."

"The wives are always the last to know, honey. Nonetheless, they need to go. Inanimate people are only allowed at Christmas and Halloween. And they must be holiday appropriate. No Santa sneaking down your chimney in October."

"I don't even have a Santa."

"Let's keep it that way." Ms. Gilford went back to cutting her roses and Elsie went back to loading her car.

She was already behind, and Ms. Gilford's interrogation had cost her precious time. Claire was at the venue and the party was scheduled to start in barely under two hours, and Elsie had at least two more trips across town. Her mom was there helping Claire "visualize her desired reality" and Harriet was DJing a bar mitzvah in Vancouver. Leaving Elsie to round up her plastic zombie army alone.

She checked her phone and wondered what the time limit was before Claire was justified in publicly poo-pooing Elsie in front of the magazine editor. Not long, she imagined, since Claire had already called about Elsie's ETA twice that afternoon.

She tried to slip the signs in between the blood and foam headstones but they didn't fit, so she flipped them flat and laid them on top of the boxes. She wouldn't be able to see out of the back, but it was better than being late to her first real job in Portland. Guiding them in straight, she slid them back. Halfway in, they got stuck. Going up on her toes, she leaned on them and pushed. And pushed.

"Shit!" They didn't budge. She stomped on the ground a few times and kicked the tire, then took a deep breath and tried to recenter herself so she could think through the sleep-deprived haze.

Maybe if she stacked the mannequins like a Tetris puzzle, she could drop down one of the back seats and make it to the party in one trip.

Elsie moved the mannequins around, stacking one upside down on the other and then, not wanting to fight with getting the last mannequin back in the SUV again, she merely crawled on the doll, then reached in the back to grab the signs.

"Is this a strict quintuple or are you open to a sextuple? Asking for a friend."

Elsie looked over her shoulder, not surprised to see Rhett, his eyes twinkling with amusement as he held open the passenger door to watch the show. What was surprising was the annoying flutter that started low in her belly and bubbled upward.

The man was a menace to female hearts everywhere and he knew it.

"People put bells on their pets' collars for this exact reason," she said.

He peeked his head in, smiling as he took in the dolls next to her in the recognizable 69 position, then looked at her as she straddled the blonde doll like it was a mechanical bull. "I've never been into collars, but I'm always open to new things."

"Go away," she said, turning her attention to the back seat and away from his million-watt smile. Because divorcées who couldn't make it work with a background musician had no business getting hot and bothered by the front man.

"And miss the show?" he said. "I'd lose my man-card for that."

"How about the gentleman card?"

He gave her a crisp salute. "You're right. I should be helping. Tell me where to put my hands." She leveled him with a look. "Are you preparing for a zombie uprising?"

"I'm doing a themed party. And don't you dare try something cute, like making a surprise appearance; this is an important night to me. My mom will already be there, I don't think I can handle one more person making a scene."

"Don't worry, Red, I'll be right here in *my* house enjoying the peace and quiet," he said. "And I didn't know you did parties."

"I don't. Well, I mean I am. Just this once. My mom committed me without my permission. She forgets sometimes that I renovate, not decorate."

"I'm sorry she doesn't listen."

She shrugged casually but she felt anything but casual on the topic. In fact, she felt discouraged and like a failure. "Most people don't."

"I do."

She swallowed hard. "I remember."

Their gazes locked for a long, heated moment, then he smiled. "Does this party happen to take place at a strip club?"

"No," she said primly, then leaned further forward to tug the sign, placing her breasts in Lola 2.0's face. The sign still didn't budge. "And where are you going?"

"I was actually going to work, but I thought you could use this." He held out a to-go cup of coffee and she nearly moaned as the scent of hazelnut and vanilla wafted into her car. It smelled like morning sun and angel tears.

She'd had a cup at five that morning but had been so busy she hadn't had time to refuel. He handed it over and she nearly ripped his arm off getting it. She took a big sip. "Thank you."

"You're welcome."

Her unexpected hero wore dark gray slacks and a tie, looking fit for the cover of *GQ*, with a leather jacket that added a touch of edge to the rock star, and a pair of ocean-blue eyes that did something to her belly. They'd always reminded her of a calm, crystal-clear lake. Today they were warm, like hot summer nights.

"Now, why don't you hop out and let me see if I can help. If it doesn't fit, we can take my Rover."

She eyed him but didn't move.

He ran a hand down his face. "Good God, you are the most suspicious and stubborn woman I've ever met. I saw the other boxes in the hallway, know that you are stuffed to max capacity, and that this party is important to you otherwise you wouldn't have agreed to do it," he said. "Why did you agree?"

She closed her eyes and took in a deep breath. Here it went. "*Modern Masterpiece* magazine is dedicating an entire issue to interior architects in Portland and the senior editor is going to be at the party."

"That could be huge. Congrats. Why didn't you say anything earlier?"

She waved a hand. "Nothing's concrete and it's such a long shot."

"Els," he said in a tone that brought her right back to that weekend. Right back to the moment she told him about her dream to be a world-class interior architect featured in *Modern Masterpiece* magazine. As if his mind had taken the same nostalgic journey, he said, "You're looking at a long shot, remember? Who knew back then that I'd be this now?"

"I did," she said honestly. "Even back in college. The moment I heard you on stage I knew you were special."

He flashed her that bad-boy grin. "You think I'm special, huh?"

"Don't brush it off." She put a hand to his chest and pushed. He didn't move and neither did her hand—which stayed steadily on his pec. "I'm being serious."

"So am I." He placed his hand over hers and she shivered. The jolt was enough to have her pulling it back. "Just from your sketches and what you've done to this house," he said in a tone that carried a genuine belief. It made her wonder if maybe she did have a legit shot at being chosen. They were going to choose ten people, why not her?

He looked over his shoulder and she followed his gaze to her house. It represented three years of her life.

Three years of hard work and passion. She'd invested every last dime of her inheritance, every spare hour, doing as much of the renovation as she could, even laying the tile in the kitchen and sheet-rocking the entire downstairs. She'd mainly bring in crews when the task was too big for one person. It was how she spent her time when Axel was on the road for long stretches. Every year marked another milestone, taking her one more step closer to her goal of creating a showcase home that was worthy of her dream. And it was almost complete.

But she couldn't get there on her own.

"I need your help then," she said, her stomach churning over the fact that she had to, once again, rely on a man.

"Shoot."

"If I am chosen, the house I'd enter would be yours." And here came the hard part. "They'd need your permission to do a shoot here."

She waited for him to make some crack about her finally admitting it was his house, waited for him to reject her plea immediately like Axel would have, but as she waited none of that came. Instead, his gaze gentle with understanding and a flicker of pride—for her. "Then permission granted."

"You know what you're committing to. A couple days of fifteen-plus people overtaking every corner of the house. There'd be equipment everywhere, and they'd be loud and intrusive. I know how sacred a musician's space is when they're creating."

"It can't be any worse than Big Pete."

She grimaced. "Full disclosure. I may or may not have told Big Pete to come at six instead of eight tomorrow."

"Full disclosure, I paid him a hundred bucks to use the kitchen as the new thoroughfare."

She bit back a smile. "You know he got sawdust and tiny chinks of Sheetrock all over my foam house. I had to re-glue the steps leading to the studio twice."

"He's drilled and banged through my writing time for six days straight. Today makes seven." His expression turned dead serious. "Red, I have four weeks left to pull an album out of my ass and it's already not going well."

She felt a punch of guilt. "I didn't know or I would have reined in Big Pete."

"I know."

"But I have been trying to make sure that they are following the plans precisely so there won't be any surprises, like a staircase that leads to nowhere. Which takes me to my offer." She pulled in a deep breath. "If I'm selected, the house needs to be finished. Big Pete will still be here for another week and I can act as the general contractor, keep them in line and quiet. Most of the work from there, I can do myself and do quietly."

"In return?"

"In return I get to stay here until I close escrow on my new house and if I'm selected, you'll vacate the house while they shoot. A favor for a favor, so we're square."

"And if we have a disagreement on style choices?"

Naivete had Elsie's heart hammering. While plotting her elaborate plan, she'd never imagined a situation when Rhett wouldn't like her choices. But if this were to work, she'd need control of the direction—not complete control, but the freedom to make the right choices for the project.

"I will, of course, update you on every decision, but if you give me creative control, anything you don't like I will buy back from you when the house is finished and photographed."

Had she just said that? It was a huge commitment. She was placing her financial future on the miniscule chance that she was picked for the article. Then again, she was going to have the house photographed for her portfolio anyway, and she knew Rhett's style. She could do this.

"This project will need to be carte blanche," she said with as much bravado as she could muster.

"Deal."

Excitement and surprise filled her every cell. "Seriously? You'd give me complete control?"

"What can I say? I'm a sucker for a woman in leather pants," he said. "Plus, you're that good, Red. Magazine quality good."

She swallowed back the emotion that was building. "Thank you."

"I'd say let's seal it with a kiss, but we both agreed that would be a bad idea."

"Lola 2.0 might get jealous," she said, pointing to the mannequin in the car, still dumbfounded by his confidence in her.

He winked. "Back to the problem at hand, will you get over yourself and let me help load up so you're not late?"

Before she could answer, he shouldered past her and easily lifted Lola 2.0 by her hips and placed her in the center seat.

"Be sure to strap her in. I don't want to risk getting a ticket."

"Noted." He straightened and rested his arm on top of the door, bringing himself right up against her. "How was your date? I mean, you didn't even leave time for the carriage to turn back into the pumpkin."

She could go two ways with this. Tell him it went fantastic so he'd leave it be, or tell him the truth and open herself up to a possible onslaught of B-team jokes. But he'd just been so honest with her, she decided to meet him on the same level. "It went awful. The music was awful. And loud. The venue was standing room only and Pierce was, well, he was sweet and boring."

"He seemed like a nice guy."

"He was a bit too nice and broke rule number four on my *Why I'm never dating* list."

"And what's rule number four?"

"He used lofty words."

"Says the girl using the word *lofty*."

"Well, if lofty language doesn't bother you, I'm sure he'd say yes to a date. He spent the night saying how sublime it was to meet you."

Rhett didn't laugh, instead his expression became serious and heated. "What are the other rules?"

She swallowed. "Rules?"

"You said rule four. What are the other rules? Again, asking for a friend."

♥

"You sure you don't want to sit in back with the rest of your girl band?" Rhett asked, sending her a sidelong glance.

"In your dreams," Elsie said, holding a box of rubber body parts, her lips pursed as if trying to hold back a smile.

God, she was prickly as a pissed-off porcupine when stressed. And she was stressed. But knowing that all she could have on beneath that prim posturing and skintight Lara Croft–esque leather pants was a thong was a total turn-on.

Elsie had been wise to turn him down. While she took risks in her designs, in her personal life she played things safe, and there was nothing safe about their history or the sparks flying between them. Which was why he was determined to keep his distance. They were both licking their wounds and trying to find themselves and had no business complicating that with a kiss. No matter how badly he wanted a replay.

They were wrong for each other. She was building her life here in Portland, working hard to create stability, and Rhett's life was chaotic and unpredictable. The only thing that would come from crossing the line would be someone getting hurt, so he'd decided to back off, work on his music and avoid her as much as possible.

Then he'd found her on the losing end of a battle with some sex dolls and there he was reorganizing and reloading her crap into his Range Rover.

"My dreams will include you, leather, and that ax. In case you were wondering." Leaving him wondering why he was so bad at following his own advice.

Thankfully, she ignored this. "Are you sure you don't need your car?"

"Nope. I've got a ride." Who was twenty minutes late. Not that he cared, he'd rather listen to Big Pete jackhammer his way through Rhett's floor than fulfill his obligation.

She gave him a once-over. "Is there an award show I don't know about?"

"No, Steph is doing a pop-up boutique today and I said I'd be there." He held his arms out and did a little spin, and when he looked over his shoulder, he caught Elsie staring at his ass. Good to know she was having as hard of a time as he was when it came to their attraction. "It's a tie-required event."

"Isn't that weird? You going to an event with your ex? I mean, the last time I was in a room with Axel had been at our divorce proceedings and I nearly stabbed him with a pencil."

Not for the first time, Rhett found himself trying to reconcile the picture Axel had painted with Elsie's story. "I promised her before the divorce was official. Plus, the sponsor said they'd pull out if I didn't show."

Elsie handed him three foam signs and he easily slid them into the trunk. "It's clear she's using you for your name to bring more people to her event."

He shrugged. "I agreed to go."

"Before she left you."

She hadn't actually left. She'd been in Tokyo on a shoot, and he'd been in New York when she said she wanted out. They hadn't seen each other for weeks and he was about to get on a plane to go spend the weekend with her, to tell her he wanted to give it a real go, to fix things. He'd already cut back his tour schedule, canceling several dates and moving around studio time to be with her.

In the end, it hadn't mattered. She wasn't willing to make the sacrifices he'd made, then she'd dropped the bomb that she didn't want kids and that was something he couldn't sacrifice.

It wasn't a "later" or "not the right time," she'd changed her mind completely. He knew she didn't have the best of childhoods and that her parents' split had really affected her outlook on marriage, but while they'd been planning their wedding all she could talk about was starting a family with him.

Hell, he wasn't even sure when it all changed, but it had and it simply confirmed what he'd suspected over the years—that people aren't always who they say they are.

"I can't control how she acts, only how I do," he said. "I made a promise. I don't go back on them."

"I forgot that about you." She held out a box but when he went to take it, she didn't let go. "I forgot a lot about you."

"Ouch."

"All I mean is that we were with other people back then."

"What happened between you and Axel?"

"Besides the whole 'Girls marry their fathers' adage? My dad was pretty absent growing up. Okay, he was fully absent, so I promised myself that if I ever married it would be to someone who loved me enough to stay." She snorted. "Then I married a guy whose job it was to be gone."

Rhett went quiet. And problem number two presented itself. He was gone more than her ex. That was the nature of the business. Unfortunately, being wrong for her had never felt so right.

He shoved in the last box and sat on the end of the cargo area. "What's it like being married to a musician?"

"Lonely."

"Then how did you guys make it work for so long?"

"I did. I made it work. I made sure that when he was home things were perfect, easy. All he had to do was show up. In the end even that was too much." She hopped up next to him. "What's it like from your perspective?"

"When I'm on the road all I can think about is home and when I'm home all I can think about is the road. Or at least that's how it used to be."

"How is it now?"

"I'm home and I can't even imagine going back on the road." Even talking about it made his chest squeeze uncomfortably. Caused anxiety to build in his lungs. "At least not until I figure out whatever this thing is that's holding me here."

Something deep down, that he refused to recognize, hinted that what was holding him here was looking at him now through those mossy green eyes.

"I hope you figure it out. I really do."

"I hope I do too."

CHAPTER TEN

Dating Tips from Elsie Dodd
*Beware of dates who sneak
up on you.*

"It's even better than I imagined," Faye said, looking around the party. They were sitting on the back porch of Claire's house, which had been turned into a butcher shop freezer, complete with dry ice and animated zombies hanging from meat hooks. "It's stunning."

"I don't know if stunning's the right word, but thanks," Elsie said, a bubble of pride warming her chest. It wasn't often that her mom doled out compliments. She was more of a Motivational Guide kind of mom.

"When I asked Claire to bring in a decorator with a limited track record, she had her concerns, but, as always, my instincts were spot on."

"You *asked* Claire to hire me?" Elsie was going to kill her mother.

"You needed work, she needed a worker bee, I merely made the suggestion. It was as simple as that." Faye raised her champagne flute and toasted herself before taking a sip. "And now you are one step closer to establishing your own business."

"As a glorified party planner?"

"Well, whatever one does it should always be glorified."

Glorified was how Faye lived her life. She oozed confidence and sophistication and had this charisma that became more potent with age. While her clients fed off that, Elsie always considered her like a fine wine. Amazing in sips but if you drink the entire bottle you're asking for a migraine.

"You made it sound like she was desperate for a designer."

Desperation was something Elsie was feeling at the moment. The party was winding down and she had yet to meet Susan, the magazine editor. She didn't even know if Susan had left the party. Elsie mentioned it in passing to Claire, who assured her the introductions would be made, but as far as Elsie could tell, Claire had her attention on her guests. Which was how it should be. But Elsie really wanted to at least get some face time with the editor.

She was both anticipating and dreading the possibility. The anticipation came from the chance that one of the top experts in her field might see her work. The dread was because in order for the editor to see her work, she'd be putting Rhett out. He was a private man and she didn't want to be another person using him for his name, which was why it was critical that no one knew the proprietor.

"Desperation can be a wonderful motivator. From necessity comes invention. You needed a win and now it's up to you to take the opportunity to reinvent."

Elsie was mid eye roll when Faye's last words settled. She'd returned home to Portland to recapture the pieces of herself she'd lost over the course of her marriage, but maybe that was part of the problem. Maybe instead of recapturing she needed to reinvent.

"What do you mean by reinvent?" Elsie asked, and Faye's expression was one of surprise. "What?"

"You've never asked me for advice before."

"Sure I have." When her mom shook her head, Elsie rattled off a list as proof. "I asked you about how we should handle Grandma getting older or what to get Axel for Christmas or how short I should cut my bangs."

"While your longer bangs really frame your face, I'm talking about the important stuff." Faye set her flute down on the table. "People come to me for career and life advice, and I'm really good at what I do."

"I know, Mom." Faye wasn't just good. She was renowned. There was an extensive wait list of people begging to become clients.

"Do you? Because everything you just said is about other people. You've never asked for advice about your life or your career."

"When you're with your clients, you're giving advice. When it comes to me it feels like you're giving your opinion," Elsie said honestly. "And it's hard to be vulnerable when you went behind my back with Axel."

Faye took Elsie's hand. "I know and I'm sorry. I should have had your side from the start, which is why when he called the other day, I told him that while I still love him, I can't be more than his ex-mother-in-law."

Elsie swallowed past the emotion. "Thank you. It's not that I want you to disown him, but—"

"You want me to disown him."

Elsie laughed. "I do, but I also know how much you two love and care for each other, and I would never ask you to give that up."

"There you are," a zombie in a shredded suit, with half a head, asked. The guest had been following Elsie around all night. Asking her questions, offering to help, even assisting with putting together the wire fence that acted like a quarantine prison. He'd been overly attentive, something

Elsie didn't know what to do with. And while it set off some alarms, he was Claire's brother, so she figured helping was part of his role. "I was looking for a partner to help me with some fresh brain matter." He flashed his teeth which were more vampire than zombie. "Or maybe you need to join the infected. All it would take is one bite."

"One bite," Faye whispered to Elsie.

"Then how would I go back and forth to refresh the decorations?"

"We could break out of quarantine together, then go on a rampage. A real Bonnie and Clyde team. What do you think?" This time when he smiled it was sweet. Almost shy.

"Adorable," Faye said.

"First, I have to make sure that the mannequins are moved around the quarantine area so that they appear to be trying to escape."

"Well, I can easily do that while you take a moment to put your feet up." He looked at their empty flutes and smiled. "Can I get you ladies a refill?"

"That would be lovely," Faye said, then elbowed Elsie.

"Thanks, that's sweet."

"Isn't it." Faye nudged Elsie's arm and gave a *isn't he cute* waggle of the brow. Elsie rolled her eyes.

With a bow, the zombie took their flutes and disappeared, moaning, and really playing the part as he made his way through the butcher freezer and across the back lawn.

When he had disappeared, Elsie asked, "So how do I reinvent myself?"

Faye beamed. "Well, first you have to let go of everything holding you back. Past hurts, past fears, all the things that creep into your mind at night. Once you get your fears under control, it leaves room for the kind of changes you want to make."

"You make it sound easy. Like making pancakes. A cup of this, a cup of that, then whisk and voilà. You are your new and improved self."

"I never said it's easy, but it is simple. When you take away what you're afraid of, what you want is clear as day."

"How do I know what I want?" she asked, a pang of discomfort pressing against her chest. It had been so long since she'd wanted something for herself that she didn't even know what it would look like or how it would feel.

"Isn't that the question of the hour?" someone else said.

Elsie looked up to find another man, who inspired all kinds of feelings. Gone was the slick celeb from earlier and in his place was a Clark Kent of zombie hunters, complete with combat face paint and enough special effects make-up to disguise his identity. But one look at those deep blue eyes and Elsie's nipples made it abundantly clear who was standing in front of her.

"Rhett? What are you doing here?" she whispered.

"You have my car." He turned to Faye. "Hey, Ms. Dodd, it's good to see you again."

"Likewise."

Elsie expected Rhett and Faye to get into talks of days past, but Rhett's eyes zeroed in on Elsie instead. She felt a thin layer of sweat coat her palms. "I could have brought it home myself."

"Home?" Faye asked, her eyes bouncing back and forth between the two as they spoke. "Well, isn't this inspiring news."

"It's not like that," Elsie said to her mom.

"It kind of is," he said. He looked back to Elsie. "And I came to find out how it went with the editor."

Defeat rolled through her. "I didn't get the chance to meet her and I'm pretty sure she left."

"She did," Faye confirmed, and Elsie's heart fell. This was her big shot and she'd missed it because she was splattering brain matter on plastic curtains. "But I met her."

"You met her?" Elsie said quite loudly.

"Lovely woman."

Elsie's hackles went up. She couldn't believe what her mom was saying. "You didn't think to introduce me?" she asked, and felt Rhett get closer. Not close enough to touch, but his presence felt protective, made her feel safe. "You knew how important this was for me! It was the reason I took the job."

"You took the job because you're a good person," Faye said. "And before you hack me to bits with that ax of yours"—Faye held out a business card—"I considered getting you, but you were in the middle of chatting with Jake and I didn't want to intrude."

"Who's Jake?" Rhett and Elsie asked at the same time.

Once again, Faye looked between Elsie and Rhett and smiled. "Apparently no one."

"What I needed was my mom to have my back and make an introduction," Elsie said.

Faye's voice was low and tinged with hurt. "It happened naturally. Claire made the introduction because Susan is interested in hiring me. She commented on the party, and it gave way to the perfect opportunity for me to rave about how the decorator did this as a favor, but really she is one of the best up-and-coming modern interior architects in the area, who would be perfect for her magazine."

All the anger washed away, and Elsie found it hard to speak. "You said that?"

"Yes. I talked about you and showed her photos of your house, and your garden, and she wanted to see more so I asked for her card, promising I would pass it along. All you need to do is reach out to her."

"That's great, Mom," she said, but her head was already swimming with doubt. "I know you meant well, but I don't know how professional it came off with my mom bragging about me."

"She has no idea you're my daughter. I came at it from the point of being a fan of your work."

"I don't know what to say."

"Just that you'll email her," Faye said.

"I will first thing tomorrow. And I'll send her updated photos of the house."

She hadn't even noticed, but Rhett had moved even closer, his hand resting supportively on her lower back, his thumb rubbing back and forth. From that angle, her mom couldn't see; it was a connection between the two of them. His way of saying he knew she was upset and he was there for her.

She looked over her shoulder and up into those fascinating blue eyes and found herself smiling up at him like an idiot. Shaking the fuzzies out of her head, she narrowed her eyes. "Will you excuse us for a minute, Mom?"

Faye took a triple glance at Rhett and flashed a conspiratorial smile. "Take all the time you need."

Elsie dragged Rhett around the back of the patio and into a dark corner, away from onlookers. "What is it with you and barging in on my parties? And shouldn't you be at that pop-up?"

"Really wasn't my scene."

"And zombie uprising gender reveals are?"

He held out his arms to show off his costume which, okay, was the best costume there. He looked like a big, bad-ass, sexy zombie hunter coming to save the day. "And where did you get that costume?"

"I have a buddy who is a special effects artist and he did me a favor." His smile turned warm. "I spent the entire night pretending to be Rhett Easton, Rock God. I thought it might be fun to be just Regular Rhett."

She wasn't sure what to say to that.

"Plus, I figured that you might need help breaking down the party. Those zombie mannequins can really make a scene."

He was cracking jokes, playing his easy-going role, but it was clear something had him off-balance. This time when she took his elbow it was to give him that same protective connection he'd given her. "You okay?"

He ran a hand through his hair and his gaze skittered away. "Steph's pregnant." His voice was threadbare. "She told me she didn't want kids and now she's pregnant. I mean, the whole basis of our divorce was because we wanted different things."

Elsie knew how badly Rhett wanted a family. They'd spent part of their weekend together talking about family and kids and how he couldn't wait. He didn't just want a family; he was the caliber of man who was born to be a father.

"I am so sorry," she said.

"Me too." He met her gaze, his filled with so many emotions it broke her heart. It reminded her of the moment she'd discovered Axel's infidelity. It was this feeling like no matter how hard she tried or how different things could have been, there was something lacking in her that was the contributing factor.

So instead of simply saying she was sorry, she did what she'd wished someone had done to her. She walked into him and wrapped her arms around his middle, then rested her cheek against his chest. "I know that nothing I can say will make it hurt any less, but none of this is about you. This is about her choices, not yours."

She felt his arms slide around her and he pulled her into him, holding so tightly to her it was as if they were one person sharing the same devastating blow. "You're a great man who will made a great dad someday."

"How do you know?' he asked, his voice rough, like tossed gravel.

She looked up at him. "Because I know you. I might not know everything about who you are now, but in here," she tapped his heart, "you're that same guy I met at a party and spent a life-changing weekend with. And that guy, he's the one who will find his person to make a family with."

"You're... " he trailed off, and the way he looked into her eyes made her belly quiver.

"I'm what?" she whispered, desperately wanting to know what he saw in her.

"So goddamned beautiful." His hands slid up her back to tangle in her hair and she went still as a stone. The air around them became charged, as if someone threw a match on a barrel of gasoline, taking them from caring friends to forbidden lovers in a millisecond.

His gaze dropped to her lips, which parted on an inaudible breath. His fingers moved in small circles at the base of her neck and she shivered.

She was in trouble. Serious trouble.

She was about to kiss Rhett and she could see it in his eyes that he wasn't going to stop her.

She ran her hand up his chest to the back of his neck, sliding her fingers through his hair, her nails scratching as she went. He groaned and his eyes blazed cobalt blue as she tugged his head down. She waited for him to pull back but he leaned in, stopping midway. He was handing over the power. The next move was hers.

And move she did, closing the distance and losing herself in his mouth. Even the simple contact sparked a rekindling. His taste, his touch, the way his fingers tightened in her hair, it was subatomic.

Nostalgia had never tasted so good.

No. Nostalgia wasn't the right word because that implied something from the past. Everything she was feeling was in the here and now.

"Red," he whispered against her lips before going in for a deeper taste. She moved with him, into him, so close she was shrink-wrapped around him. Her arms tightened around his neck, her breasts rubbed his chest, and her lips cradled his.

The way he kissed her, gentle and reverent, turned her inside out. It took eons from one kiss to the next, but it took but a second for his hands to slide down her shoulders, her spine, the lower curve of her back and, god yes, to her ass.

"All night," he groaned. "The minute I saw you in these leather pants I thought about doing just this." He gave a gentle squeeze. "Beautiful," he repeated.

She felt beautiful. Even covered in fake blood and dressed like some kind of action hero, beneath his touch she felt sexy and desired. Two things she'd feared she'd never feel again. The last few years of her marriage hadn't just robbed her of her self-worth. The light in which she saw herself had been nearly extinguished. And Rhett had unknowingly relit her flame.

He had to feel what this was doing to her. Given the way he was holding her and savoring every kiss, she had an idea where this was leading.

Gripping his tie, she tugged him backward, far into the shadows and away from any prying eyes. He walked with her, backing her up against the wall of the garage, and that's when things got real.

She didn't know how he could drive her crazy and, at the same time, make her ache. All she knew was that being around him like this was dangerous. And for once in her life she wanted to taste danger.

She loosened his tie, her fingers moving from one button to the next, and finally the third and—

"Elsie?" a male voice called out, and Claire's brother came around the corner. Elsie jumped back and smoothed a hand through her hair. It didn't help. "There you are. I have your champagne."

Rhett looked at the flute, between the two of them, then back to Elsie. "Are you on a date?"

She said, "No," at the same time Jake said, "Yes."

"We're on a date?" Elsie asked her apparent date.

"Your grandma and my sister set us up. We were both a party of one so they decided we'd have fun being each other's plus one. Did they not tell you?" Jake asked, clearly confused.

Join the club.

Rhett stepped all the way back. "I guess I'll leave it to you two kids to figure out." And then he was gone.

CHAPTER ELEVEN

Dating Tips from Elsie Dodd
*Ignore the little tingle you get when you
like someone. It's common sense
leaving the building.*

"What the hell are you doing?" Rhett asked himself. He was next to his Range Rover, no keys, no ride. Just him and his hard-on. He hadn't meant to kiss Elsie. Was pretty sure it would have ended with them naked in the back of his car. No, he *knew* it would have ended with them naked in the back of his car.

What, exactly, was the problem with that?

How was he supposed to be her friend when every time he saw her all he could picture was her naked? And why whenever another date showed up—and there always seemed to be another one—did he feel like punching someone?

"You're supposed to be giving her room to decompress, not pressing her against the nearest flat surface."

He'd been fine all night. Doing the whole dog and pony show with Steph while wondering what the hell he was doing there. He met her new fiancé, they had a laugh, signed some autographs, and then she'd dropped the bomb. She was pregnant. After a year of saying she didn't want a family, she was expecting. It had him wondering if she'd changed her mind or if it was something about him that had her gun-shy when it came to having kids.

And before he knew it, he'd called in a favor from a make-up artist, then hailed a cab and headed across town to a party he hadn't been invited to.

What was it about Elsie Dodd?

She was complicated and stubborn and a complete mess. She was also sexy and sweet and so damn real he couldn't stay away. She was like some homing beacon, drawing him closer and closer until he forgot common sense.

She got to him, and he didn't know how he felt about that.

"I didn't know I was on a date."

He turned around and the woman he'd just walked away from stood two feet away. Her hair a mess, her eyes wild, and those just-been-kissed lips still wet.

She stepped closer—dangerously close. "I didn't know," she whispered.

"But you are," he said.

"I told him that I was working, and it was unprofessional."

"And kissing me?"

"I want it to be a mistake."

"But?"

"But I'm here." Oh, she was there all right. In nothing but those skintight pants and some medieval-looking top that was held together by a simple piece of silk ribbon. He wondered if the whole thing would unravel with a single tug. "I told myself the same thing I told Jake, that after this past year I'm not in the right frame of mind to date."

Something he'd known but he'd kissed her anyway. And it had been insanity. Sheer insanity. The moment their lips touched every problem and pressure evaporated and all that was left was pleasure.

And her.

"Now what?" he asked, because he needed to know what her plan was. And if her plan matched his. The one where they kept things simple; two friends who shared a mind-blowing, unexpected kiss that made a small hiccup in what they were building toward. Or the one where they rip each other's clothes off.

The first was the safe route, the second felt like the right route.

She stepped closer. Each step made his dick twitch. "I don't know. My plan was to get as far away from you as possible, but I guess I got turned around and ended up here."

"What happened to mixing business and pleasure," he asked, calling her bluff. One of them had to think past this moment and how their next moves would affect their already intertwined worlds. There was something more between them than this atomic bomb chemistry. Something that made him want to take her up on what she was offering in those pretty eyes.

"I told Claire I was taking a break, so technically I'm not on the clock."

"Why don't you hop in, I drive us home, and we go to our respective beds. Alone." Someone had to be the responsible party. And tonight, he guessed, it was him.

"Or," she began tugging on his tie, "we just hop in."

"And then?" he asked quietly.

She looked a little lost and a whole lot vulnerable. "I don't know. I made it this far. I hoped you'd know what to do next." Then those eyes, the melt-your-soul-and-steal-your-heart eyes filled with uncertainty and—*aw, hell*—hurt. "Never mind, I don't know what I was thinking."

She turned and before she could bolt, he took her hand and spun her back around.

"Neither do I." Then they were kissing and, *god,* what a kiss it was. Sparklers and fireworks and a nuclear reactor explosion all at once. Whatever had happened behind the garage was the buildup to the main event. The way her soft hands slid up his shirt, her fingertips exploring every inch of his chest, sent his body into overdrive.

A heat started well south of his belt line and slowly moved upward, settling in his chest.

"I want you," she murmured against his lips and *ho-ly shit.* Here he was trying to do the right thing, when the girl next door was looking at him as if she wanted to rock his ever-loving world, right there on the street.

"I've wanted you since that day in your kitchen at the barbecue, but I couldn't have you." If she looked surprised at his admission, she didn't show it. "Then there was the moment we ran into each other in the shower and knowing things had changed."

"And now?" she breathed against his lips.

Now, his hands did a little slip-and-slide further south for a little recon, to see if her ass still felt as spectacular as it looked in those pants. And, *holy Christ,* it felt even better. And then in a move that was all manufactured confidence, she backed him against the side of the SUV, and then there was a *beep, beep.*

And would you look at that, the driver's side door was open and she was loading him inside. Not to drive off, but to lift herself onto his lap and once she was there, she was giving him the same kind of lap dance she'd given Lola 2.0, only this was so much better because he was the recipient.

"Slow down. You're making it hard to think rationally."

Closing the door, she said, "Then let me help." She did a little shimmy that had his eyes rolling to the back of his head. "Let's not think at all. I just want to feel. And I want to feel you."

Who was he to deny her, especially when those soft hands slid down the front of his pants to the promised land? And the way she was stroking and cupping, he was in for the ride of his life. She sucked his lower lip into her mouth and let it go with a *pop*; his mind went fuzzy.

"Are you sure?" Her answer was to unsnap the top button of his pants. "What if someone comes walking by?"

"Then I guess we'd better get those tinted windows fogged up."

Then she was kissing the hell out of him again, and kissing and touching, and exploring—and he was doing some exploring himself. Mainly the front ribbon on her corset where, with one tug, and just like he knew, the whole piece split down the middle and her breasts were miraculously free. Next came the button on her top, which was easily removed, followed by the next, until he had complete access to her neckline, which he nibbled his way down.

It was that same intense fever that overtook them all those years ago. Like a wildfire rushing through his body, frying his brain and lighting his chest aflame.

She rose up so that he had to tilt his head to maintain contact, his hands going right to her ass, palming a cheek in each hand. Then, realization of realizations, he noticed that her cleavage was at the precise licking level, so he gave her open mouth kisses all the way down until he reached the next button. But as his hands were firmly planted on her ass and the button was hindering advancement, he was faced with the conundrum of all conundrums. Her breasts and bottom both needed attention but he only had two hands.

After a lengthy conversation with himself, he decided he'd become the most masterful multi-tasker on the planet.

"Red," he whispered against her skin, and his hand was about to go on a Lewis and Clark expedition of her body when she reached up and fiddled with the button until— bingo, a satisfying *pop*.

He met her gaze and she smiled down. "Teamwork."

"I wholeheartedly support teamwork."

"Me too."

Instead of going for the jackpot, he cupped her face and delivered a gentle, god-you-get-to-me kiss. And in case that wasn't clear enough, he said it aloud.

She pulled back and searched his gaze. *Lust*, he thought. That's what he'd let her see in his gaze. Not the other emotions that were freaking him out. Yet he must have let something slip because her expression went soft with concern and confusion. So, before she could pull the plug, he kissed her again. Hard and fast and hot enough to burn a hole right through the floorboard of his SUV.

She moaned against his mouth while sliding down his body and by sliding he meant, running her body up and down his, the pressure was so intense, he barely realized he still had his pants on. Then there were her hands, slipping between them, down his ridge and giving a little squeeze that changed the direction of his life. If he'd wanted her before, he needed her now.

Her fingers slowly unzipped his slacks as he recited all the reasons this was a bad idea. Then her hands went further south and his dick prayed she'd ask him to come out and play, because he'd clearly hadn't gotten the memo that this was not happening.

Not here. Not now. Not like this.

No. If they were going to do this, if they were going to go here, it wouldn't be a spur of the moment, to hell with it all, frantic sexcapade in the front seat of his SUV. It would be a planned, thought-through sextravaganza that started with a proper date and ended with zero regret when the sun rose.

Not that he could regret anything with her, but he knew she would. And that was enough to clear some of the fog.

"Els," he whispered, and yup that was his voice about to slow them down. Which for the record he couldn't figure out what he was saying. They'd been building to this moment for weeks. Years. And yet there he was about to slam on the brakes.

"Els," he whispered again, and this time she pulled back, her eyes lust-hazed.

"More kissing, less talking," she said, then gave his dick the stroke of a goddess. Her hand would slide down and give this little squeeze before starting back at the heart-stopping top, quickly finding her rhythm.

There was some moaning, probably from him, and groaning, most definitely from her, and then there was this tapping.

Tap. Tap. Tap.

Slide. Squeeze. Moan.

Tap. Tap. Tap.

Slide. Squeeze. Moan.

Tap. Tap. "Elsie? Are you in there?"

They both froze.

"Elsie?" the voice called out from the other side of the glass.

"Oh no," she whispered. "It's Claire." Elsie looked at her top that was practically falling off her body, then at Rhett's pants, which were all the way opened. "She can't catch me." Her eyes were wild and pleading. "Please, she can't catch me."

"Are you okay?" came the voice.

She slapped her hands over her mouth, glancing around as if there were a cloak of invisibility hidden somewhere in the back seat.

"Get down on the floorboard," he said.

"What?"

"Do you trust me?"

Without hesitation she nodded and his heart nearly exploded with joy. In one swift move, Rhett pushed the seat all the way back and shoved her onto the floorboard in front of him.

She huffed with indignation. "This is not the time. There is no way I'm going to—"

"Evening," he said as he rolled down the window just enough to see Claire. She was a buttoned-up socialite who, he was pretty sure, belonged to his mom's philanthropy group.

"Everything okay in there?" Claire tried her best to look inside. If years of being Margo Easton's son hadn't taught Rhett how to hide just about anything in plain sight, then evading the paparazzi had. Now, a half-naked, totally turned-on woman? This might be a challenge. But if there was anything he loved almost as much as a half-naked, totally turned-on woman, it was a challenge.

"Getting ready to head home."

Claire narrowed her eyes. "But this is my party planner's car."

"I know, I'm taking the first load home for her."

"You aren't on my guest list. I know everyone on the list." Claire gasped. "Are you a party crasher?"

"Just the help."

Before she could stick her nose between the tiny gap in the window, he said, "What a party. I've been to some impressive ones before but nothing like this. I can even see it trending in the Portland area."

"You think?"

"Oh, I know. Your party planner has magical hands." And those hands socked him square in the shin. He covered it with his, then flipped it over so they were holding hands. She gave his hand a squeeze hard enough to sting, then let go. "And she knows how to get the job done."

Another sock to the shin.

"You have a good night," he said and then rolled up the window.

"Pull over," Elsie said from the passenger seat, still in shock over what she'd done. Or who she'd almost done.

She'd nearly had front-seat sex with a guy who'd made a career out of one-night stands. It didn't take long after his divorce for him to revert back to his old ways and Elsie refused to be another in a long line of women.

This was what happened when she let her impulsive side take over. Which was why she needed to get out of this car ASAP.

"I'm serious, Rhett. Pull over."

"I'm not letting you out in the middle of the night to walk home," he said, not even slowing down.

"Then I'll take an Uber."

"Come on, Red. Let's talk about it."

"I don't want to talk. I want to clear my head."

"We don't have to talk then," he offered, and the sincerity in his tone made her chest feel like it was pressing in on itself. "We can sit silently in each other's company."

"I need some air. And space," she said. She rebuttoned her shirt and sucked in a ragged breath. Why was it so hot and stuffy and why did the car suddenly seem so small? "Please." She was surprised to hear her voice crack with emotion.

The blinker ticked as he pulled over to the curb. The car was barely in Park when she exploded out the door. The cool night air hit her face and she rested her hands on her thighs and dropped her head between her knees.

Breathe. Just breathe.

Her body was a jumble of need and regret.

Her earlier behavior was not just unprofessional and reckless, it could have cost her a chance at her dream. She didn't want to even imagine what Claire would have done had she caught Elsie in that car. Not that it was anybody's business what she did on her own time, but she wasn't really on her own time now was she. She needed to get back. There was still the party to break down, blood splatter to refresh, and Lola 2.0 needed to be moved to the infected zone. If Rhett had rolled down the window another inch, Claire would have gotten the story of a lifetime.

When her heart rate returned to normal, she straightened and found herself eye to eye with Rhett. "What are you doing?" she asked.

"Making sure you're okay." He bent his knees to get eye level with her. "You okay, Els?"

She was almost to Okay Land until he said her name like that. Not Red or sweetheart, but Els. It made her insides turn to goo. "Fine," she snapped. "Why did you follow me?"

He held up the corset of her costume and wiggled a brow. "You forgot this."

She crossed her arms across her braless chest. Unamused.

Rhett sighed. "I wanted to make sure you were okay."

"I'm dandy."

They both stood there on the sidewalk for a long moment, where he refused to move. She shoved him in the chest. He took a step back and his eyes filled with apology. "I'm sorry."

She blinked. "Why are you sorry? I came on to you."

"You did," he agreed. "But I kissed you first. And now you're upset, and for that I'm sorry."

"I'm not upset." She threw her hands in the air. "I'm confused. Okay, there, are you happy?"

She tried not to notice the way his face went slack at her accusation and instead she looked at the stars overhead. The summer night was showing off with a million twinkling lights and a gentle breeze carried the scent of crisp air and cologne.

Rhett. He'd moved closer. She could feel him at her back.

"Go out with me."

She spun around. "What?"

He was right there, so close she could feel the heat of his body. She looked up into his devastating eyes and her body gave a lengthy sigh.

"Let me take you on a proper date."

"And where would a date lead?" To disaster, that's where.

"I don't know, but I want to find out."

"You're leaving in a few weeks."

Elsie had come back to Portland to make her goal a reality, not to become distracted by another relationship. If she'd managed to lose sight of her dreams with a selfish guy like Axel, she didn't even want to think about what would happen to her goals with a man as gentle and sweet as Rhett. He had the power to swallow her whole.

"Then we have a few weeks to see where this goes." His arms slid around her waist. "I'm not asking for more than you're willing to give. I'm just asking for a chance."

A chance at what? Her body didn't seem to care but her mind seemed to understand. She'd tried the no-strings thing once and it left her heart a little battered. Could she walk into this knowing he would eventually go back to being a rock star? And what would their relationship look like after he left? What would her heart look like?

She wasn't sure. And that scared her. "Maybe we were caught up in the memory of the past."

"Do you really believe that?" She could tell by his tone that he didn't.

"I don't know," she admitted. "But my future doesn't have room for anyone or to start something remotely close to what you're offering. At least not right now. We're living together. In a house that could determine the direction of my life," she reminded them both. "You had a rough night with Steph. I'm still reeling from a disaster of a divorce and the adrenaline of what tonight could mean for my career. What if we got caught up and we're too close to this all to truly understand that it's a bad idea?"

"A bad idea was B-team, but you made room for him. Why is it different with me?"

"It just is." One date with a nobody that would lead nowhere was different than a date with a guy who she'd been crushing on for nearly a decade. Someone who lived in a world she'd barely escaped. "Plus, it's not like you have the room for dating. You're Rhett Easton, a guy who barely has time to sleep, let alone date."

The moment those words reached the air she felt the guilt kick in. He went silent. The kind of silent that had her heart hollowing out.

"I know what I am," he said quietly. "I guess I thought with you I could be Regular Rhett."

"I didn't mean it that way."

"I know," he said, but she could hear the hurt in his tone. "But if we're going for honesty, you have to admit that it doesn't matter which Rhett I am, this whole thing started the moment you walked in on me in the bathroom and it isn't going to stop until we get each other out of our systems."

She felt her face heat in the crisp evening air, followed by some heating in much more dangerous places. Was he right? They'd been fighting this insanity for weeks now and if anything, the pull was getting stronger. The attraction becoming harder to deny. The temptation to give in harder to resist—proof by what had transpired between them in his car.

"Whatever this crazy thing is between us…"

"So you admit I drive you crazy?" he whispered.

"I think you know how crazy you drive me," she said, tired of pretending he didn't affect her.

"If it's even half as much as me…" He trailed off as his gaze dropped to her lips. She felt a tingle all the way down to her toes.

"What if we give in and it ruins our relationship." She leaned in, going cheek to chest. "I like being your friend, Rhett. I don't want to lose that."

At her admission, she felt the tension in his body release. As if he'd been holding his breath since she brought up his more famous persona. She didn't see him as Rhett Easton, she never had. Whenever she looked into those mesmerizing blue eyes, she saw the sweet and caring guy who'd charmed his way into her heart.

"I don't want to lose it either, so how about we lay down some ground rules. I know how you like your rules."

She lifted her head. "What kind of rules? Like no PDA or warm fuzzies?"

"We've already broken rule one and as for warm fuzziness, I'm more of a hot and hard kind of guy."

She gave him a gentle shove and he laughed. But she also went weak in the knees, because while he was joking, she remembered how languid and laser focused on her pleasure he was when it came to driving her out of her mind.

"It has to be friends first." Was she seriously considering this? Apparently, she was, because she added, "Sex comes second."

"A very close, almost on the same level, second." When he spoke next, the low rumble of his voice sent a delicious shiver down her spine. "While I'm all for front-seat foreplay, I want to take a step back and go slow," he said, even as he tightened his hold, pulling her against him so all their good parts lined up. "Make sure we do this right."

"Based on what just happened, I don't think slow is an option."

"I was serious when I said I'm a date first kind of guy." She gave a disbelieving look, because they both knew that he'd been hook-up central since his divorce. He tilted her chin up and the emotions she saw shining in his eyes nearly knocked her off her feet. "With you, I'm a date first kind of guy."

"Dating sounds like a commitment."

"I'm not talking chartering a flight to Paris for dinner overlooking the Eiffel Tower."

She gasped. "You've done that?"

"Haven't you?" He teased but she wasn't sure if he was joking. "I was thinking something more casual. Like a night in, where I cook. It can be fun, and you need some fun in your life."

She snorted. "You cook?"

"If you go out with me, I can learn."

"Do you even hear what you're saying?"

"I'm as surprised as you are," he said, and his honesty scared her. Because Honest Rhett was a whole lot harder to resist than Flirty Rhett. "I don't need an answer now. Take some time to think it over."

Thinking wasn't the problem. It was all the feels he inspired. All the what-ifs and might-be-worth-its that tore at her carefully laid plans. Which was why, instead of getting back in that car with Rhett, she walked back to Claire's. She had a party to run, and she wasn't going to jeopardize her goals over a kiss.

Even if it was a blow-her-mind and rock-her-world kiss to end all kisses.

CHAPTER TWELVE

Dating Tips from Elsie Dodd
Don't do it.

Two nights later, Elsie strutted into the Whiskey Depository wearing her best cocktail dress, grout under her nails, and a smile on her face. She'd just spent the past ten hours—a very rewarding ten hours—ripping out the tile in the downstairs bathroom and not thinking about Rhett and that kiss once. Not when she'd snuck into the kitchen at five a.m. to avoid him. Not when she'd heard the strumming of his guitar. Not even when she caught a glimpse of his jean-clad ass climbing into his SUV.

Nope, she didn't even think about him eight hours later when he still hadn't come home. Not that she wanted him to. He'd given her a proposition, one that was as ridiculous as it was tempting, and she needed more time to think it through—really think it through. Which was why she'd called her friend Carla to meet downtown for drinks.

Carla was recently divorced but, unlike Elsie, she was managing singlehood like a ninja. She took to single life like a fish to water, while Elsie was floundering. So who better to give some expert advice on her situation?

And she needed advice.

Rhett had given Elsie an interesting proposition, then acted as if nothing had changed between them, leaving her confused and a bit angry. Sure, she could have confronted him, but she handled confrontation like most people did dentist appointments—procrastination, procrastination, procrastination.

The moment Elsie walked into the restaurant she spotted her friend sitting at the bar. Carla glanced over her shoulder and when she caught sight of Elsie she smiled, big and bright, then waved her over.

"You're here!" Carla gave Elsie the best hug. "And you're not wearing overalls. I'm impressed."

"I might have a light layer of sawdust in my hair, but I wore my new shoes." Elsie held out her foot and wiggled her leg.

"You look amazing." Carla turned to the man next to her, who was dressed in a smart-looking suit, tie, and warm smile. "Doesn't she look amazing."

Mr. Suit took in Elsie and her dress and smiled a smile that had *Interested* written all over it. "Stunning."

Carla waggled a brow and whispered to Elsie, "He said stunning."

Mr. Suit was good-looking in that boardroom badass kind of way. Clean cut with broad shoulders and the prettiest hazel eyes she'd ever seen. The exact steady nine-to-fiver she'd imagined she'd date—when the time came that she was ready. And yet not a single flutter or zing. In fact, her hormones seemed to have gone on strike.

"Elsie, this is Keith. He's a commodity broker, likes the opera, and sings off key." Carla stepped back. "Keith, my best friend Elsie who has formed a recent allergy to musicians."

"Good thing I can't even hold a tune." Keith stuck out his hand and they shook. He held on a moment longer than random-meeting etiquette required and an unsettling feeling started to nag deep in her belly. "Nice to meet you. Carla here told me that you're an architect. That sounds fascinating."

"Fascinating," Carla repeated again.

"Interior architect and I love what I do."

"That makes all the difference," he said. "Now, what can I get you two drink?"

"Oh, I'm fine," Elsie said at the exact same time Carla said, "She'll take a margarita. On the rocks. No salt. And a martini for me. Extra dirty."

"You got it," he said with a wink. Again, zero flutters. "I'll be right back."

Elsie pasted a polite smile on her face until Keith was gone. She grabbed Carla's arm. "What are you doing?"

"I'm doing you a favor," Carla said.

"By setting me up with some stranger at a bar?"

"He's not a stranger. He's a coworker who likes long walks on the beach, top-shelf whiskey, and he isn't battery operated."

"Then why don't you go date him?"

"I already have a man waiting. He's twenty-two, a rugby player, and into older women. Did I mention he's a god in the sack?" Carla patted a hand to her chest and sighed. "I wasn't suggesting you date Keith. Just fuc—"

Elsie coughed to cover up Carla's *suggestion*. "Shhh. And I'm not a one-night-stand girl. Plus, Keith isn't my type."

Carla snorted. "Fine, make it a summer fling for all I care, but make it something." Carla took Elsie by the shoulders and spun her on the bar stool. "Take a look around the bar and tell me who is your type. There are fifty fine specimens to pick from and if you say the guy playing the piano, I will smother you."

Elsie didn't even bother to look. Yes, there were a sea of steady suits in the crowd, but she was already trying to balance one guy, an occasional suit who mostly wore jeans and vintage tees and had a schedule about as steady as a boat during a hurricane. "Piano guy doesn't do it for me."

"Well, then who does? Because you need to get laid, girl."

"Why does everyone keep saying that?"

Carla laughed. "If you could see your face right now, you'd know the answer to that question."

"What makes you think I'm not already dating someone?"

"Are you?"

She plopped on the bar stool and sighed. "Maybe."

"Define maybe."

"I might, possibly have a proposal, a strictly summer fling, friends-with-benefits proposal that could lead to an orgasm." She thought back to their weekend and there were those flutters she'd been looking for.

"Could or would?"

"Definitely a would situation." Rhett was a multiple "would" kind of lover. He was giving and tender and attentive—with a small dash of kink. Then there was the cosmic connection. From the word go, there had been this unexplainable *thing* between them that still burned hot. Proved by the fact that every day that passed, the more seriously she considered his proposal.

"Then why are you here with me and not out getting some would?"

"Self-preservation," Elsie said, thinking back to the other night. "With this guy it would be easy to mistake the benefits with something more."

"What's wrong with more?"

What *was* wrong with more?

Right. More led to feelings which led to possibilities which led to heartache. Elsie had lived that cycle too many times to count. It had been a wash, rinse, and repeat variety of heartache and she liked to think that she'd learned her lesson.

"I'm not looking for more. I have enough on my plate without adding *more*." But an orgasm here and there wouldn't be so bad. "I'm in the middle of a renovation."

Carla's sharp gaze landed on her. "Work is no excuse."

"I just got out of a marriage."

"You've been separated for more than a year," Carla countered. "Which means you are way overdue for a some man-made woulds."

"Then there's the fact that my mom and friends keep setting me up on random dates and sucking up any free time I have."

"Keith!" Carla shouted over the patrons. "Sorry, buddy, she's potentially in a '*benefits*' kind of way."

"Can you not announce to the entire bar my current dating status."

"Ah, so you admit you're dating."

If she'd said yes to Rhett, was that what they'd be? Dating? He did say he was a date first kind of guy and the thought of a dinner with him had all those hormones shouting at her to go for it.

"Thinking about it."

Carla studied her for a heartbeat, then grinned. "You like him."

"No. Maybe." Elsie plopped her elbows on the bar top and let her head hang. "I do. More than I should for a temporary, can't-go-anywhere fling. Every time I'm around him my clothes practically melt off my body. And then there's the way he kisses."

Carla lifted a brow. "So you've kissed."

Oh, they kissed, all right. They'd nearly blown the roof right off the car. And more.

She grimaced. There was that *more* again. "We kissed, then he asked me out on a date, and I panicked, then ran like a big fat chicken."

Carla flapped her arms like a bird. "*Cluck. Cluck.*"

"Now, I'm avoiding him, which is harder than it sounds since we're practically living on top of each other."

Carla gasped, covering her mouth with her hands. "It's the new homeowner! You are totally going to boink the new owner."

"Again, with the blasting my dating status."

"Sorry, it's just all so exciting. Who is he?"

Elsie went mum.

"Fine, what does he do? And please don't tell me he's another musician. Remember, you're allergic to them."

Elsie mimed zipping her lips and tossing away the key.

Carla sighed. "What's with all the secrecy? And since when do we keep secrets from each other?"

Elsie allowed herself five seconds to think about how she'd bring up Rhett without mentioning his name. It wasn't that she didn't trust her friend, they've shared everything over the years. But she felt protective of Rhett's privacy. Also, she wanted things to stay between the two of them. The last thing Elsie needed was to agree and then have things go sideways, only to have to face all the pitying looks from her friends wanting to know all the details.

"I don't want to say anything until I know I'm going to say yes."

"You're going to say yes."

"How do you know?"

"Because you have moon-eyes."

Elsie snorted. "What are moon-eyes?"

"That sappy-happy look people get when they're crushing. And you are crushing hard."

"I am not." Elsie looked at herself in the mirror behind the bar and, *oh my god*, she had moon-eyes. "Plus, in a few weeks, he's leaving for an extended work thing that could be up to a year. And what happens then?"

"You celebrate that you're no longer a divorcée but a single woman on the town. All the lingering anger from the divorce will vanish and then you'll get your fresh start. Trust me. Rebound sex is the best therapy one can get."

"No lingering here," she said, then paused. Every time she thought about how Axel had duped her, first by the affairs and then by selling her house out from under her, it got her blood boiling. She'd had a few fantasies where Axel lost everything and had to start his life over like she had.

He still had no idea how hard it had been to keep her chin up while he squashed her like a cockroach. "Okay, maybe a tad bit of lingering. In fact, I may have stolen his drumsticks."

Carla's mouth dropped open. "The ones Dave Grohl gave him that he had framed in his studio?"

"The ones I had framed." Axel had been "too busy" to do something as domestic as buying a frame, so Elsie had surprised him. "The judge said I could take anything from the house that belonged to me. I framed those suckers, so technically the frame belongs to me and, I figured, what's inside was up for grabs." So she'd snagged them when packing her personal belongings. It was petty and immature and felt liberating as hell. How she saw it was that he'd stolen eight years of her life, so she'd stolen his most prized possession.

"You stuck it to him by stealing his sticks?" Carla clapped her hands. "How poetic. I knew you had a little rebellious side in there. And maybe that's who you need to channel. That inner wild child."

Elsie hadn't been in touch with her adventurous side since that weekend with Rhett. Her heart had been so bruised she'd decided the safe route was more her speed. But playing it safe by marrying a man who openly spoke about marriage had bruised more than her heart. It had fractured it.

Not totally broken, she realized. Just a hairline fracture.

"If this is going to work, I need to set some rules." Some concrete, unbreakable, keep-her-heart-safe rules.

"Oh, for god's sake. How many times do I have to tell you? Rules are like kale, full of regret."

"Rules keep people safe."

"Oh, babe. You went the marriage way, and you were miserable for years. Maybe it's time to give fun a try. Who knows? You might actually find yourself smiling like you were a minute ago."

Wasn't that exactly what Rhett had said? And what did it say about her that the two people she spent the most time with thought she was unhappy? "I guess it's just dinner and seeing where it leads from there."

Right to the bedroom, her inner horndog said. And would that be so bad? *Yes*, her warning bells rebutted.

"Leap and the orgasms will come."

Elsie covered her eyes and grimaced. "Can we talk about something else? Anything else?"

"Fine. Only because I know that you're going to say yes."

Elsie rolled her eyes. "I got an email back from the editor at *Modern Masterpiece*."

"You did not!"

"I totally did. This afternoon. And it turns out the architect who lands the cover also wins a three-year lease on a downtown studio and fifty-thousand dollars to set up shop."

"This is your big break, Elsie! This is the moment you've been working toward since I met you." Carla studied her seriously. "Why aren't you smiling?"

"There are still a lot of hoops to jump through. Being considered is a dream come true, but making the cut, let alone landing the cover, is still a pie-in-the-sky thing for me to wrap my brain around."

Carla took both of Elsie's hands. "Stop undercutting your talent. You are cover worthy. You just have to believe in your work. Visualize yourself with a thick wad of fifty grand and a sweet studio downtown."

"Visualize?" Elsie chuckled. "You sound like my mom."

Carla made a face. "While that is an insult, maybe this one time she's right. So what's the next hoop to jump through?"

"The editor wants to see more pictures of the house."

"That's easy."

"Like ASAP. I still have some work to do"—so much she was insane to think she could pull this off—"but the house is really coming together, and I think if I can get to the next step, where they actually do a walk-through, then I might have a chance."

"There's my girl."

Elsie set her head on Carla's shoulder and looked up at her with a dramatic eye flutter. "Which means I need a kick-ass photographer to help me capture the house in the right light. Know of anyone?"

Elsie could snap some decent shots of rooms, but she wasn't a trained photographer. And she needed a trained, talented, and not too expensive photographer if she was to make it to the next level.

"I know quite a few. But one comes to mind."

Carla was a real estate agent who knew how to sell a house. She also knew photographers who knew how to capture living spaces in ways Elsie never could. She was a designer with a good eye for composition, but this was too important for an amateur.

She kissed her friend on the cheek. "I know they're probably slammed and that my ask is short notice. And they probably charge way more than my bank account will allow, but maybe they'd be open to a trade swap. I can—"

"Do nothing but sit back and let me do my thing. And before you say something stupid that will offend me and diminish our friendship, I have some favors I can call in."

"I don't want you to waste a favor."

"*Waste* and *Elsie* could never be used in the same sentence. This is what family does, Elsie. And you and me? We've been family since that first day when you let me cry on your shoulder over some guy I can't even remember. You didn't even know me, but you knew I needed a friend. Because that's the kind of person you are. So let me be that person for you."

Elsie felt a tug in her chest at the reminder of how it felt to be around a good friend. She'd had a lot of friends in her lifetime, but never ones like Carla. She was genuine, giving, funny, and loyal to a fault—a person much like Rhett. And Elsie needed more people like that in her life.

CHAPTER THIRTEEN

Dating Tips from Elsie Dodd
Unless you're an undercover operative,
go easy on the interrogation.

Early Monday morning, Rhett walked into The Easton Agency to help his brothers finalize the lineup for Portland Live. This year the family's bar was hosting their twentieth annual music festival where ten up-and-coming musicians, who were looking for their big break, could play a set in front of industry execs. Founded by Rhett's dad, the festival was a fun way to give back to the community, and it had played a big part in Rhett's success. Being able to jam with the old-timers during rehearsals and hone his skills in front of a live audience had given him the drive and experience to stand out in a sea of talent. Nowadays, this event was designed to showcase talent as much as it was paying tribute to the man who'd believed in his sons before they knew how to believe in themselves.

Rhett could use some of that belief right then. It had been three days since the roadside kiss and he'd barely seen Elsie. She was avoiding him and he was letting her. He'd promised her space to think about his offer, but he hadn't expected her to stew for so long.

He didn't get it, she'd gone out on three dates with three different guys, none of them even remotely a match for her, but she needed three days to decide if she wanted to have dinner with him. He hadn't gotten down on one knee, and he wasn't asking for forever. He was just asking for a little of her time, to see where this unbreakable connection could lead them.

He got why she was hesitant. There was a lot at stake. After years of dodging her, she was finally back in his life and he didn't want to lose her. He'd rather have her as a friend than sever what was between them. Problem was, when it came to Elsie, friendly was the last thing he felt.

He knew he was a failure at relationships. His job made things impossible. It was why he'd only ever had one meaningful, let's-go-the-distance relationship in his life. And look how that turned out.

He'd seen his parents, with how deep their love could go, just like he'd seen how quickly it could be stolen. One day his dad was fine and well, smiling that smile of a man who had the entire world at his fingers, the next he was sick. Seeing his dad deteriorate had torn Rhett apart.

That weekend with Elsie had been a bright light during a rough time in his life. The sex hadn't been just amazing, it was surface of the sun hot. Even more, she'd been, to date, the most incredible woman he'd ever met, making him laugh and feel something other than grief. His dad had been dying, his mom drowning in sorrow, and in the middle of that heartache came Elsie, who provided this reprieve, a safe haven where nothing mattered outside of her apartment.

Almost immediately after meeting her, his dad passed and he'd channeled all that anger and mourning into his career. His grief was so consuming, he didn't have what it took to be in a relationship, not one that would be fair to the other person.

Elsie was the kind of woman who deserved someone's entire heart, and Rhett's was shattered. How could he be happy when his family was in so much pain?

Then a day became a week, and a week, a month. He'd kept that gum wrapper with her number on it for nearly a year, but with all the changes happening in his world, he'd never found the right time to call. And then he'd run into her with Axel and like that, his time was up, so he told himself to move on.

And he did, it just took a while. Steph wasn't the first woman he'd had a long-term relationship with, but she'd been the first one who tempted him to walk down the aisle.

Just as quickly as he'd fallen for Steph, their marriage had fallen apart. He wasn't sure he wanted to go through that again. That's why his proposition to Elsie was simple—a friends with benefits offer that came with zero expectations, zero strings, and zero chance of breaking his heart. They could spend the summer getting the other person out of their system in a win-win situation.

So what was her holdup?

He'd done his best to keep out of her way. A hard task since they shared the same square feet, including the master shower since the guest bath was currently under renovation, leaving his bathroom smelling like a unique mixture of sawdust, paint thinner, and lavender. He never took Elsie for a flower kind of woman, but the scent of lavender would forever give him a hard-on.

So he'd kept himself busy, spending a lot of time not doing what he'd come home to do. And that was write. So last night he'd stayed on his boat, with only his guitar and the faint hint of lavender on his shirt for company, determined to put something to paper. And what he'd come up with was the beginnings of something decent. Better than decent, it had the potential to be a hit. Which was why he was at his agent's office.

Holding Littleshit, he strode down a hallway lined with signed sports paraphernalia and platinum records. Half of those records belonged to Subtle Warfare. Rhett was looking to put a few up there with his solo album. He was over being a pussy, over writer's block, and over letting his old insecurities, which came from his divorce, define him. He was ready to get down to work.

Arf.

Littleshit looked up at Rhett and panted happily, his tail swishing so hard his entire backside wiggled. Rhett gave him a ruffle behind the ears. The dog might be a menace, but he was Rhett's menace. Plus, he'd come to like the ball of floof. The mutt was the only constant in Rhett's life at the moment.

He was hoping to change that.

"Hey, Holly," he said to Gage's secretary, setting Littleshit on the floor and choking up on the leash.

"Long time no see." Holly stood and came around to give him a welcoming hug, which was big on the welcome. She was tall, stacked, and slid up against him in a blatant invitation.

A few months back, they'd shared a night and it had been a good time. So good he'd been looking for another opportunity to see her. The expression flashing on her face said she was open for a replay.

A few weeks ago, it would have been go time. But suddenly, Rhett wasn't feeling it.

Problem was, he hadn't felt it for another woman since Elsie moved in. It was one thing to go without when you were locked away in a basement, it was another when the opportunity was staring you in the face and there wasn't even a stir.

He checked in with his dick, willing it to do something, but it was silent on the subject. Holly must have sensed the change because she stepped back with a *well isn't that a shame* smile.

"Is Gage in?"

"Yes, but…" Her eyes fell to Littleshit, who was dressed like a backup singer for Britney Spears. Thanks to his ex, the dog wouldn't leave the house without wearing some brand of critter couture. "There's a strict no dog policy on this floor of the place." She pointed to a poster of a dog with a big red X through it—with Littleshit being the poster pet.

At the sight of his face on the sign, negative or not, Littleshit barked and Holly jumped back in fear. Eyes big and wary, arms crossed protectively around her waist, she said, "Maybe you should leave her in the car."

Littleshit went apeshit, his little legs pumping to get to Holly, straining against the leash, determined to break free and gnaw Holly's heels right off her feet. "*He* isn't big on being left alone. Plus, Gage would love to see his nephew." He looked down at Littleshit, who ran around in excited circles. "Isn't that right, boy."

Yip. Yip. Arf.

"I don't think that would be a good idea," Holly said as Rhett ignored her and strode to the closed door, Littleshit following in his wake. "Plus, Gage is in an, um, meeting."

"I know."

Against Holly's protest, Rhett opened the door and—

"Jesus!" He looked away against the image of Gage getting up close and personal with his wife, Darcy.

163

"Seriously?" Rhett said, lifting the dog and shielding his eyes.

"Sorry, bro." Darcy was trying to untangle herself from Gage like it was an Olympic sport, but Gage wasn't so fast to let her go. "But in my defense, you didn't call."

"I need to call to see my brother?"

Gage pointed to his watch. "At eight in the morning? Yeah."

"Eight?" Darcy said, buttoning the top button of her dress. "I'm supposed to meet a new couple at eight thirty. I'm going to be late." She smoothed down her hair, which did not help one bit. "How do I look?"

Gage tucked a stray hair behind his wife's ear. "Like you just got lucky."

"Rhett?"

Rhett held up his hands. "I plead the fifth."

Darcy was a wedding planner, who owned one of the most popular venues on the west coast. She had taken a run-down old mansion and turned it into the destination for the who's who of Celebrity-ville. Rhett and Steph had been some of her first clients.

She and Gage were proof that love could conquer all, and not just because they'd once been bitter enemies. In addition to being a runaway bride, and leaving Gage's twin brother, Kyle, at the altar, she'd also kept it a secret that she was carrying Kyle's baby. It wasn't until years after Kyle was killed in a car crash that Gage had discovered they'd had a niece. Gage fell hard and fast for Darcy, but it took the rest of the family some time to come to terms with things. The Eastons were lucky Darcy didn't kick them all out of her life for good.

Luckily for them, while most of the Eastons sought blame, Gage had the forethought to see an opportunity to heal their family. And Darcy had a big enough heart to give them all a second chance.

Darcy gave him a long, hard look that had him squirming in his shoes. "If I weren't so late, I'd get to the bottom of this roommate you're hiding."

Rhett gulped. His sister-in-law had gained more confessions from him and his brothers than a Catholic priest.

"You wouldn't want to keep true love waiting, now would you?" she continued. She gave Rhett a knowing smile and gave Gage a parting kiss. "See you after work, sweetie."

When she shut the door, Rhett lifted a brow. "Sweetie?"

"You sleeping with anything but an ugly-ass dog lately?"

Littleshit went ballistic, lunging for the jugular. Rhett released the kraken and the dog charged under the desk. Just when he was about to attack, he lifted his leg and peed on Gage's shoe.

Gage shot up. "Are you kidding me?" He shook his foot. "I have a strict no dog policy."

"He isn't a dog, he's an icon. Has more followers on social media than me."

"He's a demon."

Said demon strutted proudly back to papa and Rhett picked him up. The dog walked around in three exact circles on Rhett's lap, then lay down and closed one eye—the other was eyeballing Gage, as if ready to attack at any sudden movements.

"And apparently a cockblock too," Gage said, taking off his shoes with disgust.

"What does that mean?"

Gage leaned back in his chair, then kicked his sock-clad feet up on the desk. "You're living with a beautiful woman, who you've had a boner for since college, and you're still sleeping in your own bed."

He might still be in his own bed, but he was on her mind. And that was more important than a one-night stand.

"I don't want to talk about it."

"You don't have to. I can tell you're about as close to getting laid as Clay is to getting Jillian to marry him."

Clay and Jillian had been dating for over a year and while Clay would love to tie the knot, Jillian didn't see the need to follow society norms. Not that his baby brother minded; Clay was happy just to make the love of his life happy.

As if remembering the time, Gage asked, "What are you doing in my office this early? Shouldn't you be doing something very rock star, like sleeping until noon? Or, I don't know, maybe writing?"

"As a matter of fact, that's part of the reason I'm here," he said. "I've got something."

Gage flashed his teeth. "What kind of something."

"A fan-fucking-tastic kind of something. It's not ready yet." Rhett was very private about his work. A lot like someone else he knew who had to have it perfect before having others weigh in. And while most artists didn't go to their agent for creative direction, Gage was more than his agent and brother. He was the guy who stepped up when their dad passed and put all his confidence and belief in Rhett and his music. "But it's practically writing itself."

"What changed?"

"What do you mean?"

"How did you go from brain fart to fan-fucking-tastic?"

Elsie, a little whisper said. It started that morning they'd sparred in her bed while she'd been in nothing but a pink thong, then grew stronger after that kiss—or should he say kisses.

Rhett lifted a shoulder. "Maybe being home is what I needed."

"So you're thinking of your tax shelter as home?"

Was he? Even under renovations, the place felt warm and welcoming with a distinct feminine feel that softened the creative vibe, which was fine by him. Maybe that vibe was what was making the notes flow. Was it his home? He didn't know but it felt like a hell of a lot more than a simple investment.

"It's coming along," was all he was going to say on the matter. "Speaking of coming along, how is Portland Live going?"

"Good, why?"

"Well, I wanted to talk about the final lineup."

Gage looked at his watch. "At eight? On a Tuesday?"

"I thought today we were going over the logistics of the event." He looked at the door. "Where is everyone?"

"Probably in bed with their wives since the meeting is scheduled for *tomorrow* at eight. And since when do you help with the event?"

"I help every year."

"No, you give me a list of musicians, then leave the rest up to the rest of us. You haven't helped with the logistics since you started dating Steph."

Had it been that long? And since when had he become the guy who left his brothers hanging? Steph hadn't been all that big on spending time with Rhett's family. After the way his mom treated her during the planning of the wedding, he didn't blame her. But it was one of the points of contention during their short marriage.

But he'd been divorced going on a year now and he still hadn't been pulling his weight. And that was on him.

"Well, I want to do more." This year he needed to be around family. Needed to play a bigger role, to feel a part of something instead of being the something. "I've been thinking about mentoring some of the musicians. Help them pick their music, really give some one-on-one advice."

His brother's eyes went wide. "What about your schedule and your writing? It sounds like you're on a roll."

"I am, but I really need this album to pop and I think I can do that better by going back to a time before everything changed. To work with musicians who are still hungry and raw. Remember what it was like to jam with some of Dad's old cronies at the bar. I want to give to these kids that same chance I was given."

"Does this sudden change in your involvement have anything to do with the roommate whose party you crashed?" Before Rhett could deny anything, Gage said, "Shawn of the Dead?"

Rhett groaned. "I didn't really crash it, I was helping." Then he'd gone and kissed Elsie and she'd nearly ripped his clothes off. God, he could still taste her on his lips. "How do you even know I was at the party?"

"You're an Easton, bro. The minute you ditched an appearance to go to a gender reveal party, the women in the family started talking. All it took was a few calls for Mom to get to the bottom of it."

"Mom made some calls?" God, he hoped Claire didn't put two and two together and come up with Rhett de-corseting Elsie in the front seat of his car. Even worse, he didn't need his mom sniffing around his personal life.

"What did you expect her to do. The woman could get Castro to give up his deepest darkest secrets."

Margo's love was fierce and unwavering, but it fed into her habit of inserting herself into her sons' private lives. She'd nearly chased off every one of his brothers' wives and girlfriends. Elsie was already relationship-shy, the last thing he needed was his mom poking around and giving Elsie one more reason to say no.

"Shit."

"Is that a problem?" Gage asked.

"Maybe," he said. "I don't know." Rhett rubbed a hand down his face. Jesus, when was the last time he'd slept through the night? Not since his divorce.

"You don't know, or you don't want to talk about it?"

"Both."

Gage dropped his feet to the ground, leaned forward and rested his elbows on the desk, with a *You stepped in it* grin.

"What?" Rhett snapped.

"Nothing. Just the great Rhett Easton has found the one person in the world who won't give in to his charm."

"Not for a lack of trying."

"So you tried and...?"

"It didn't go as planned."

"Usually, you'd move on. What's different?"

She was different. Elsie got to him in ways that nobody else had. Not even his family. "I don't know what it is about her, but I can't seem to walk away." Even when it was the smart thing to do.

"Then why are you in my office instead of at home with your pretty redhead?" Gage asked. "We could have worked all of this out over email."

"I asked her out and she said she had to think about it. And based on the radio silence, there's a lot to think about. She said she was off men, but she's already been on a few first dates with some other guys. Lame ones, too. Not worthy of her."

Gage bit back a grin—the asshole. "And you are? So let me get this straight. You asked her out, she said no, and now you're hiding out in my office?"

"I'm not hiding out. She didn't say no."

"But she didn't say yes," Gage so helpfully pointed out.

"She said she needed time to think things through." Why did he sound so defensive? "I'm giving her space. I don't want to rush her. This is a big decision."

Gage crossed his arms in consideration. "Define 'big.'"

"Big enough that I'm here talking to you." Because that's why he'd come. Yes, he wanted to play a larger role in the event and, yes, the idea of mentoring kids was inspiring. Then there was the fact that he'd spend more time around his family. But he'd come here this morning looking for direction because when it came to Elsie, he was so damn lost.

He knew what he wanted. *Her.* He just wasn't sure how to go about it.

If asked, Rhett could list a hundred-and-one reasons for why this should be a slam dunk. There was but one reason to walk away. He didn't want to hurt her. They'd been down this road before and he'd put an abrupt end to things and disappointed her. They were in the same place, but this time there was more at stake. And the sexual awareness? It burned hot enough to scorch the earth.

"If it's that big, why aren't you talking to her?" Gage asked.

"She needs time to weigh the pros and cons."

"She said that?"

"Yeah, well, actually no." Rhett had said it. She'd asked him if he was serious about becoming a *them*, even if he was leaving for LA in a few weeks, followed by the end of Subtle Warfare's tour. He'd been so afraid she'd tell him to eff-off, he hadn't let her answer, then he'd avoided her for a few days. *Shit!* "I think I screwed up."

"We're Eastons. It's what we do. You want to know what you do?"

"Not really."

"You please."

"What the hell does that even mean?"

"You give everything you have to everyone. It's part of the reason you're so successful in an industry where everyone fails. You're a pleaser."

"And here I thought it had to do with talent and hard work."

"Those too, but you're like Dad in that you'll keep on giving even after your well is tapped. One," Gage held up a finger and ticked off the ways Rhett was supposedly ruining his life, "you give your fans what they want." Another finger. "Your band what they need." A third finger joined the others, "And your family your unyielding support."

"And that's a bad thing?"

"In your professional life? Hell no. But in your personal life? You're so focused on everyone else's needs, you forget yourself."

Rhett held up a finger of his own. "I'm stepping out on my own with this album."

"Which is great. Seriously, I'm excited for you. It's been a long time coming," he said. "But take your divorce, you gave Steph everything she asked for without question or hesitation. It's no wonder why you're in burnout."

"You're saying the past few years have been hell because I'm too nice?"

"Maybe."

"So I should become a prick?"

"I'm not Yoda, man, but take stock of your past year. You're homeless, burnt out, and the proud parent of a dog you never wanted because it was easier to give Steph what *she* wanted than to tell anyone what *you* wanted." Gage got really quiet. "What do you want, Rhett?"

Rhett could name a dozen things that he wanted, and they all centered around a prickly redhead. His brother sat back with a smug grin. "That's what I thought."

CHAPTER FOURTEEN

Dating Tips from Elsie Dodd
No expectations, no disappointments.

Elsie stood in the music room, gritting her teeth, trying to contain her temper as the county inspector, who was there to sign off on the new plumbing in the guest bath, hemmed and hawed. It wasn't that there was anything wrong with the work, *Stan* was expecting to deal with Big Pete. Except Big Pete had moved on to his next job and Elsie was finishing the remodel, including the guest bath, on her own.

She'd located a refurbished, 1960s chest of drawers converted to a modern vanity. Made from teak, it had sleek, clean lines and curved edges, with two square brass handles located in the middle, making it look more like a piece of art than bathroom furniture. She'd also planned on replacing the flooring with narrow, rectangular stone tiles and adding an extra sink, which was where the inspector came in.

In order to turn the single sink vanity into a double, they'd needed to move around some piping, which introduced the need of an inspector. All she required was his signature, then she could repatch the wall and begin the install.

Stan was going on and on about needing to see the original plans Big Pete had used, which was a problem since Big Pete, she'd learned, was more of a go-by-touch sort than a by-blueprint contractor. He got the job done, and it was good work, it just didn't always follow the layout to the letter.

Stan's lips were flapping about why protocol was important and how wasting the county's precious resources should be punishable by law, and something about eating into his lunch hour—she couldn't be sure since she was yawning.

Yesterday, after her time with Carla, she came home feeling confident in her decision. She'd wanted to talk to Rhett, but he'd been a no-show—which left her uncertain. She tried to tell herself it wasn't any of her business what he did, they weren't committed. Heck, they hadn't even agreed on what that kiss meant or how his proposition would work. Did it leave room for other women? That would be a hard no for her. Then again, she didn't see Rhett as a woman juggler like Axel.

What did she know? Maybe he made these kinds of offers all the time. Who was to say she was the only woman to capture his short-term interest? The idea sent a shot of white-hot jealousy crashing through her. Silly because they'd engaged in a little touching and a little kissing. Nothing more. She had zero claims on him.

But you want to.

With idle hands and all of that, Elsie had worked well into the night preparing the subflooring for the new tile. This morning she'd awoken at dawn to put the first coat of paint in the music room so it would be dry enough for its second coat.

"The next appointment I can give you would be a week from Tuesday, assuming you can get a hold of the contractor," Stan said.

That snapped her wide awake. "I am acting contractor, completing the renovations myself. And a whole week would put me behind schedule."

Dangerously behind schedule. Carla was coming on Saturday with her photographer to shoot the new rooms and Elsie needed the house looking pristine, just in case the impossible became possible.

"Until I can get the contractor to sign off on the work he did do, I'm kind of stuck."

"I did the work." Big Pete had been securing the three wooden beams to the ceiling in the music room and prepping the walls for paint. Elsie had taken over the bathroom.

Stan scratched the balding spot on his head with the tip of his pen, leaving behind a blue line. "You the owner?"

Wasn't that the question of the hour. The truth was, today was closing day and she wasn't sure if escrow had closed or if she was still the owner. She'd received a call from Axel and two from her banker, but she'd sent them to voice mail. Her gut told her that the house was no longer hers, but *hearing* those words would change everything. She would be nothing more than a hired gun renovating a beautiful house that was no longer hers and that Rhett was now the rightful owner.

She'd even brought out a bottle of bubbly she'd been saving for her last night in the house. She'd imagined it would be her alone, saying goodbye to an old friend. Instead, it was a celebration of Rhett closing on his new house. It was hard to let go, but she was discovering it was even harder to hold on.

"No, as of today I'm not the owner," she said honestly. "But the owner and I have an understanding."

"So he hired you?"

"Not really. More of a favor."

He didn't look like he believed her.

She flashed a smile. "Carte blanche was the term used." She'd used the term, not Rhett, but what Stan didn't know wouldn't hurt him.

With a sigh, Stan flipped through his clipboard at the stacks of inspection sheets he still had yet to complete. She knew she was losing him.

"Okay, so here's the truth. Up until twenty-four hours ago this was my house. But my cheating bastard of an ex sold it right out from under me. Now I have this once in a lifetime opportunity to be featured in *Modern Masterpiece*. You heard of it?"

Stan crossed his arms across his chest, looking unimpressed.

"It's a magazine and a big deal in my world. If I'm chosen, and that's a big if, then this house will be showcased in their Portland edition."

"Like one of those showcase homes they show on television."

"Exactly." Only in a magazine. How were people missing the point? "So you see my problem. If they pick me, then this house would need to be ready in a little under three weeks. A delay, even as small as a week, could jeopardize everything."

Stan looked at her as if she were crazy.

"Are you married?" she asked.

"Divorced. She took the house and the dog. Man, I loved that dog."

"Then you know how these things go. All I'm asking for is for you to look at my work, then tell me if it meets code."

"Is the owner home?"

No, no he wasn't. In fact, she'd spent so much time mulling over his proposal that she'd overthought him right out of the house—if his empty bed this morning was anything to go by.

"He's right here," a familiar voice said from behind.

She turned her head and watched as Rhett strode into the room, gracefully navigating the crates of tiles, electric tools, and stacks of lumber. He was dressed in a pair of cargo shorts, a blue tee advertising his band, flip-flops and dark glasses—looking deceptively casual. Which was in direct contrast to the confident swagger in his gait.

Her mouth went dry, which worked since he looked like a tall, cold drink of water.

Three days, her body reminded. Three days they'd been avoiding each other. She'd blamed him but she'd been at fault as well. She'd distracted herself by working her ass off on getting the renovations complete, which served as a valid avoidance tactic. And he'd been content to let her, but the way he was looking at her now said *time was up.*

It said a whole lot more, the kind of more that had her thighs quivering.

"Nice to meet you, man." Rhett stuck out his hand and, to her utter surprise, Stan pumped it enthusiastically. "I'm the owner."

Elsie's heart sank a little. So it was true. Escrow had closed. She tried to look away, to blink back the wave of sadness. She'd hoped to conceal her roiling emotions, but nothing got past Rhett. His direct gaze locked on hers and warm understanding passed between them.

"I'd heard someone big had bought the place. My kids are going to freak," Stan said, and that's when Elsie realized he wasn't waffling because he doubted her work, he wanted to meet the new celebrity tenant.

She rolled her eyes and—*whoops,* caught. Rhett looked at her over his sunglasses, delivering a panty-melting grin.

"Would you mind taking a picture with me? To show the guys at work."

Rhett smiled easily but Elsie could see past the casual façade. He didn't want to take the photo and she knew why.

"Actually, Stan. I imagine Mr. Easton would want to keep his privacy a little while longer. At least until he has time to move in," Elsie said.

Stan blushed so bright the tips of his ears flamed. "Of course, I didn't even think."

"I don't mind," Rhett lied, and stood next to Stan, who was grinning like a fool. He handed Elsie the camera. "Elsie, would you...?"

Her look said, *you sure?* When he nodded, she took the phone. "On three. One, two, three." She snapped a few pics, then handed back Stan's camera. "Now, about that permit."

"Everything looked fine to me." Stan scribbled his name and checked off some boxes. "I'll file this with the county, and you should be good to go."

Elsie folded her arms. "That easy?"

"That easy."

"Thanks for coming out," Rhett said. "And I'd appreciate it if you'd keep those photos under wraps for a few weeks. You can show them to your family, but let's let the guys at work sweat it out a little while longer."

"You bet," Stan said as if he met legendary superstars every day. "When you're ready for the final permit on the remodel be sure to ask for me." He pulled a card from his pocket. Elsie reached for it, but he handed it to Rhett. "I'll make sure everything is handled in a timely manner."

"We appreciate that," Rhett said, purposefully handing the card to Elsie, which made her heart do a little tap dance, then he walked the inspector out, chatting away the entire distance from the bathroom to the front door. Rhett laid on his usual charm and Elsie wondered how tiring it must be to manage extreme expectations, while placing others' wants in the forefront. When people met Rhett it was one of the highlights of their lives—a fact that Rhett took to heart. It was why he was so generous with his time.

She'd once heard that he'd sat for twelve hours straight at a music festival to make sure he signed something for every fan who'd turned out to see him. That was on top of being the headline act. She didn't know how he did it, but part of his success came from his kind and generous spirit. And tenacity. Something she needed to adopt if she wanted to make this business of hers a success.

A trait that, had she used it during her divorce, might have saved her the Greenhill house—and her pride. Axel had taken a lot from her, things that she was slowly coming to understand. The house was the tip of the iceberg.

Carla was right. She did need to move on—be open to some fun.

She could hear Rhett and Stan talking about speaker installation and rolled her eyes. He'd talk until Stan was ready to leave, it was in his nature.

Elsie picked up the paint roller and began painting over Big Pete's Igloo Frost walls. She didn't know why she was so ticked. If Rhett hadn't shown up, she likely wouldn't have gotten the sign off. But maybe that's what irked her. That she hadn't been able to get it done. This was her project, her house—at least until a few hours ago—and she couldn't even convince the city inspector that the perfectly executed plumbing was up to snuff.

After a long moment she realized that someone was staring at her back. She didn't turn to meet his gaze.

"Thanks," was all she said, but even to her ears she sounded defensive.

"The guy was an ass," he said, directly behind her. So close she could feel his breath skate down her neck. Then his hands rested on her shoulders and he began to massage away the stress from the day. Mindlessly, she melted under his touch.

"I didn't have everything buttoned up like I should have."

"He was an ass," he repeated.

"He was right. I should have thought to have Big Pete here since I knew the inspector was coming and might have questions. Is it true?" she asked casually, proud that her voice didn't betray her. To prove she was holding strong, she bent over and rolled the roller in the deep blue paint, a color that was more Rhett than the original color she'd chosen. "Did escrow close?"

"Yes," he whispered.

Her chin dropped to her chest. It was official. The house was no longer hers. Yes, she'd get to finish it, and wasn't that what she'd wanted? Suddenly, it didn't feel like enough.

"I know this isn't what you imagined and I'm sorry for the role I played."

She lifted a very tired shoulder and let it fall. "I was out-manned and outmaneuvered. With Axel's legal team, my divorce was like David versus Goliath." She turned to face him. "None of that is your fault. And if the house had to go to anyone, I'm glad it's you."

And she meant it. More than even Grandma Harriet, Rhett knew what this house represented to her. He might not keep it the exact way she designed it, but he'd respect and appreciate the finished product.

He stood there silently regarding her, absorbing her words. "Els—"

Swallowing past the pity party, she waved him off with a big, fat smile on her face. "It's not your fault, Rhett. Plus, we should be celebrating. You're the official owner of your dream home. Or at least your new home."

"This is actually my first home."

"Ever?"

He shrugged. "I lived on the road so a house of my own seemed a waste, so I'd stay with one of my brothers when I came to town. Then there was Steph, who made every decision down to the color of stain on the garage door. So they'd never felt like mine."

He'd never had a chosen home of his own and he'd chosen hers. Warmth washed through her. "Why this house, then?"

"At first, I told myself it was nothing more than a convenient solution to a pressing problem. I needed to establish residency, Axel told me about the house, which has a recording studio and privacy; it was an easy yes. But now, looking around, being in the space, I think I bought it because it reminded me of a time when things were simpler, happier. A time when I loved my music and my job."

"You'd only ever been here a handful of times. And every time, the house was under major renovations."

He reached out and tucked a strand of hair behind her ear. "It made a lasting impression."

Gone was the guy who'd been letting her avoid him and back was the confident, irresistible guy from the other night.

"I know the feeling," she admitted quietly.

He took the roller out of her hand and placed it on the paint tray sitting on the tarp directly behind them, then cupped her hips. His eyes were open and locked on hers even as he got closer and closer, her heartbeat beating faster and faster, bordering on stroke levels. The sexual awareness burned hot enough to melt the icecaps.

He descended, his speed was slow but steady and then there he was, their lips a breath away. "What are you feeling now, Red?"

She grabbed the hem of his shirt. "Safe." Tugged the shirt from his shorts. "Sexy." She slid her hands higher, her fingers exploring the soft skin and hard muscle beneath the cotton. "Combustible."

His nostrils flared and, gaze never wavering, his mouth crashed down on hers. It wasn't a tentative kiss. It was hot and heady and languid all at the same time. It didn't take her long to catch up to speed, wrapping her arms around his neck and plastering herself to him like a koala on a tree.

When they finally came up for air, he rested his forehead against hers. "I missed you." He cradled her head with his big, strong hands. "I tried to be patient, waited for you to make your decision, but I can't wait anymore. I need to know if you're in this."

Her heart was saying yes, but her head was telling her to slam on the brakes, throw that baby in reverse, and burn rubber out of there. Because, no matter what Carla had said, getting into something with someone who was destined to leave was crazy.

Based on the way her fingers were sliding around to explore the sinew of his back, her body was already committed. Her heart was warier. Lust was a powerful motivator, but she'd always been cautious when it came to letting people in.

Because they always leave, she reminded herself. But she knew the deal, knew the rules, had even written them down in case this thing was to progress.

Oh, who was she kidding. It had already progressed. She'd thought of nothing else since his proposition. Even when telling herself not to think about him, she couldn't help but think about him. Which was why, last night, after she'd returned home from the bar, she'd made a list of a few hard and fast rules that could never ever—even if she wanted to, like in the throes of an orgasm—be broken.

She removed her hands from his person and took a centering breath. "Are you in this?"

She met his intense blue gaze and a flash of white-hot lightning hammered in her chest at the conviction she saw there. "You already know the answer to that."

She did. It was right there in his eyes, burning dark and making her heart pound wildly.

"If this is going to work—"

His hands slid down her spine to the curve of her back— and lower. "Oh, it'll work."

"There needs to be rules," she said primly. She took a tiny step back, out of his arms, and nearly bumping into the freshly painted wall. "I can't think straight when you're touching me, and I need to think right now."

"Is 'no touching' one of these rules? Because, honey, you blew through that rule a second ago. Plus, that won't work for me."

She reached into the back pocket of her jeans and pulled out a piece of paper. She unfolded it and cleared her throat. "If this is going to work," she repeated, "we have to agree that there will be no expectations beyond this agreement. No changing the rules midgame."

"No expectations, but the game plan is negotiable."

"No, no negotiations, Rhett," she whispered. "I need to set firm boundaries, so no one gets hurt." Namely her. "At some point you have to get back to your life and the road and I don't want to be waiting here for scraps of your time."

"I've been walked away from too. I'm in this for as long as you'll let me," he said with a gentle directness that made her heart catch.

"I'm in this for as long as you're home."

"So are you saying that afterward we what, go our separate ways like nothing happened?" Now he sounded disbelieving and something else. Angry?

"I hope we part friends," she said, wondering if a with-benefits relationship could become a platonic one. If, when their time was up, she could walk away and still not want him.

Which is why the rules are there, she reminded herself.

A cut-and-dried agreement where they can give in to the want and get each other out of their systems and then move on to their regularly scheduled lives.

It would tear them in opposing directions but that was the point. She had too many dreams that had been put on hold for too long to ask for more. And he had his career, which was a lifestyle she'd already lived and lost out big.

"Which brings me to number two. We both have to be honest about what we want."

"I want you."

Oh boy. That simple, three-word sentence had the power to melt her panties right off. Then there was the way he was looking at her with that all-consuming, hungry gaze. She felt herself being pulled into the relationship trap.

"No moon-eyes," she said affirmingly.

His lips quirked with humor. "What's moon-eyes?"

"You know, the sappy, *aren't we cute* look that people get when they're in a relationship, because this will never be a relationship."

"No expectations, honesty, and no moon-eyes. Got it."

"No words of affection. Public or otherwise. And that includes during sex." She felt her face heat, but this was an important rule. The intimacy that came with sweet nothings or caught-up-in-the-moment admissions could turn this from a with-benefits to *more*. And she didn't want to accidently fall into more.

"If I remember correctly, when it comes to the bedroom, you're the chatty one. In fact, you liked to call me babe. Actually, you'd scream 'Oh babe.' 'Yes, babe.' 'Harder, babe—'"

She smothered his mouth with her hands. "I did not."

"Number two. Honesty. Remember?" He kissed the inside of her palm and when she moved to pull away, he took her hand in his. "And I like it when you call me babe."

She liked it too. She also liked how his eyes would go soft when she called him that—soft like moon-eyes. "Okay, but only in the bedroom. I don't want anyone else to know about us."

"Does that make me your dirty little secret?"

"We're each other's secret. The last thing I want is to answer more questions about relationships ending." She went serious. "I want this thing between us to be fun and freeing and I can't do that if, when this ends, a line of people will want all the juicy details. I went through that once, I don't want a replay."

"I'd never do anything to hurt you, including sharing private moments between us," he said softly. "However, if we're being honest, I need to tell you that my brothers already know."

She groaned. "How?"

A boyish grin spread across his face. "I may or may not have let our weekend slip years ago, so when my brother

Gage found out we were living together, he put two and two together. By now I'm sure it's blown through my entire family tree."

"We're not living together. We're sharing space. And your *whole* family?"

"Probably even the bad apples. It's the downside of having a big family."

"Are there upsides?" she found herself asking.

His smile said it all. It was bright and nostalgic and carried an emotion she'd never known. Being an only child had its perks but mainly it just left her feeling lonely. When her dad walked out, her mom buried herself in work, leaving Harriet to raise Elsie. And she loved her grandmother fiercely, but Harriet couldn't be all things all the time.

"More than I can count. Like pointing out when you're too dumb to acknowledge what's right in front of you."

Note to self: avoid Rhett's family at all costs. If their BS meters were that attuned, she didn't want to be anywhere near them. Because then they'd see that, no matter how casual she was playing this, Elsie *was* crushing hard. And she needed to know upfront how he felt about her.

"What's right in front of you?"

"You." He leaned in and ran his lips over the outer shell of her ear. "I like you, Red." He gave a little nip to her lobe. "I liked you back then and I like you now. And I'm okay with keeping things between us quiet so long as there's an *us*."

A thrill raced through her, sparking a chain reaction of warm fuzzies and something more complicated that she wasn't willing to dissect at the moment. Something that could jeopardize their no-strings agreement.

"I like you too." *A lot.* "Which brings me to the fifth and final rule. No sleepovers. After we, well you know, then we go to our respective beds."

He looked around the room as if cataloguing every flat surface, wall, and nook that was still in play and her toes curled. "Does that eliminate morning sex?"

She quivered at the thought. Oh, how she enjoyed morning sex. It was lazy and languid and, with Rhett, it was a religious experience.

"You can climb into bed with me in the morning, but once we're done there's no lingering."

He trailed a finger down her neck to the start of her cleavage. "You like it when I linger. And, this being an equal opportunity situation, what if I want *you* to climb into *my* bed?"

Her heart sank and every reason that this was a problem started to bubble to the surface. "I won't ever go in that bed again," she whispered, humiliation igniting in her belly. "He brought other women here, in our bed, and I just can't—"

Rhett brushed a gentle kiss over her lips. "Your bed it is."

That was it. No questions asked, no further explanation needed. Just a simple acknowledgement of how bad Axel's betrayal had been.

"Thank you."

He tipped her chin. "He's an idiot, Els. He was lucky to have you and a fool to lose you."

Her heart shifted in her chest. Logically she knew this, knew that it wasn't her fault. But sometimes the betrayal went so deep it was hard to look in the mirror and not question her part in what had transpired over the past few years. Wonder why she was so easy to walk away from. To lie to and hide things from. Which was why her last rule was the most important.

"There's one more thing."

"You said five," he teased, but she didn't smile.

"This isn't a guideline or a rule. It's a dealmaker or breaker, there's no in the middle," she said. "I can't handle lies or empty promises of any kind. This is about more than honesty, it's about keeping my heart safe. If you don't feel it, don't say it. If you can't deliver, then don't bring it up. Trust is hard for me, like really hard, but I'm willing to give this a try if you are."

His eyes searched hers for a long moment but said nothing. When he finally spoke, she could hear the gravity in his voice. "I will never lie to you or disappoint you. I've been on the losing side, too, and I know how bad it can hurt. How it can make you question your own judgment. Your trust is safe with me."

"And yours is safe with me," she said. A sense of intimacy fell over them and the world fell away. The past heartache and disappointment vanished, and Elsie allowed her walls to lower and her heart to open. "How about you? Any rules?"

"Just one. As long as we're together, you're mine. No more first dates. No Walking Dead, no Mr. Lofty, no one else."

She didn't know how she felt about the possessiveness of being someone's "mine," but when he said it, it sounded more like a vulnerable admission than someone staking claim. It was the uncertainty in his eyes, she decided. An uncertainty that reached out to her and pulled her in—all the way in.

"And what about you? Are you just mine?"

"I've been yours since that morning in the bathroom."

She blinked. "So you haven't been with anyone—"

He shook his head. "Since the bathroom," he repeated, and her heart slammed against her chest. She wasn't sure what that meant but her belly fluttered like a thousand butterflies took flight.

"Just you and me," she said, and his smile went wicked.

"Then, grab on to me, Red, because this is going to be one hell of a ride," he said, resting his hands above her and nudging her up against the wall.

CHAPTER FIFTEEN

Dating Tips from Elsie Dodd
Don't forget your pleasure passport.
There are so many places to explore.

The ride hadn't even begun, and Elsie was already wet. From her head to her toes and all the spots in-between.

"I just painted this wall," she said as he peppered kisses down her throat.

"My bad." With a mischievous look, he took his hands off the wall and placed them on her backside. His paint-covered palms cupped each cheek and gave a squeeze, leaving two Rhett-sized prints on her ass.

She squeaked. "These are my favorite jeans."

He gave another squeeze. "Now they're mine."

"This is my favorite shirt of yours." He looked down and frowned when he realized he was wearing a faded U of O shirt. "It reminds me of that first night we met."

"Had I known, I would have worn it the first day in the shower." His hands went to her waist, and he popped the button of her jeans.

She looked around. Yes, the ground was covered with tarps, but everything else was bare. "We're going to get everything all dirty."

"We can't have that." With just his thumb and forefinger, he expertly pulled down her zipper, leaving behind not a single trace of paint.

"What happened to being a date first kind of guy?"

"There's bubbly in the fridge. I brought home takeout. Close enough for me. Now, about how dirty you are." He tugged at the waist and slid her jeans efficiently down her legs and she stepped out of them. Next went her hoodie, which he unzipped—with his teeth—exposing a sliver on bare skin as he went. Her body trembled with anticipation.

He languorously kissed his way down her neck to her collarbone, the valley between her breasts, stopping short at the red lace of her bra. With an appreciative groan he nosed the zip-up sweatshirt to the side, producing one beaded breast, then the other as the hoodie slid down her arms.

"Where to begin?"

He nuzzled one breast before paying equal attention to the other, going side to side, his mouth hovering over each nipple, over the soft cotton of her shirt, never once coming into contact. In fact, besides his breath, he wasn't touching her at all. His paint-covered hands hung at his sides, his body a scant inch from brushing hers, his mouth taunting.

"What are you doing?" she asked.

"I can't get you all dirty, now, can I? Lose the shirt, Red," he commanded. She lost the shirt. "Now the bra." She reached back for the clasp and he kissed her valley. "Slowly. I want to watch the lace reveal just how much I turn you on."

Her fingers trembled as she followed his instruction, nearly going into meltdown as she watched him watching her with rapt attention.

"Where to start? Maybe here?" He licked her liberated breasts before sucking them deep inside his mouth, his tongue toying with her nipples, his teeth tenderly scraping and sending her careening down a path toward pleasure. The harder he sucked, the tighter she squeezed her thighs together.

"Or maybe here." He kissed the soft patch of skin right below her navel, lingering, letting her know that he remembered all her favorite spots. "Oh, I know." He sank to his knees, pressed those broad shoulders between her legs, and looked up at her. "You want me here."

Yes. Yes she did. She wanted him right there with his talented mouth that had driven her crazy for an entire weekend. She knew what came next—and it would be her.

He still wasn't touching her, but he was watching, intently, seeing everything. "It's not just the paint that's wet," he said, his voice rough. "Are you wet for me, Red?"

Before she could answer, he kissed her, right in the middle of her lace. Her head fell back on a loud moan as that kiss became a lick. He pulled back, and blew gently, his breath brushing against her core and then his mouth was on her again. Nipping and licking and driving her out of her ever-loving mind. It was like the years between them fell away; he remembered exactly how she liked it. Even more, how she loved it.

That talented mouth of his worked her until she was about to wobble over, so she did as he'd recommended and held on, threading her fingers through his hair and gripping him for dear life as he tortured her. The suck and draw of his mouth, the gentle graze of his teeth, the lust that flooded her body. Her core ignited like a nuclear reactor moments before a meltdown.

"Rhett," she said it again, but more frantic, her hips pushing against his mouth. "I need—"

Before she could finish, he proved he knew exactly what she needed and gave it to her. Over and over as she rose up toward that precipice, tightening and contracting until she was exploding in record time. When she came crashing down, she was lying on the tarp with Rhett over her, his elbows resting beside her head.

"Welcome back," he said, kissing his way up her navel and snagging her lips in a languorous kiss that had her stretching out beneath him like a sated cat.

She'd just had the best orgasm of her life and she was still in her panties; he hadn't laid a finger on her. And suddenly getting dirty had never felt so erotic.

"That was new," she said, breathless.

"Oh, we're going to explore a lot of new tonight. In fact, it will probably take all night just to get through items one through five. Tomorrow we'll start on six to ten."

Her lady land raised its flag in surrender.

"My turn, and I know where I want to start," she said and reached over and dipped her hand into the paint pan. His expression lifted in challenge and, oh, how she loved a challenge. She rubbed her hands together, then reached between them and palmed his crotch, leaving a handprint on his shorts.

"I figured this was a tit-for-tat situation," she said, and he burst out laughing. She found herself laughing with him. A genuine, warm to the core laugh that felt like a ray of sunshine had penetrated her carefully built wall.

"Tit for tat, huh?" he said, and before she could move, he was straddling her with her hands pinned above her head. "If you say so."

With a gentle stay-put squeeze of the wrists, he dipped his hands in the paint. She could have squirmed away if she wanted to. Only, she liked being pinned beneath him, spread out for his viewing pleasure. A realization that was as shocking as it was exciting.

He placed a single finger in the hollow of her throat. The chill of the paint against her hot skin made her shiver.

His gaze dropped to his finger as he traced a feather-light line right down her middle, between her breasts, dipping into her navel, and when he was hovering just above her panty line, he fanned out his hands, spanning her entire waist. His thumbs rubbed in hypnotizing circles, spreading the paint higher and higher as his hands traveled, and sending her pulse racing until her breath was coming in short, hard bursts.

He took his time retracing his path north, gliding over each rib, his fingers slippery, the paint heating under his touch. His hands were so big in comparison, his fingers spanned her entire width. Then they zeroed in, moving on a direct course to pleasure, and when his hands glided over her breasts, his thumbs scraped against her nipples, creating a delicious bite of pain, and she arched up off the floor.

He sculpted and weighed her breasts, painting until she was panting as he once again brought her close to the edge—and he wasn't even inside her. What he was doing to her felt better than anything she'd ever experienced before.

"Rhett," she pled.

But he wasn't listening because his hands switched course and headed further north, running up her arms, her wrists, painting as he went until finally lacing his fingers with hers. He didn't look away, didn't move, holding her captive with those all-knowing eyes that had haunted her dreams for nearly a decade.

"You steal my breath." He captured her mouth in a searing kiss that, *oh no*, had her heart turning over. It was the way he was holding her, she decided. Reverent and protective, demonstrating a raw vulnerability that made her want to open herself up to all the emotions rushing between them. Emotions that had no place in a with-benefits relationship.

Gah. They hadn't even sealed the deal and already she was thinking in terms of relationships. She needed to bring this back to that biological urge surging between them.

"Off," she said, yanking his shirt over his head and when it fell to the ground her breath caught. The warm summer sun cast a soft glow over his solid jaw and generous lips. He was gorgeous.

She'd been around a lot of tens in her lifetime. Being married to a man who worked in an industry where being a ten was a requirement made her an expert on attractiveness. But never had she seen someone as handsome as Rhett. Sure, there was the award-winning butt, the rock-hard abs, the dimple-packed smile. But it was those piercing eyes that melted her heart and right then they were looking at her as if nothing else in the world mattered.

She shoved him onto his back, now the one straddling him, and sank her hands into the paint and smiled. He met that smile with one of his own, a *give me what you've got* kind, even smugly folding his arms beneath his head.

Elsie started painting those rock-hard abs and felt her way up his entire torso, loving every single inch. He let her explore, take her time, and admire all the hard work he spent honing his body. When she reached his shoulders, those broad I-can-handle-anything shoulders, she found herself needing to take things deeper, so she cupped his jaw and brushed her lips to his.

She wanted this. Wanted him. No, she needed him with an urgency that scared her.

"I'll be right back."

"Whoa." He grabbed her before she could sneak off. "Where are you going?" He studied her gaze and that's when she saw it, an uncertainty that broke her heart a little. He thought she was leaving—that she'd changed her mind.

"I need to get condoms. They're in the bedroom."

A grin spread across his face. "When did you buy condoms, Red?"

"On the way home from Claire's party."

"You mean, I've spent the last three days in agony for nothing?"

"All you had to do was ask." With a smack to the lips, she shoved at his chest to get him off, but he didn't move, except to reach in his back pocket and pull out a roll of condoms. "I bought them the next morning."

"So we both—"

"Wasted three whole days that could've been spent finger painting."

"Which is why we both have to be open and honest about what we want," she said, repeating one of her rules.

"I want you. Now."

"Then lose the pants, babe."

"I like it when you call me babe." He stood, dispensed with his clothes, and came back by her side.

"Lay on your back." She nudged him and he rolled over so that she could straddle him. Which she did, after taking the condoms from his hand. She tore off one and opened it, gently gliding it down his length.

She positioned them and right before she slid down, he said, "Wait," and framed her face with his hands. Then he did the most romantic thing possible, he took her mouth in a kiss that was reverent and tender and all the things that spoke of something much more than sex. When he filled her, it felt like their worlds had collided into one.

"You feel incredible," he whispered, then moved ever so slightly.

Incredible didn't even begin to describe what was happening to her. A zing ricocheted around her chest like a pinball machine, lighting up every sensor it hit. Then there was the lightness in her body, as if some heavy weight had been lifted and she was finally able to breathe without the fear of agonizing pain.

"You okay?" he asked, and she realized she'd rested her forehead to his.

"It's just been a while," she confessed.

"Then we take it extra slow," he said and rolled so that she was tucked beneath him.

Man of his word, he took it soft and smooth and so incredibly good. Then their bodies started to glide. Slick from the paint, they moved like they'd been together forever, completely in sync, as if too tired to continue the fight to resist.

Rhett set a steady rhythm with deep thrusts and even slower withdrawals, nearly backing all the way out before filling her so completely a sense of rightness washed over her. Her heels dug into the floor and her back arched so that she could take all of him. And when that wasn't enough, she wrapped her legs around his waist and squeezed.

"Red," he whispered into her ear, so she did it again. This time when he whispered her name, he whispered her real name and a warmth started in her chest and radiated out. Her throat began to tighten and her eyes burned; she was on the verge of letting this moment take her under. Something she'd promised herself wouldn't happen. But it was—happening—and she didn't know how to fight it.

The pace picked up, the emotions between them intensified and she knew, without a doubt, he was feeling it too. Then she opened her eyes and found him looking back. What she saw there undid her.

"Rhett!" she cried as the orgasm tore through her, a million miles a minute, the power of a comet, it shattered every wall she had put in place. He was right there with her, she realized, because as she squeezed tightly, he gave one last thrust and then he was calling out her name as his body shuddered.

As she was coming down, her breath still lodged in her throat, she felt herself being moved so that she was cradled beside him, his arm wrapped tightly around her. He kissed her temple and whispered soothing things in her ear, something that sounded like, "I can't believe you're finally mine."

And he's yours, her heart said. At least until he wasn't.

CHAPTER SIXTEEN

Dating Tips from Elsie Dodd
Spooning leads to forking.
Use condiments.

"Come to bed," Rhett said, patting the empty spot on the mattress next to him. Elsie gave it a longing look, like she was seriously considering it, then shook her head. "Before you say no sleepovers, I promise there won't be any sleeping."

"You're forgetting rule four," she said sternly, batting away Rhett's hands when he reached for her. "No public displays of affection."

"Says the woman who sweet-talked me into a little back-seat foreplay," Rhett said, and he couldn't help but smile.

She gave the mattress a little nudge and wrinkled her nose in the air. "It's a little soft, don't you think?"

"So you're looking for something harder. I've got you covered. Come over here and let me show you." Sitting, he tugged her between his legs and ran his hands down the backs of her legs.

"Someone might see?" But she didn't back away. In fact, she stepped closer.

"Who? The store's closed." He'd bribed the owner to let them in before opening so that they could look for a new bed and a few other pieces of furniture to finish off the master.

Elsie had put some serious hours into the house. The guest bathroom had turned out spectacular, the music room was in its last stages, and all that was left was the master—the main reason for their little trip downtown.

As far as Rhett was concerned, they could burn down the master and start from scratch, but since he didn't want to deal with insurance, he'd agreed to donate the furniture. That had been a week ago and he was desperate to get Elsie into his bed. Oh, he didn't mind how creative they got with her twin-sized bed or the full-sized one in the spare room, but he needed some space to show off his best moves.

Plus, he needed to see what she looked like with her hair spread out over his pillows, her body snug against him. He knew why she'd put the no snuggling rule into place—just another layer of protection around her heart—but he was hoping to change her mind.

Hell, he was hoping to change her mind on a lot of things.

"What about the manager?" she said.

"Went to grab coffee."

"The windows?"

"Tinted."

"What happened to you needing peace and quiet to work?"

He gently strummed his hands against her thighs, his fingers dancing beneath the hem of her skirt. "I am writing. Plus, I'm getting to the point where I can show someone what I have."

And that was the truth. The more time he spent with Elsie, the easier the music flowed. Her drive to chase her dream was inspiring and made him want to recommit to his. But he wasn't all that certain what his dream looked like anymore. Oh, music was definitely a driving force, but he began to wonder, not for the first time since Stephanie, if maybe his life could be more than just his career. He'd been working toward a stadium tour from the beginning, but it felt good to be writing again and tap into that passion inside.

"Have you shared it with anyone yet?" she asked, moving to sit on his lap.

He shook his head. "I usually show it to Gage first, always have. It's been kind of our thing. He's my quality meter, always being straight up and telling me when it's a hit or when it's B-side material."

"And you don't like B-side material?"

"Nope." He knew a lot of musicians who used subquality songs to fill an album, but that wasn't Rhett's style. He liked to think that every song could be a hit. "But I'm almost there." He could feel it. Feel the album coming together and it felt amazing.

She felt amazing. Just like this, in his arms, so soft and pliant, as if she were his. He knew he was leaving in just under two weeks' time and while part of him knew their lives didn't match up, the other part wanted to fight for a world where they could both have what they wanted and still have each other.

"I shouldn't have blackmailed you into coming here. You should be in the studio working. Or preparing for Portland Live."

"I have a few sessions later this afternoon."

She flicked the bill of his ball cap, sending it falling to the mattress, then ran her fingers into his hair. His eyes closed in pleasure. He loved it when she touched him. "How are you liking mentoring?"

"Actually, a lot. When I first brought it up, it was to reconnect with my roots and authenticity, but it's also given me a chance to show my brothers that I can pull my own weight. Now that I'm in it, it feels really good. There are some really talented kids. Too many."

"What do you mean?"

"We start at three in the afternoon and go until closing, so there's barely enough time for ten sets, but there's this kid, who I met through a friend, and he's really talented."

"He reminds you of you," she guessed.

"How did you know?"

"The way you're talking about him. It's the same way you sounded that first weekend we met."

"He's really good. And there are a few other musicians who didn't make the cut but should have and I don't know how to help them."

"Your faith in them and the time you're giving them is changing their world."

"I wish I could do more."

"What would you have wanted back when you were starting out?"

"A chance to play with some of the old-timers."

"Then give them the chance to play with an old dog."

He tickled her side and she giggled. "Are you saying I'm old?"

"Maybe." She cupped his face. "I'm saying you're a good and generous man, Rhett. You'll figure it out."

"How much can I actually do? I'm only here for another couple of weeks."

"Then make them count." He knew that they were no longer talking about the festival. "So we're really alone?"

He kissed her neck. "All alone.

"Then the manager won't mind me touching this."

Rhett lay back, elbows folded behind his head and waggled his brows. "Oh, he won't mind. Touch all you want."

Instead of touching him, Elsie walked to a bed, two rows over that was on a display stand. She stepped up and ran a hand over the top of the wood. "It's beautiful," she said in wonder. "Look, it's made of reclaimed teak and mango tree wood and handcrafted by a father/son team. Oh, I remember them," she said brightly. "I met them at a furniture show last year. They specialize in one-of-a-kinds, but I've never seen a piece this stunning before."

Rhett stood and walked to the bed. He liked the look of the wood and the bold lines of the frame. It was artsy but masculine. "I'm actually into it."

She looked at him over her shoulder. "What do you mean you're 'actually into it'? You make it sound like you haven't liked anything else I've shown you." She blanched. "You haven't liked anything else I've shown you."

He came up behind her and wrapped his arms around her waist. "I've *liked* everything you've shown me. But I'm actually really into this. Like, I can see it in our bedroom."

She pretended she didn't catch his slip, but her pretty blush told him otherwise. "I'll have to talk to the owner, but I bet he can have this delivered this week."

"I bet I can get him to deliver it today." Hell, with the right incentive Rhett could probably get the guy to deliver it this morning. Then Rhett could spend the rest of the day in his stunning new bed with his stunner of a woman.

"I can already see it in your room. I can see it on the cover of *Modern Masterpiece*. It's... oh my god," Elsie said, stepping out of his embrace. "I didn't see the price or I never would have suggested it. I'm sorry."

"Hang on. For what?"

"Well, here I am talking about how great it would look in the magazine when I'm not the one fronting the bill. And trust me it's an insane bill."

She held up the price tag, but he didn't even look at it. "And?"

"And I would never want you to think that I'm taking advantage of our relationship to advance my career."

Well, hell. Most people wouldn't even think twice about what something cost as long as he was picking up the tab. And here he'd given the woman a blank check and she was afraid he'd think she was taking advantage of him.

"If I were another client with the same budget, would you hesitate to recommend this bed?"

"Probably not," she admitted. "But you're not just any client."

He cupped her hips, nudging her closer. "I like that I'm not just any client. And I like that you worry about me. But I hired you for your talent and taste. So if you think it will look great, then I want it."

He mainly wanted it to look great for her. Sure, he was going to sleep in it and, sure, he liked nice things, but he loved watching the expression on her pretty face light up when she found another piece to her puzzle. He wasn't blowing smoke up her ass when he paid her those compliments; she was talented and seemed to know his taste better than he did.

"No lies, remember?"

"I remember," she whispered.

"Good, then in the spirit of honesty, I really want to kiss you." So he did, and when they both came up for air they were breathing heavy.

"What do you think about the end table they paired with it?"

"I like it."

She gave him a little shove. "You *like* it but you're not *into* it."

"I'm into you." He framed her face. "Really into you."

"Yeah?" she breathed.

"Oh yeah." Before she could come up with another way this could somehow be PDA, he kissed her. Slow at first, walking them backward until she ran into the mattress and tumbled back onto the bed. He didn't break contact, following her down. He left a little room between them so she could push him off if she desired, but apparently she desired him more because she ran her fingers into his hair and squeezed, causing a little sting to his scalp.

"I love it when you do that," he groaned.

And then because he was the luckiest son of a bitch on the planet, she wrapped her legs around him, her mile-high heels cutting into his ass. Her hands moved down his chest to the bottom of his shirt and she tugged it up.

"What are we doing?" he asked, because he needed to be one-hundred percent certain that they were on the same page.

"We're testing out the mattress." She gave a little wriggle that gave her breasts a small bounce.

"I'm all for tests."

"We should first test it for firmness." She ran a hand between their bodies and down the front of his pants and, *holy Mary, mother of God*, slid all the way down to the base before giving a squeeze.

"Test passed," she said. "Next, we need to know that it will hold up over time. No one wants a mattress that gives out halfway through its warranty."

Before she could give another tempting squeeze, he caught her hand and tugged it back out, sliding it over her head as he laced their fingers together. "It will go the distance and then keep going and going and—"

She kissed him. "Lucky me. Now, how about its design?"

"You tell me, Red. Do you like its design?"

Her eyes roamed over his face and down his body and back. He could tell by the hunger in her gaze she liked his design just fine.

"I like its interior the best."

This time she kissed him, hot and hungry and showing no signs of stopping. The owner had given him a whole hour in the showroom, so as Rhett saw it, they had fortyish minutes left, which was enough time for a double-the-trouble kind of outing. Except her phone rang.

She didn't move.

It rang again and she let out a frustrated groan.

On the third ring she flopped back on the mattress. "It could be my mom or grandma."

He let her fish her phone out of her purse, then kissed her on the corner of her mouth, then down her neck.

"It's an unknown number. I should get this, it could be a client."

"Don't miss it on my account." He made his way down her throat to the gentle curve of her shoulder.

"Hello," she said, and she sounded thoroughly turned on. He gave a little nip and her eyes closed. "Uh huh. This is her." She sat up straight and shoved Rhett aside. "No, I'm excited to hear from you."

There was a long pause, where Rhett assumed the other person was talking. Then Elsie was on her feet pacing, her free hand smoothing down her hair as if the person on the other side of the phone could see her.

"Wow, that's great. Next Friday?" She looked at Rhett as if to concur, like he knew what she was talking about.

She seemed to need someone in her corner, so he nodded. "Friday works."

She gave a few more unintelligible sounds and several more thanks and then hung up. She spun to face him, her eyes a little wild. "That was Susan from *Modern Masterpiece* magazine. She saw the photos I sent over and she wants to do a walk-through on Friday." She threw herself into his arms. "Can you believe it?"

"Yes, I can. You're exactly the caliber of designer they're looking for."

She pulled back. "And what kind is that?"

"Talented, educated, with your own twist on the expected. And sexy."

She laughed. "I don't think sexy helped me any. But thank you to the rest of it."

"I mean it. While you held me hostage at first, I wouldn't have said yes if I didn't love your work."

"This doesn't mean I've actually landed the article." She walked out of his arms and paced. "It means that they're interested in finding out more about the house."

"They're interested in finding more about you."

She stopped, and the look she gave was so vulnerable and uncertain he wanted to punch Axel. And not for the first time. Every time she second-guessed herself or gave in to the insecurities that he knew Axel put there, the impulse grew.

"You think?"

He took her hands and drew her in. "I know." She gifted him a small smile. He cradled her face. "Whatever he told you was a lie. It was his way of making himself feel like the big man of the house. None of it was grounded in truth."

She worried her lower lip and her eyes went a little glassy. She was killing him. "It's hard sometimes to remember that, when so many people, who I thought were in my corner, jumped on the Axel bandwagon." She met his gaze and this time it was filled with hurt. "Like you did."

"Oh, Els," he whispered, hating that she was right.

He'd bought Axel's "she fleeced me" story—hook, line, and sinker. Maybe it was because Rhett had just gone through a divorce and it was nothing more than male bonding. Or maybe he'd been looking for a reason—any reason—to keep his distance when it came to Elsie. Whatever the reason, it was clear he'd hurt her. Deeply.

"I was an idiot who was stupid enough to take a liar at face value. I should have known better. There are a lot of should'ves that I'm not proud of when it comes to you, but I promise I'll never make another should've where you're concerned."

She studied the ground. "No empty promises," she whispered.

"This promise isn't empty." He tilted her chin up to meet his gaze and when their eyes locked, neither looked away. He wasn't sure what she saw in his expression, but hers went from disbelieving to hopeful and then right into wary.

"Why didn't you call?" she asked. "After that weekend. You said you'd call and then you didn't. Why?"

He took a step back and ran a hand down his face. There were so many reasons he didn't call. His dad's health being one. Benji passed a week after he'd met Elsie. Then there was his career that was taking off and he was putting everything he had into it. But then there was the real answer, the one she deserved to hear.

"You scared the shit out of me, Elsie. I knew what my life was going to be like and it didn't match with a hometown girl who clearly had big dreams too. My dreams would lead me around the world and yours would lead you eventually to a forever home. I didn't want to take that life from you."

"I've been walked out on my entire life, so when you did it I thought that maybe that was just how things would go for me."

"God, no." His heart cracked open that he'd been just another in a long line of disappointments in her life. He kissed her lips gently. "At the time, I thought I was making the best decision for the both of us."

She considered this for a long moment. "In retrospect, it was. We both had a lot of things we wanted to accomplish in life, but you still broke my heart. I didn't date for nearly a year, waiting for you to call."

He ran a hand through her hair to cradle her head. "I kept that gum wrapper with your number on it until the day I ran into you and Axel. I never stopped thinking about you." And this was the part of his admission where he sounded like an asshole. "Even though you were with him, I kept thinking of you as mine. Which was why, after your wedding, I had to create some distance."

She nodded ever so subtly. "You said I scared you. What about now?"

"I'm still scared shitless that I'll somehow screw this up." He closed his eyes and groaned. "Like tonight. I know we talked about dinner, but I have to meet with Gage about some sponsorship stuff, which means I won't be home until later. So don't wait on me for dinner."

She tilted her head. "I can wait a few hours to eat with you."

He shrugged off her offer. "I'll be late."

"I know. I can wait." She said it like it was no big deal. Like it was part of being an "us." "Maybe we can eat snuggled on the couch watching a movie."

"Is movie code for sex? Because then I'm all for a double feature." She gave him a playful shove. "Seriously though, I don't want you to wait for me."

Otherwise she'd be waiting a lifetime for his life to match up with hers.

Her features softened as she studied him. "It's just dinner, and whatever Steph told you or didn't tell you, you're worth waiting for, Rhett."

A lump the size of Oregon filled his throat, rendering him unable to speak. All he could do was kiss her, show her exactly what her words meant to him. But instead of him kissing her, she was kissing him, gentle and tender, and filled with so much compassion he knew he was in deep.

Too deep to pull himself out.

Chapter Seventeen

Dating Tips from Elsie Dodd
It's not the walk of shame.
It's called exercise.

The final meeting for Portland Live was held in a large conference room at Gage's office. Each of the Eastons was present, including all the women. When Rhett walked in late, Gage and Owen grinned like they knew why.

Rhett didn't care what they thought. He'd awoken with Elsie wrapped around him like a pretzel, both nothing but a tangle of sated limbs. The second she'd fallen asleep last night, he'd known he should have awoken her, but she'd felt so good pressed into him he'd promised himself five minutes. Then he accidentally dozed off.

When his alarm sounded, she'd opened her eyes and all but scrambled off him, racing out of the room claiming she had a presentation to finish for a potential new client. It wasn't exactly a lie; she had landed a meeting with someone from the gender reveal party who was looking to make a major addition to their house, but she was using it as an excuse.

She'd need space to sort it out. Hell, he needed space. When he'd looked in the mirror he'd had, embarrassingly enough, moon-eyes. He'd never seen the look so close up before and now knew why she'd banned them from their relationship. Which left him with a single problem.

What to do about Elsie.

After their morning at the furniture store, they'd decided to test the full capacity of his Rover, knocking down the back seats as they went. And when they'd gotten home, he'd felt this tingle to get into the studio, which proved to be time well spent. He'd managed to get an entire song written in under an hour. He spent the rest of the week really polishing it.

He couldn't remember the last time a song had come to him so easily. Actually, it was back in the beginning of his career, right after his dad died, when he'd started taking things seriously.

After he'd come up for air last night, he was certain he'd be sleeping alone, except he'd stepped into the kitchen to find Elsie dressed in a pretty sundress and a pair of those heels he loved, her hair loose and silky. He nearly wept. Then there was the dinner she'd made of a dozen different kinds of finger foods. Which they fed to each other on the couch while watching the latest superhero movie.

They barely made it halfway through before they were completely naked. They'd spent the first part of the night on the couch and the second part rechristening every inch of their new bed. Which was how they'd wound up breaking rule five—no sleepovers.

"Rhett?" he heard Piper, Josh's wife, ask. When he looked up, he found the entire room staring at him in question.

"What?" was all he said, but he knew he looked sex drunk. And everyone in the room knew it. His clothes were wrinkled, his hair finger-combed, and his grin was impossible to hide.

"I was just saying that your new master looks cozy," Piper said, biting back a smile.

"You were in my house?"

"Turns out Elsie and I have a mutual friend. Elsie let me in so I could photograph the place. Pretty."

Rhett wasn't sure if she was referring to the house or Elsie, but he had to agree on both. But the idea of one of his family members being at his house, possibly interrogating Elsie, made his warning bells sound.

"Don't worry, I only gave her my first name, and I didn't give her the third degree. I kept it strictly professional."

"Uh huh," Rhett mumbled, knowing he was going to have to possibly apologize for his nosy family. "Change of topic, please."

"How about the surprise of you being here," Gage said. He was in his usual slacks, button-down shirt, no tie, leather jacket—and a know-it-all smile.

"The meeting starts at eight, right?" Rhett asked. "It's eight so we better get started."

"It's eight twenty," Owen said, looking at the wall clock. "But who's counting?"

"He wasn't the only one who was late," Abi, Owen's fiancée, said. The look she gave Owen told the room they'd been late for the same reason as Rhett. "So be nice."

Abi nudged Owen, who pulled her in for a kiss.

"Not in front of the children," Josh said. He was dressed in his usual smart suit, but with one of those baby slings around his neck and a sleeping baby Lily tucked inside. His eyes were bloodshot, his hair on end, and he looked as if he hadn't slept in weeks. Then he met his wife's eyes and Rhett saw it—moon-eyes.

In fact, as he looked around the table, he noticed that every one of his brothers wore the same goofy look. And, not for the first time, Rhett felt like the odd man out. Even Owen, his last ride-or-die bro, was blissfully in love.

He wanted that, he realized. And he wanted it with Elsie. He just didn't know how to go about it. Not that love hadn't come with hardships for his siblings. But at least they all lived in the same zip code while figuring out their futures. Rhett's future ended in a little over a week when he was expected in LA to start laying down tracks, and he didn't know how to make it work in the long term. Not without one of them giving up on a dream.

Shit.

Not wanting Clay to do his see-behind-the-walls thing, Rhett flipped through the agenda, which was a zillion pages long, and sighed. It reminded him why he usually skipped these kinds of meetings. He was more of a hands-on guy, but he wanted to spend more time with his family, and right then that meant helping with the event.

"You still want to be here?" Gage asked.

Rhett smiled. "Wouldn't miss it for the world."

They discussed everything from budget to sponsors to logistics, and by the time they arrived at the lineup Rhett was dozing off.

"We have the final order?" Gage said.

"About that," Rhett said, suddenly awake, and Owen groaned.

"I told you one of us should handle it."

"I have it right here." He passed around the single piece of paper. It had a double column with fifteen names on it.

"Can't you count to ten or do we need to go over addition again?" Owen asked.

"Hear me out. I was going through the demos and realized what the problem was."

"That you can't count to ten?" Again with Owen bringing the smartass.

"That there were more than ten people who deserved a shot," Rhett countered.

"The night is set at ten because Saturday night barely has room for ten," Josh so helpfully pointed out.

"Which is why I was thinking that maybe we make it a weekend thing," Rhett suggested, and the table went silent. "We leave Saturday for the current lineup, which you'll see is in the second column, and then we add Friday. They can be opening acts of sorts. They get to play one song each."

"I think it's a great idea. For next year," Gage said.

"A year is a long time in a musician's world." A year can make the difference between playing for a living and waiting tables. A die hard would never give up their dream, but being able to gig for a living, even if you're living on ramen and mac 'n' cheese, is the dream.

"That's a lot of work to put together between now and then," Josh pointed out as Lily started to cry. Josh stood and paced the room, gently bouncing the baby.

"This change would require a lot of time," Gage said. "There's getting the permit, making sure the bar is properly staffed, getting word out so there's actually a crowd expecting music and not sports."

"I can help with the permit," Piper said, taking Lily from Josh and holding her to her chest, giving a little bounce. Josh put a hand on her lower back. "I know my way around city hall and the permit process now. As long as you're not asking for a liquor permit, then I'm your girl."

"We've got a lot going on," Josh cooed. "Don't we, sweet pea."

"I can help with the staffing," Abi said. "I know that there are a few employees desperate for more hours. Offer up time and a half and we'll have an overflow of staff."

"There's still a matter of getting the word out," Clay said.

"Which is why I'm offering to MC the event."

It was as if the air was sucked out of the room with shock. "You hate MCing," Gage said. "You specifically have it written into every contract you sign."

"This is important to me and if it takes me stepping out of my comfort zone, then out I step." He couldn't help but smile. Elsie would be proud of his idea. Hell, he was damn proud of his idea. "I also want to do a small set at the end of the night play one of my new songs." Rhett looked around the room; everyone looked back. Still silent. "What?"

"It's just you've always said that releasing a single in a small venue is a waste of what could be a big PR event," Gage said.

"That was Subtle Warfare's policy. This is just me, and Rhett Easton used to play at his dad's bar every weekend. Maybe it's time to get back to that."

"I don't even know if the label will sign off on that. And what about additional security?"

"I have a bulldog of an agent who I bet could make those things happen."

Gage's smile widened to cover his entire face. "You haven't even played anything for me. You have a new confidant we don't know about?"

"Oh, he has a lot we don't know about," Piper said, biting back a laugh.

Rhett thought back to Elsie and their conversation the other day and had to smile. Yeah, he had a new confidante and it felt good. Not that he'd played her even a string, but she'd given him the exact advice he'd needed.

"Like a new confidante?" Piper continued. "Red hair, about yea high, couldn't stop smiling."

Rhett just shrugged. He neither confirmed nor denied a thing. He'd promised Elsie privacy and he was going to give her that—even when it came to his nosy family.

"What song are you going to play?" Gage asked.

"I haven't decided yet," he lied. He knew exactly which song he was going to play, it was the one he'd started that first morning when he'd awoken in bed with a very pissed off Elsie. And his gut told him it was a hit, through and through. He just knew it had that inexplicable quality that made listeners play it on repeat and sing it in their cars with the windows down. It was the kind of song that would be played at weddings and ball games.

It was the kind of song he'd set out to write when he'd decided to go solo.

CHAPTER EIGHTEEN

Dating Tips from Elsie Dodd
Be you.

R hett couldn't look away.

The main music room was done. And it was perfect. The modern lines of the space juxtaposed the gentle curve of the guitars, which were hung in glassless frames, making them look like art, while allowing easy access. Acoustic, electric, vintage, his entire collection hung around the room, creating a 1960s British-rock vibe. The floors were glossy wood, the walls a deep blue, the ceiling slightly domed for acoustics. In the corner, by the massive line of windows, sat an oversized leather chair, with his first six-string propped up on a stand.

In the center of the room was *his* piano. Not the piece of shit Axel left behind, but a restored mahogany Steinway Rhett bought at auction three years ago and never had the space to display. He didn't even know how Elsie discovered its existence, since the only person in the world who knew he owned it was Gage.

Goddamned Gage.

Rhett smiled. Two of his favorite people were conspiring for him.

The end result was a sophisticated space with a unique edge, which was a reflection of him and his music. He didn't know how she'd nailed it, but she'd nailed it.

Rhett walked over to the armchair and tried it on for size. It was the perfect fit. Its buttery leather high arms were the perfect configuration to play guitar, which he picked up. Memories rolled through him as he cradled the present his dad gifted him on his sixteenth birthday. The family didn't have a lot of money back then, so Rhett cherished the second-hand instrument.

Even though he hadn't played it in years, one chord and it felt as if his world righted. Like sitting around the family room and tinkering while his old man acted like Rhett had composed something on the scale of Jimi Hendrix.

He rested the body of the guitar on his knee, placed his hand on the neck, and grinned. Even after all these years, it was the perfect fit. The groove where his palm rested, the way the curve hugged his thigh.

He strummed the strings and laughed. It was completely out of tune. Sitting back in the chair, he spent some time tuning it and reacquainting himself, a real get-to-know-you-again kind of moment that resonated with a piece of himself he'd forgotten about. The hungry musician who lived and breathed music.

He closed his eyes and pictured the sounds in his head, every color and detail of each note as his hands glided over the strings. He played one of his old favorites, a Johnny Cash song he and his dad loved, then one of Rhett's old songs, and before he knew it, he was playing his new song, the one he'd been tinkering with for weeks now. And wouldn't you know it, it just came rushing through him. The words, the melody, even the slight break in his voice came naturally. He wasn't dialing it in, he was in the music.

So deep he didn't notice he wasn't alone until he looked up and saw beautiful standing in the doorway, dressed in a pretty sundress, no shoes, pink painted toes. The fading sun cast a warm glow around her and even from the distance he could see those emerald-green pools, warm and open. She was letting her walls down for him.

"I didn't mean to interrupt," she said with a shyness to her voice that made him smile.

He set the guitar on the stand and patted his lap. "You aren't interrupting. In fact, you were just who I needed to see."

She padded across the floor, her smile tentative and nervous as she grew closer. "It's beautiful."

He rested his hands on her hips and drew her between his thighs. "You're beautiful."

"That's the song you were playing the morning after my divorce party," she said, and he was reminded what a good ear she had for music. "You finished it."

"I did." He ran his hands down the backs of her thighs and under the hem of her dress, just barely, but far enough to get a small taste of that silky skin.

"What's it about?"

His fingers glided higher. He couldn't seem to keep his hands off her. So he pulled her onto his lap. "You."

She swallowed. "Me?"

"It's about you." He took her wrists and slid her arms around his neck, gliding his hands down her arms to her waist.

"I used to listen to your song 'Time Lost,'" she said, referring to his first hit. She leaned into him, her eyes locked on his. "And wonder if it was about our weekend."

"Red, half of that first album is about that weekend." She opened her mouth and he stopped her. "And before you remind me you were with Axel while that album came out, I didn't care. I don't care now."

"I was going to say that was my favorite album," she teased, and he laughed.

"Hey, what about my other albums?"

"All outstanding, as proof of the many awards." She pointed to the trophies hanging on the walls. "But they were more Subtle Warfare and less Rhett Easton. I missed the Rhett Easton part."

No one had been this honest with him about his music. Not since his dad. Even Gage, who rarely sugar-coated anything, tiptoed around things sometimes.

"And what I just played?" he asked.

"Emotional, raw, visceral." She brushed a barely-there kiss to his lips. "One hundred percent you."

"I was going more for tender, real, sexy," he said. "Which is one hundred percent you."

She rested her head on his shoulder and melted into him, even tucking her feet beneath her, until he was her chair. "Play it again," she asked.

He rested his guitar against her hip and played the song. Not the lyrics, just the melody, and he could feel her heartbeat wash through him and slowed the rhythm to match. There it was, the one thing he was missing, the slow, steady tempo, which was the heart of the song. *Her* heart.

When he finished, he waited for her to say something, but she remained quiet for a long moment. He was about to ask her what she thought when she whispered, "It's Rhett without all the noise. It's not me about me, it's you."

He turned his head to meet her gaze. "Maybe it's us."

His heart leapt at the word. It was simply two letters but it meant a hell of a lot more. He not only wanted "us," he wanted to take this confusing heap of a relationship and nurture it into something more. Something rare and beautiful, something akin to what his brothers had.

She searched his gaze. "Us is a scary thing."

"I'm not scared, Elsie."

And he wasn't. Not anymore. The one thing he was afraid of was that she didn't feel the same. That she would be the one to walk away. He wouldn't blame her. His life was crazy, and hers was finally settling down.

Once the reprieve was over and he went back on the road to finish the second half of the tour, he'd be gone weeks on end. Sometimes even a month at a time. How could a relationship as new as theirs withstand that?

She must have seen the panic in his eyes because she ever so softly cupped his cheek. "Neither am I."

She captured his lips in a gentle, probing kiss that kick-started his heart. Slowly she took his lower lip between hers, cradling it before slowly pulling away, only to go back in for more. He wasn't sure how long they sat like that, with her on his lap, their lips brushing back and forth in what had to be the most real connection of his life. No hands, no tongue, just a gentle coming together.

A minute, an hour, hell maybe it was a year later something shifted, heated. She twisted on his lap and pressed herself all the way into him.

"Elsie, when you say us, do you mean—"

This time when she kissed him, she gave his mouth a little nip, followed by a harder one. And suddenly he wasn't all that interested in talking. Us meant us as far as he could tell. A clear indicator that they were both on the same page, which, *hallelujah*, it had taken them years to arrive at and now here they were on the precipice of something special and—

Oh yeah, she was no longer running her hands over his pecs. Her hands went all the way down and she was using those elegant fingers to stroke him. First on the outside of his jeans, then, *bingo,* right down his pants and, thank god, he'd decided to go commando.

"Elsie—" he groaned, his eyeballs rolling to the back of his head.

"Uh huh," she mumbled, and with a simple *zip, rustle, shove,* his jeans were around his hips. "Lift up," she commanded, and who was he to deny a lady's wish? So he lifted up and she dragged his pants lower and lower still until... until... finally they were on the ground and so was she—kneeling before him looking like she'd waltzed right out of last night's dream.

She looked up at him and, *hot damn,* that look on her face meant that he, Regular Rhett, AKA the luckiest son of a bitch on the planet, was one hundred percent about to get lucky—if his jeans weren't already an indication.

She rested her hands on his chest and with a single push he was leaned back—all the way back—in the chair, his full monty upright and ready for a game of kiss and blow and, *holy god,* one lick from her mouth and he nearly came off the chair.

She gripped him at the base and gave another lick before taking him in her mouth. He told himself to play it cool, let her set the pace—until he found his hands in her hair. A move she was fully on board with since she moaned, the sound reverberating through him. She went in for a full base-to-tip motion and his lungs stopped working. Black spots started around the periphery of his vision and when she went in for another taste he nearly blacked out.

"Red," he whispered, tilting her head up to meet his. "I want to come so bad, but I want to do it inside you."

Without one last pump of the hand, she stood, just out of reach, and unbuttoned each button of that sundress, shoving it off her shoulders. Her breasts. A pair of black panties—see-through black panties that made his mouth go dry—then, *poof,* the dress went bye-bye, leaving her in nothing but black lace and matching fuck-me pumps.

He reached his arms out, but she shook her head. Reaching behind her, she undid her bra, letting it fall to the floor, then slipped out of her thong. In a move that had his heart fist-bumping his ribcage, she pulled her hair from the ponytail band and let it spill around her. Long, silky auburn waves falling to nipple length, playing a game of naked peek-a-boo.

She started to step out of her heels and he held up a hand. "Leave them on."

Only after she was completely naked did she strut toward him in those dick-teasing heels, her hips swaying with the confidence of a woman who knew her worth. A woman who knew exactly what she was doing to him. A woman he hadn't seen since emerging from her divorce.

The sexy, confident, take-what-you-want woman from his past was front and center.

He froze for a brief moment, his brain skittering to a halt as uncertainty crept in, making him wonder, not for the first time, if he was worthy enough. Before he could ask or even find the answer himself, she was straddling him— in his chair, surrounded by all his guitars, looking like a wet dream. He'd imagined a scenario like this for nearly a decade, yet reality far surpassed his imagination.

His hands slid to her very naked ass and she rose slightly so he could get a better hold before sinking back down. Her hands went to his chest, gripping his shirt, and disposing of it with what was by then a well-practiced move. Then she kissed him and every second of that weekend came rushing back. The feelings, the emotion, the love.

Love?

Where had that come from? Like? Yes. Lust? Hell yeah. But love? Is this really what it felt like? He'd only ever felt it once before, with Elsie in her blink-and-you'll-miss-it apartment, but he'd shrugged it off as raw hunger and youth. That night he'd followed her back to her home for one reason: to get lucky. He'd stayed because he couldn't walk away. Then he'd run, fast and hard in the opposite direction because he knew leaving was the right call. It was the hard call, but the right one all the same. And he still believed that.

But now their paths had crossed once again, and what if this was the universe's way of providing them a second chance to get it right? But they still weren't on the same path—it was more of a meeting at a crossroads where their lives intersected for a few blissful weeks.

What would happen come Monday when he left for LA?

"Elsie," he said, loving the way her name sounded on his tongue. She must have liked it too because her mouth went from his neck to his chest, gifting him a sweet kiss right over his heart. And while he wanted to see where this game of Candyland would end, he cupped her face and brought her gaze to his.

Before he could speak, or at least ask her if she was open to more, she put a silencing finger to his lips. "No empty promises," she said, emotions thick in her voice. "It's easy to say things in the moment that are taken back when the world rights itself."

"What if I still feel the same when the world rights itself?"

Her eyes were glassy, she was looking at him so intently, as if she were trying to see inside his head. *Don't do it,* his alarm bells screamed, *back away and protect yourself from what could be the biggest disappointment of your life.* But his head and his heart were at war, battling it out. His heart was adamant that this was the time to open up and let her see what he'd been hiding all this time. Let her see the hurt and anguish and disappointment and all the raw emotions from his dad's death, then Kyle's, and finally his divorce that he kept hidden from the world behind his "I'm good" grin.

Not even his brothers knew the extent of the baggage he'd piled up along the way, and then Steph's walking away reconfirmed that he might not be enough.

Rhett made himself hold her gaze and then the way her expression changed had him feeling edgy and out of control. "There were rules for a reason. We agreed for a reason. And we have to trust that reason," she said.

That was the wrong answer, and he knew she could see it in his gaze.

"I'm sorry if that isn't enough, but I made myself a promise and I vowed never to break another promise to myself. But if it's not what you're looking for..."

"You are what I'm looking for."

"I want you so much." She rose up on her knees taking just the tip inside her and he forgot what they were talking about. "Tonight, right here in this chair, I don't want to think or reason or second-guess, I just want to feel."

Then feel was what she was going to get. He was going to put every single feel into making her lose her mind. And then tomorrow he'd try again. And again. He'd missed his chance once, he wasn't going to miss it again because of logistics.

If she didn't feel it, she didn't feel it and it would break his heart. But if it was fear that had her waffling, then that he could work with.

He understood why she was afraid to put herself out there. She'd done it twice and twice she'd been burned.

Gripping the backs of her thighs, he lifted her up until she was kneeling fully. "Scoot closer, Els."

"Scoot to where?"

He put pressure on her thighs and she toppled over his head as he scooched even lower.

"What are you doing?"

"Making you feel," he said, then positioned her directly above him. Without repeating himself he ran his tongue between her folds, loving the way she gasped. So he did it again and he felt her wobble.

He took her hands, which were on his shoulders and lifted them to the back of the chair, waiting until she gripped the leather before letting go. He nudged her legs further apart and made himself right at home, pressing a series of open-mouthed kisses. First on her inner thigh, then the other, waiting until she was quivering before he kissed the motherland.

"Rhett," she sighed, and he could tell her head had fallen back because her back was arched in the sexiest position known to man. This time he went in full force with a kiss followed by a sharp nip, then a soothing glide of the tongue. He did a replay of the triple-threat and she bucked into his mouth.

"Easy." Gripping her thighs, he held her still as he drove her right to the edge and backed off, loving the way she squirmed, trying to break his embrace and push further onto his face.

"This is torture." He could hear the frustration in her tone.

Welcome to the club. Rhett had a Tortured by Elsie card in his back pocket somewhere. Had been there since that first day in the bathroom.

"God, you taste good," he said, sucking her and then when she was sliding down the chair and the only thing keeping her upright was his hands on her ass, he went in for the kill. He moved one thumb around to press on her sweet spot, giving a pressured lick in the right spot, and she went off like a rocket.

He felt her tighten, then contract, and then she was moaning and pumping, and he rode it out with her, gently bringing her back. And when her orgasm softened and she opened her eyes, she was straddling him with her arms limply wrapped around his neck.

Had he ever felt like this? So wild and out of control. So close to another human being that he could hear their heartbeats sync.

The answer was yes. He'd felt it once before, but it hadn't been this intense or all consuming.

He lifted her head and brushed away a strand of hair that had stuck to her forehead. "Grab my condom out of my back pocket."

She did and he was wrapped and ready in no time. He lifted her again, but this time let her set the pace and she went for reverent. Resting her forehead to his, they locked eyes as she gently slid down his length. When she got to the bottom, they both sighed.

"You fit so damn perfect," he whispered.

Her response was a kiss. A gentle *I'm yours* kiss that shattered his heart. It was clear she was ready for him, but she didn't move and neither did he. A thin sheen of perspiration broke out on his forehead from holding back and then, thank the universe, she started to rock against him, taking him even deeper.

Gripping her hips, he lifted her up and all the way back down, controlling the speed and taking his sweet time to memorize every second of him inside her. He lifted her again, but this time when he lowered her, she tightened her core, creating a friction that blew his mind.

"Rhett," she said, heat in her eyes. He loved the way she looked at him like that. And he loved looking at her too. Watching the way her expression went lax when he moved inside her. It was the most beautiful thing he'd ever seen. "I need all of you."

Something in his chest shifted because he knew she wasn't talking about sex anymore, she was talking about his heart. And that, he decided right then and there, was hers for the taking. Now, the question was: would she take it? He hoped to god yes. But she was so commitment shy she might just break his heart in the process of figuring out this push and pull connection between them.

So he decided not to think—about his heart, about promises, or about the future and what would happen after Monday. He decided to do what she was doing and just feel. The rest could be dealt with later.

At least that's what he told himself.

"You got me," he whispered, slipping a hand between them so that as she rose up he could double the fun with a squeeze. Her voice caught and finally they found their rhythm, their blessed, unique-to-them rhythm that sent his head spinning.

They reached the edge at the exact moment, as if this had already been written in the history books. When she came down, he pushed up and the pressure was too much to contain, so he held her above and pumped hard into her, loving every gasp of pleasure he created until the gasps stopped and the breathing became labored.

"Let go, babe," she said, and his heart boomed at the forbidden term of affection. If she noticed the slip, he wasn't going to say a word—or maybe it was because she was too busy coming. And she came hard, milking him and sending him shooting off into oblivion.

When he came back to reality, they were a tangled heap on the chair, her arms slack around his waist, her head in the curve of his neck. His arms were around her back, making gentle passes up and down her spine. He couldn't stand if his life depended on it, then again he wasn't looking to go anywhere fast.

He wanted to stay like this forever. Now he just needed to figure out how to make that happen.

Rhett woke to an empty bed. He reached his hand over to feel the sheets. Still warm, which meant she'd spent the night, she just didn't want him to know.

That made him smile.

She couldn't have gotten far, so he threw on a pair of jeans and went in search of his wavering bachelorette. He found her with her arms wrapped around her middle, looking out the window, her body language dialed to devastated.

He walked up behind her and slid his arms around her. She didn't flinch, which meant she knew he was there.

"It's morning," was all she said. "I fell asleep again and broke rule five." She rested her head back against his chest. "Your arms are like my kryptonite, rendering me stupid whenever I'm in the vicinity of those biceps."

He flexed and she gave a little laugh, but it was fleeting. And that broke his heart. Last night was the best thing to ever happen to him and it had left her distraught.

"You okay?"

She looked over her shoulder and he could tell she'd been crying. Crying! Jesus, if he'd stuck to the rules she wouldn't be upset.

It was understandable why she wanted to stick to the rules, she didn't want to crash and burn. Neither did he, but he was willing to risk it. And while she had every reason to be scared, they were already well past some silly set of rules. He wanted to put a spotlight on their fledgling relationship, but he wanted her by his side and in his life.

"Not really," she answered.

"You want to talk about it?"

She shook her head, so he rested his chin on her shoulder, both of them looking out onto the manicured lawn and dogwood-lined drive, while the sun rose over the green hills in the distance. Neither spoke. But the silence was deafening. He didn't know how long they stood like that, only that he waited for her to make the first move. When she leaned further back into him and rested her hands over his, pulling his arms tighter around her middle, it gave him hope.

"I heard back from Susan at the magazine," she said so softly he barely heard. But the emotion he was able to catch didn't bode well for her dream and that broke his heart. "She emailed me."

"And?"

"And they want me." She sniffled.

He turned her in his arms, but he had to tilt his head down to meet her gaze. "That's great! Isn't it?" Then her body sank in on itself like it was the worst thing possible.

"It's everything." Her eyes were teary, her nose red, and he wanted to sweep her up into his arms. "There's a condition."

"What's that?" What possible condition could have her this upset?

"They want you in the article. And a photo of you in the music room. I have no idea how they even knew that this was your house." She looked at him, her eyes wide with worry. "I swear I didn't tell anyone. I'd never do that to you. I know how much you value your privacy. But they won't run the article without you in it."

"Okay, so I give them a few shots of me in the house. Maybe in my new bed," he teased.

"I'm being serious."

"So am I." He nuzzled her cheek.

"I won't use your name like everyone else does," she whispered.

"It's not using if I agree."

"Then everyone will know where you live."

"The inspector knows. Big Pete and all his ninety-seven minions know. Escrow closed. I give it a week before the media figures it out and everyone knows where I live. And why shouldn't you get your work celebrated just because some asshole bought your house out from under you?"

She snorted. "You did buy it right out from under my nose."

"I know." He tucked her hair behind her ear. "And I'm sorry for that."

"I'm not. If you hadn't bought it, we wouldn't be here."

They wouldn't, and wouldn't that be a shame. Rhett loved it here almost as much as he loved Elsie. The singular thing about this whole situation he was starting to tire from was keeping things a secret. It wasn't that he wanted their business plastered across every media outlet in the country. But damn, he missed the days that he could take a beautiful woman to dinner and have it be nothing more than two people sharing a meal.

"First, call Susan back and tell her I'm in."

"But she only wants to do it because of you. If it were anyone else's house they'd pass."

"You don't know that. And so what if they did? They aren't going to say yes unless they love your work. Which they clearly do."

"But your privacy. Are you sure? Like really sure. Because remember rule two: Honesty."

"Here's honest then. I want you to come with me to Portland Live."

Her mouth parted on a breath. "Is that safe? I mean, one photo and we're outed."

He took both her hands. "It doesn't have to be more than friends, but this is important to me and I want you there. Even if I have to keep my hands off you."

"No moon-eyes," she teased, but he was pretty sure he couldn't keep that promise, which broke her cardinal rule, so he said nothing. "Susan is walking the house on Friday to get ideas for the shoot."

"I know." He knew what he was asking of her, and it was more than a simple friend-supporting-friend question. He moved closer. "Even if it's just for a few minutes, go with me."

She thunked her forehead to his chest. "It breaks rule four."

"I am aware, but I figure that we can overlook it for one night."

Now that he'd said it, he was nervous. Nervous that she'd say no and nervous that she'd say yes, because either answer would determine the direction their relationship would take.

"Can I think about it?" she asked, worrying her lower lip.

"Just don't think too long."

CHAPTER NINETEEN

Dating Tips from Elsie Dodd
Become the best version of yourself.

Elsie was dressed to impress. In her favorite blue blouse, a pair of smart-looking slacks, and lucky heels, she was ready to take her career to the next level. Besides the faint smell, no one would even know that she'd just slathered on the last coat of paint in the bathroom.

The house was finally finished, and it was gorgeous. Sharp and sophisticated and as beautiful as any home that had graced the cover of *Modern Masterpiece*, it was magazine worthy. She knew how her portfolio would look, just like she knew her career was about to take off. She'd no longer be the interior architect without a stunning portfolio.

More importantly, Rhett loved the end product. Unlike most modern designs, she'd chosen comfort at every step. So when he'd said that it felt like home, a wealth of pride welled up.

He liked the stark difference between the warm, deep walls, minimalist and fashionable aesthetic, and inviting furniture that made you want to take your shoes off and cuddle up. And cuddle they had. On the couch, one of the barrel chairs, each and every bed. They'd even *cuddled* in the shower twice that morning before he headed off to help his family set up for Portland Live.

Elsie felt as if her new life had finally fallen into place and she wanted to soak in every moment. She was one yes from making her longtime dream become reality. Didn't mean that when a knock sounded, her didn't heart thunder with nerves.

She was confident in her work, but behind that proud voice was a little whisper of doubt. A little whisper that started with her dad and echoed by Axel when they both treated her as if she wasn't good enough. But she squashed that whisper and instead listened to the part of her that had taken a risk, worked tirelessly, and finally expelled all that doubt to make today a success.

Smoothing down her blouse, Elsie opened the door and, instead of a face, she was greeted by the largest bouquet in all the Pacific Northwest. Dogwood and peonies.

Her favorite.

A warm rush of something too special to label rolled through her.

"I wasn't snooping, they were at your doorstep when I arrived," Susan said.

Elsie took the bouquet and opened the door wider. "Please, come in."

Susan stepped inside the foyer and closed the door behind her.

"Let me set these down. I must have been in the shower when they were delivered." Elsie placed the vase and flowers on the entry table, and it was as if they had been created to match the colors and feel of the entry.

Rhett, her heart sighed. Of course they were the perfect fit because he was the kind of guy who paid attention to details. When he made a gesture, it was specific and unique—from the heart.

She smelled one of the petals and closed her eyes at the beautiful scent of romance.

"Husband?" Susan asked.

Before she could think of her answer, "Boyfriend," slipped out. Then she remembered their "no label" rule, but instead of feeling off-kilter or cornered by the term of endearment, a calmness overcame her. A rightness.

They may not have put a label on things, which was her doing, but in her heart she knew that's what Rhett would have said if asked the same question.

Elsie picked up the card, then paused. "Do you mind?"

Susan waved a hand. "Please."

She opened the card and her heart melted to goo.

Els,
You take my breath away.
Today and every day.
You've got this.
R

"He was wishing me luck today."

Susan laughed. "I got a similar bouquet this morning from my husband. Wishing me luck for my first walk-through."

Elsie was taken aback. "This is your first walk-through? Like for the Portland edition?"

"Like ever. I'm new at the magazine and this is my first big project, which is why I'm so excited to be here. If your house is half as beautiful as those photos..." Susan faded off as she glanced around the entry, taking in everything.

And Elsie couldn't be positive, but she could have sworn Susan gave a soft, "Incredible."

"Well, then we're both experiencing a first," Elsie said. "Which means it's the perfect time to pop the prosecco I have cooling in the fridge. Why don't we start in the kitchen for a toast and I can show you around from there."

"Sounds perfect."

Elsie headed toward the kitchen with Susan following, but the woman's head was turning this way and that, her lips slightly parted in awe. Elsie gave herself a mental high-five.

She pulled out two stemmed glasses and topped each off with bubbly.

"I love how you've staggered the floating shelves. It gives them a geometric and innovative feel."

"Thank you." Elsie beamed. "They're made from reclaimed redwood that I purchased from a broker in Pennsylvania. The wood comes from a hundred-year-old barn. I saw it at an antique shop and fell in love with the movement of the grain. A little historic character to offset the sleek metals and sharp lines."

"I love the square copper chandeliers. Even though they give off an industrial vibe, they also add a bit of playfulness."

Elsie couldn't speak. That was exactly what she was going for.

Susan turned to look at Elsie. "Are they antique?"

"Actually, no. They're custom. I couldn't find a fixture that had more open space than metal, so I designed them, then hired one of the best ironsmiths in the area, Milton Hunt, to meld them."

"I'm already blown away."

Elsie handed her a glass and held hers up. "To firsts."

"To firsts."

After a never-going-to-forget-this-moment toast, Elsie walked Susan through the rest of the house.

Susan hadn't just loved the house, she'd commented on some of the big choices Elsie had made in her design, like the living wall that was by the span of windows, which blended the indoors and outdoors. But she was also impressed by the small details that pulled the house together and made it a showcase.

Susan had actually said that. A showcase home. A thrill of pride zinged off every one of Elsie's ribs.

Then Elsie walked her into the last room, her favorite room—the music room. She'd put her heart and soul into this room and was so proud of how it turned out. It was also Rhett's favorite room. If they weren't together, he was sitting in his leather chair writing. In fact, he'd written a total of five songs over the past week. All of them amazing.

They entered the room and Elsie realized that Susan had stopped at the threshold, her eyes wide—as if taking it all in. Elsie knew how the woman felt. Every time she walked into this room she had to pause in appreciation for how well it came together. It was her masterpiece. And she could tell by the look on Susan's face that the woman agreed. But she wasn't sure if Susan was impressed because of the design or because it was obvious that this was where the guitar prodigy made magic.

"Where did you come up with the idea to frame the guitars? It's inspired."

Any insecurities that Elsie was holding that the magazine's interest was because of Rhett evaporated. It was clear, Susan had chosen the house for its design. Susan had chosen her. And based on the comments over the course of the tour, Elsie was fairly confident she was in the running.

"I wanted each of them to be appreciated as art. Guitar luthiers spend hundreds of hours creating each piece and I wanted to honor that while also allowing them to be used as the instruments were intended."

Susan steady gaze met Elsie's. "To say I'm impressed would be an understatement. When Claire told me about you, I was hesitant because you are new to the area and the business."

"I might seem new, but I've been working toward this day for years and I finally got my shot at my dream."

"Well, you shot it out of the park. This is the exact look and feel we like to feature in our magazine. My team is going to die when they see this place."

Susan commented on the specific elements she'd loved about the house, did a second walk-through, taking pictures of the spaces she imagined her boss would want to display in the article, and promised to get back to Elsie within the week.

Three hours later, Elsie showed Susan to the door.

"I don't want to jump the gun because I still have a team to report to, but Elsie, I think your music room could be our cover shot."

"Are you serious?" Elsie asked, and she could hear the barely suppressed emotion in her voice.

"Absolutely. I know a stunner when I see one and you have created a space that resonates with people. A space that will convey something special to our audience."

"What's that?" Elsie held her breath.

"You don't know?" Susan asked with a smile. "Elsie, you've created a unique and sophisticated space that somehow feels like coming home. I want to share that home with two million readers."

"What does that mean?"

"That my legal team will be reaching out to you with the specifics, but Greenhill House will be featured in our fall edition."

"Oh my god! Thank you." When Susan reached out for a parting handshake, Elsie pulled her in for a hug. "Thank you so much," she whispered.

They said their goodbyes and the minute the door shut she jumped in the air, pumping her fist, followed by a celebratory touchdown dance in the hallway. Everything had gone perfectly, the only thing missing from the experience was Rhett.

She walked upstairs to change out of her #LikeABoss attire and spent the next hour trying on every piece of clothing she owned—looking for the perfect outfit for the benefit. She'd nailed the pants and heels, it was just the shirt that was missing.

Light-bulb moment, she dug through her T-shirts and pulled out a well-worn Subtle Warfare shirt. Next, she uncovered her sewing sheers and went to work. She cut the hem off the bottom, then got rid of the collar by cutting a deep V down the middle. It wasn't too drastic, but low enough to show off her girls.

It screamed obsessed fan. And she was obsessed. With Rhett. His touch, his smile, even the way he smelled—like moon lit kisses nights and sexy man.

She was applying her lipstick in the master bath—since that's where she and Rhett both got ready—when the doorbell rang. Giving a last pucker, she walked downstairs and answered.

"Mom?" she said, surprised to see Faye on her doorstep. "What are you doing here?"

"I came to see my daughter on her big day," Faye said, then she lowered her voice. "I didn't barge in, did I? Is Susan gone?"

Elsie opened the door wider and waved Faye in. "She left about an hour ago."

"How did it go?"

"Amazing. I mean, it couldn't have gone better. I'm going to—" Elsie started to tell her about how she was going to be featured, but stopped. She wanted Rhett to hear it first. "I'm going to hear back from her team this week."

"That's fantastic. You must be so proud," Faye said, and Elsie noticed that she hadn't said, "I'm so proud." She considered asking her mom if that pride extended to her but was unwilling to risk a Faye-ism.

Faye must have taken her pause for something more, because she hadn't budged from the doorstep. "I'm sorry for barging in, but I wanted to give you this." Faye held out a box—eggshell blue with a white bow.

"You aren't barging in."

"I know how you like a little notice before having visitors."

Faye still held the box and Elsie realized she looked nervous. Her high-powered, take-life-by-the-balls mother was on unsure footing. Elsie didn't know what to say. It was clear that Elsie's need for control and order had somehow given her mom the impression that she wasn't wanted. Elsie knew how that felt and it broke her heart that she'd made her mom feel the same kind of uncertainty when it came to doing things that mothers were supposed to do—like drop by their daughter's house just because.

"Why don't you come in. I can make us some coffee."

Faye took a step back. "It looks like you're headed out and really I wanted to drop this by." Faye handed her the box and Elsie looked down. It wasn't actually wrapped, there was just the bow. So there was nothing to conceal the fact that her mother had brought her a mini-architect building kit. "It isn't anything big. More of a gag present really. But when I saw it at the art store, I thought that my interior architect of a daughter might get a kick out of it."

Elsie's eyes stung at her mother's words. She hadn't said decorator or designer. In her own way, Faye was acknowledging what Elsie had accomplished. And while she didn't voice it, Elsie could tell her mom was proud.

Another first in her life. And one she'd cherish until the day she died.

CHAPTER TWENTY

Dating Tips from Elsie Dodd
Show up and let yourself be seen.

For such a rule maker, Elsie had become an expert rule breaker. And she was about to break a big one. If she could get in.

She stood outside Stout in what had to be a line of fifty people deep. The event had already started. She could feel the bass thumping in her sternum, had heard Rhett introduce two acts thus far. She was still wearing the perma-grin from her meeting with Susan. And a warm lightness from her talk with her mom.

Bouncing on the balls of her toes and rubbing her arms to get the chill off from the crisp summer night, she craned her head to look down the street and take in the never-ending que. At this rate she'd get in after the show was finished and Rhett had performed his new song. Which would be a shame because she really wanted to be there for him, wanted to hear which song he'd picked. There was finally an album-full to choose from. So would it be the one about them or a different, not so personal one? In addition, she really wanted to see the look on his face when she walked in wearing the pair of mile-high heels she'd worn the other night in the music room and her upcycled T-shirt.

Then there were her pants—leather, tight, and fitting her body like a glove. She'd agreed to show up in a strict friend capacity, but her outfit screamed sex buddies. Which broke yet another rule—keeping things private. In fact, the one rule they hadn't broken was no empty promises. And she knew in her heart that Rhett wasn't the kind to make a promise lightly.

He'd been careful with what he'd asked of her, what he could offer and what he wanted—which was more time—and that terrified her as much as it secretly thrilled her. But when she'd shrugged off his offer for more—because she wasn't sure she could do more once he left to go back on tour—he'd respected her decision. Yet now, with mere days before he left for LA, she was wondering if she could go through with it and actually call it quits. She's never said a man-free diet, she'd said a dick-free diet, and Rhett was as far from a dick as Axel was to husband material.

Rhett was respectful, honest, gentle, and kind. He was also a man of his word. He may have ghosted her ten years ago, but they'd been kids with dreams that would take them in different directions and it had been the right call. Problem was, she didn't know what was right for them this time around. They both had big dreams—dreams that conflicted and took them in opposing directions.

"Elsie?" a man who looked like Jason Statham with tattoos said, walking on the outskirts of the line and stopping in front of her.

She looked over her shoulder, to see if there was another Elsie standing behind her, because she had zero clue who this guy was. Then she noticed the piercing blue eyes and knew he was an Easton.

"You're Elsie," he stated. "I'm Owen, Rhett's brother. He's been peeking out the window for the past hour looking for you."

A combination of excited flutters that he'd been waiting collided with guilt that he'd been waiting. "I'm sorry I'm late."

"Oh, you're just in time."

"I got stuck in line."

"You were on the list."

Her heart fluttered. "I didn't know."

"That's okay." Owen put his hand on her lower back and guided her past the long line and toward the entrance. "Watching him stress was priceless. So thanks for that. We have a poll going on just how long he'd wait before ditching the concert to go looking for you."

"Does he know about the poll?"

"He gave himself ten to one odds that he'd bail at halftime, leaving me to host. So thanks for showing. I hate playing the jester."

Rhett would make an excellent MC. He's funny and real and knows how to work a crowd. So then, "Why is he stressed?" she asked, concerned. "Is he reconsidering playing?"

Owen mumbled something like, "He's reconsidering something," but it was hard to tell over the noise.

They entered through the front door and were immediately assaulted by the stench of beer, the loud chatter of the audience, and the crush of people—she nearly turned tail and walked out. This scene was so achingly familiar. It was everything she hated about her marriage. Elsie standing on the sidelines while Axel got to live out his dream. Then there were the women, filling the front two rows and lining the walls—waiting for their moment to pounce.

Before Axel's infidelity Elsie had never been bothered by groupies nor had she been jealous, but after his betrayal—his multiple betrayals that spanned most of their marriage—seeing the women watching Rhett ignited something inside Elsie that she didn't like.

A wave of uncertainty washed over her, nearly taking her breath in a riptide of jealousy. What was she doing here? And how did she think this was going to end? They'd go their separate ways, then what? Rhett would be back on the market, and she'd have to watch him shuffle through a rolodex of women. While Elsie stood from the sidelines yet again—her feelings insignificant.

It would be just like her divorce, but worse because his conquests would be plastered on every tabloid and magazine in the country. At the bookstore in town, the checkout line at the Hub and Grub, even her hair salon.

"Maybe I should go." She began to turn around, but Owen caught her hand.

"I didn't take you for a coward."

She bristled. "You don't even know me."

"Maybe not," Owen said softly, "but I know that look. And I've watched my brother waver between knowing you'd show and fearing that he'd be left standing alone. He has this stupid idea in his head that he isn't worth fighting for. Are you the kind of person to leave him hanging?"

His question hit hard, like thunder rattling her brain. She didn't want to be another walk-out in his life and hurt Rhett like his ex had. She knew what that felt like. But she also didn't know if she could go through feeling like just one in a crowd of many.

"No. I'm not a coward," she said, feeling like the Lion in the *The Wizard of Oz*. She looked around the intimidating room and a thin sheen of perspiration glistened on her forehead. She thought back to what her mom would say in this situation, her favorite Brené Brown saying, "Courage starts with showing up and letting ourselves be seen."

And Elsie was ready to be seen. She glanced around, searching for a seat, but the place was standing-room only. There were the lucky few who'd snagged seats, probably because they'd camped out overnight, then there were the dedicated fans who'd chosen to fill any available space, the VIP section, and finally the family area. Then there was Elsie somewhere in the middle. "Where should I stand?"

"Rhett saved you a seat." Owen took led her through the room to the bar, using his big body to shelter her from the sardine can of people around them. He guided her to a single chair that sat behind a roped off area, in the middle of four women, who all looked at her the same way Owen had.

Like they knew her. And one did.

"Piper?" Elsie said.

"Uh, surprise! I'm sorry I didn't tell you before, I didn't want to freak you out," Piper said.

"Like we're doing right now," a brunette beside her said.

Elsie's palms began to tremble, so she put them behind her back.

"We won't bite," one of the women, with blonde shoulder-length hair, said. Owen laughed.

Elsie gave a forced laugh and took a seat. "Hi, I'm—"

"Elsie," a woman with a southern accent said. "We know."

"Not a lot," Piper said, and it was nice to see a familiar face. "All we know is that Rhett doesn't want us to know anything about you."

"You could have asked me about it at the photo shoot, which by the way I totally owe you for, because the photographs turned out amazing."

"My pleasure," Piper said. "And the other day was business. This is girls' night and that means gossip is fair game."

"So he really hasn't told you anything?"

"Not a single word," the blonde said assuredly.

Elsie released a relieved breath. She should have known Rhett would keep his word. He'd already warned her that his family knew they had history but that their current situation was private. The women looking on were interested in the second half.

Elsie squirmed in her heels. Man, she knew she might run into his family, but she never imagined she have to stare them down in one big bestie-pack.

"Which is why we were hoping you'd tell us everything," one of the women said, offering Elsie a flute with champagne. "I'm Jillian, by the way, the nosy one. And this is Darcy and Abi."

The four women couldn't be more different, but somehow they all gave off the same look. The look Elsie recognized as a woman in love. Uncomfortable and feeling out of place, she glanced away, wondering why Rhett had seated her there. Did he hope they'd all bond or did he not give it even a thought?

"So what doesn't he want us to know?" Jillian asked.

"I guess you already know that we met in college. He was, well, he was Rhett just younger, and we almost had a thing, then we didn't. The next time I saw him I was engaged. End of story," she lied.

"Thanks for giving us the highlights," Jillian said. She clearly wasn't buying it. "But we want to know what happened between almost having a thing and you being engaged."

Elsie thought about how to describe what had happened and for the first time she felt right about everything. Even though College Elsie wouldn't have let Sweet-Talking Rhett off that easy had she known why he ghosted her, Big-Girl Elsie would have understood and would even be thankful that he made the tough call. It didn't mean she approved of his method, but his heart was in the right place.

After telling Axel the basics when they'd had the unexpected Rhett run-in, who'd brushed it off as "things happen,"—talk about red flag—Elsie had never really spoken about that weekend with anyone. At first it was because it was so special that she wanted to keep it between the two of them. Then she'd been too embarrassed, and after she'd married Axel it was too awkward. Now, she didn't want anyone to think she was bragging about bagging America's Sexiest Man. She also did not want people probing her about what happened between them when their time was up.

Because between her goals and his commitments there would come a time, likely soon, where they'd have to admit that things weren't going to work out in the long haul.

"We had just one weekend, but it was a *weekend*," she said, and even she could hear the swooning in her voice. The women exchanged a knowing look, which Elsie promptly ignored. "I thought maybe I'd found my person, but the next thing I knew he ghosted me."

All four women gasped.

"He did not," Piper said. "What a dick."

"What a total Easton thing to do," Darcy said, rolling her eyes. "They try so hard, but they tend to make a mess of everything." She rested her hand atop Elsie's. "Their hearts are always in the right place; they can't help themselves."

"I think it's a Y-chromosome thing," Piper said. "They can't help that the leg fell off the X, rendering them temporarily stupid at times."

The group laughed.

"Rhett definitely suffered from temporary stupidity." But that was years ago. In fact, since their unexpected reunion, he'd been a rock. Strong, steady, supportive—all the things that made a man a *man*. And all the traits that made Rhett the man who had stolen her heart.

Wanting to know more about him, she said, "I didn't know a lot about what was happening in his life when we first met, but later he told me it was around the time his dad passed."

"All the boys were devastated. They are a tight-knit family, so close nothing could tear them apart until their dad died. Benji was the glue, the dad we all wished we'd had. The world as they knew it shattered with him. Their mom mourned Benji for nearly a decade and I think each son still mourns him in their own way," Piper said.

"I didn't know," she said. Elsie wasn't sure how she'd feel if her father died; she'd never had that kind of parental love. Not even with her mother. The closest she came was Harriet, whose love had its own unique flavor.

That wasn't fair. Earlier, she and Faye had taken a step in the right direction. Oh, Faye had dropped a few Faye-isms as Elsie tried to give her a proper hug, but the gesture was what mattered.

"It was bad," Darcy said. "Then Rhett went after his career full force. It was his way of honoring his father's unyielding support."

"I knew his career was taking off, but I didn't know the rest." Rhett had confided pieces about his dad's health, but she had no clue as to how sick Benji really was. That he passed within days of her and Rhett's time together made her heart ache for him even more.

Abi reached out and rested her hand over Elsie's in a sign of support. "You said end of story, but your expression says something different."

Too tired to keep up pretense, Elsie said, "The story picks up a month ago when I found him in my house, which is now his house. He let me finish the renovation because it's going to be featured in a national magazine."

"*Modern Masterpiece*," Piper chimed in. "It's a huge deal."

"Congrats." Abi held up a flute and they all tinked glasses.

"Thanks, it's exciting." And Rhett was a big part of her dream coming true. "We made an agreement—I'd finish the house making as little noise as possible so he could write and he'd let me stay in the house while I finished it—but then things became intertwined."

"How intertwined?" Jillian rubbed her hands together like she was about to learn next week's lotto numbers.

"What did he tell you?" Because if he told them about their sex-buddies arrangement, she'd die of embarrassment.

"My husband mentioned Rhett's relationship to your ex," said Jillian.

"Nothing more," Piper said again, and smacked Jillian's hand. "He hasn't said a word to anyone about anything. Jillian's just filling in the blanks like she always does."

Jillian held up two fingers. "I swear. I didn't mean to pry."

"Liar," the three women said in unison, then burst out laughing and Elsie found herself laughing too. She also felt herself brought into the fold of what seemed to be a special bond between these women.

"We all did and we're sorry," Darcy said.

"I didn't," Piper said.

"It's okay. I'd be curious too." Elsie explained the situation with the house, and how Axel bamboozled them both, and then more about their arrangement. Just the part about living together, not the "benefits" part. "It's a temporary thing born from a shitty situation."

"We offered to have him stay in the cottage. He declined," Darcy said suspiciously.

Elsie tried to be angry on the matter but thinking back to earlier that morning and waking up in his arms, how he'd wished her a good morning, not once but three times, she couldn't. It was as if she'd landed right where she belonged.

She looked up to find all four women looking back. "My new place won't be ready for another few weeks. Rhett has been very generous by letting me stay."

Jillian took an innocent sip of her bubbly. "So, how's *that* going?"

"He's leaving for LA next week and we're trying to leave the past in the past. But sometimes the past seeps into the present," she said honestly.

Darcy snorted. "Gage and I tried that, but it didn't work."

"Why not?"

"The harder we tried to keep apart, the stronger the pull," Darcy said. "Did Rhett ever tell you how I met Gage?"

"No."

"I was a runaway bride."

"And you ran into his arms?" Elsie said with a sigh, because how romantic was that.

"I wish. That would have made the transition so much easier, but it wasn't our time. I was actually engaged to his twin brother, Kyle."

"Oh my god." Elsie covered her mouth. That topped any complications Elsie had in her life. "How does that even work?"

"I found out Kyle was cheating on me, so the day of the wedding I asked him to choose between me and his co-worker. He didn't have an answer, but that was all the answer I needed."

Darcy shrugged like it was no big deal, but Elsie imagined at the time it was a huge deal. She knew how crippling infidelity could be.

"I didn't find out about my husband's cheating until eight years in."

"I am so sorry," Darcy said. "Then you understand how hard it can be to trust again. But I promise, with the right person it can work."

"So you were able to trust again?"

"First, I bolted. Right out of the church and never looked back. That same night Kyle was killed in a car crash." Elsie could tell there was more to the story but didn't ask. "The family blamed me for his accident and made my life hell."

"Even Rhett?" He was such a gentle soul, she couldn't imagine him being vindictive to anyone. Then again, she never imagined Axel would come at her so hard during their divorce.

"Even Rhett. In his defense, no one knew about Kyle and his side-piece. They also didn't know I was pregnant. Keeping my daughter a secret from the family was wrong, but their mom, Margo, can be overbearing and downright mean, and I refused to put my daughter through that."

"But you seem so happy now."

"That was Gage. Once he found out he was an uncle, he did everything it took to make things right again. He was patient, supportive, and loves my daughter like she's his own. More than that, he puts us first."

"My ex didn't even consider other people's needs. He put himself first at every turn." It hadn't always been that way. There had been a time when he'd made her feel as if she were the center of his universe. Once he set his sights on something he pursued it with singular focus.

With her father walking out and her mom so dedicated to her career, Elsie never felt like a priority, and Axel treated her as if she mattered. Until he didn't. There had been warning signs along the way that she'd ignored because he was so attentive, and she wanted so badly to be chosen, to be a priority, that she overlooked so much.

But things were different with Rhett. He didn't just put her first, he listened and respected her wishes, even though she was beginning to think she wanted more. Hell, she did want more. More than some stupid set of rules.

"Look at us prying," Piper said, giving the other women the eye.

Darcy held up a hand. "You're right. It's none of our business. Being in this family has made me a busybody. It's almost contagious in the Easton clan. We're always up in each other's business, especially the men. They're the worst."

"I don't think anyone could be more of a busybody than my grandma," she said, and the women laughed. "She's been playing matchmaker since I came home. She somehow missed the 'I'm off men' memo."

"And now?"

"I don't know." *Liar.* "A big part of the reason my marriage failed, besides my husband was a cheat, was that he was constantly leaving. It's scary to invest my heart into someone who has the same lifestyle."

"I struggled with the same thing," Jillian said. "I'm a mom of a nine-year-old boy so my Me Time is nonexistent. When Clay and I first started flirting I told myself there was no way to make it work with a guy who lived in another state. But we somehow make it work. Actually, he puts the time in every day to make it work."

"How?" Elsie found herself asking.

"We both gave a little and met in the middle, and he decided to put us first before everything. He even retired"

Was it possible to meet in the middle with their wildly different commitments and lives without one of them giving up their career? "And now?"

Jillian lifted a brow. "Temporary became forever. And trust me, it took a lot to get me to come around. I'd gone through a hellish separation and an even worse divorce. I was so off men, I didn't even think the Hemsworth brothers were worth my time."

"Been there. Still reeling," Elsie admitted. "My husband and his legal team tore me to shreds. But I picked up the pieces and now I'm starting fresh, with my life and my career."

Abi lifted a brow. "So, there's no room for more?"

"I'd like to know the answer to that question." Elsie turned to find Rhett directly behind her. He was dressed in dark jeans, a ball cap, his worn U of O shirt, and a lush black leather jacket. He looked like backstreet musician meets rock star.

"Hey," she said, and it was almost a whisper. She couldn't take her eyes off him. She was certain the other women were making all kinds of assumptions, but she didn't care.

His gaze roamed down her body and his expression said anything but friends. Just like her outfit.

"Can I borrow you for a moment?"

He didn't wait for her to answer, just took her hand and led her around the bar and into a back storage room, where he kicked the door shut with his foot, then pushed her up against it.

Her belly flipped, then flopped at the possessiveness in his touch. She'd never considered possessiveness a good thing, but with him it felt more like he was asking her to be his.

Yes, her mind screamed. Her hormones screamed something else when she saw the raw hunger in his eyes.

"How did it go with Susan?" he asked, and she loved that, even though it was his big night, the first thing out of his mouth was about her big day.

"I'm in! She loved the house," she said. "She's even talking the music room being a possible cover image."

"I am so damn proud of you, Red. So proud," he said lowly.

"Thank you. It couldn't have happened without you."

"No way." He tipped her chin up. "This is all on you. You made this happen."

A shiver ran through her entire body at his words, and she rubbed her arms to heat them up. She looked around the room, at the baskets of fresh produce, jars of fresh herbs, and shelves of ingredients. "Are we in the refrigerator?"

"It was the closest place I could think of where no one will bug us." He took off his jacket and put it over her shoulders. She tugged it around her. Still warm from his body heat, the scent of yummy man engulfed her. "I can find someplace else?"

There was a wildness to his eyes that she hadn't seen since their first kiss. "I'm not going anywhere."

"Good answer." His mouth came crushing down on hers in a full-on assault. It didn't take long for her to melt into him, slide her arms around his neck, and give in to the fire. His hands were everywhere all at once.

"I love this top," he said, kissing his way down her neck and taking advantage of the low V of her shirt. "It checks off another one of my Elsie Fantasies."

"Because it's your band on the front?"

"That too," he said as he licked the cleavage between her breasts.

"I like yours." He ran his tongue across a peaked nipple and her head fell back against the wall. "It reminds me of the night we met."

He looked up with a boyish grin. "I know. That's why I wore it." He looked down. "Nice heels."

"That's why I wore them."

He was back to kissing her, long and hard like he was breathing her in. His hands went to the backs of her thighs and he lifted her weight, caging her between his hard body and the door. She locked her legs around his waist and he moaned when her heels bit him in the ass.

She tugged at his shirt, pulling it up so she could slip her hands beneath. The sensation of her fingers gliding over warm skin was erotic. He hummed his approval.

She felt the door behind her jar a scant inch and rattle, then slam shut.

"Come back," Rhett said against her mouth.

The door jarred again, and Rhett pressed his forehead to hers. "What part of 'come back' did you miss?"

"Um, you're up in two minutes," Owen said from the other side of the door, and she could hear the humor in his voice.

"Everyone will know what we're doing," she whispered.

"Do you care?"

She thought about that, then took his mouth. She didn't give a shit if his family knew they were making out in the back of a bar.

"I'll take that as a no," he chuckled. After another kiss he asked. "Do you?"

A little dazed from all the kissing, she asked, "Do I what?"

"Have room for a man?" he asked quietly.

She opened her mouth to say no, then snapped it closed because no wouldn't be honest and that was one of two rules she'd never break. "I don't know, but I want to try."

"I don't want to leave on Monday and walk away from this. I know that we have a lot to figure out but I'm willing to try." He framed her face.

She thought back to what Jillian had said, and the look of love in her eyes, and smiled.

"The question is, are you? Because when I look at you all I see is my future," Rhett said.

There was a pound on the door. "Seriously, bro. Sixty seconds."

He gave her a quick kiss and set her on her feet. "I have to go, but I want to finish our talk. Okay?"

Still in a daze, Elsie nodded. Then watched Rhett walk out of the refrigerator. She stood there for a moment, absorbing what he'd just said. He wanted to try and if she really asked herself that question, she came up with a resounding yes. More than her space and her silly rules, she wanted to try at a future with Rhett.

Grin a mile wide, Elsie walked out of the room and was brought up short when she saw Owen.

"It looks good on you," he said.

"What?"

"Whatever it is you just decided," was all he said and then disappeared, leaving her with her thoughts. Thoughts of what a future with Rhett would look like.

She knew that there was the possibility for devastating, gut-wrenching disappointment and heartbreak, but hope sprang eternal. And she couldn't ignore the fact that life with Rhett could be as freeing as it would be exciting. So what if he shared the same profession as Axel? They weren't the same person. And Rhett knew, firsthand, what it felt like to be overlooked and underappreciated. His ex had treated him with the same callousness as Axel had treated Elsie. So if anyone knew how awful it felt to be lied to and taken advantage of, it was him.

He'd been honest and open and always in her corner. Even when she'd been stubborn and fickle, giving him every reason to walk away, he'd stuck it out. Never once showing her anything other than honesty. He was the sort of man a woman could fall in love with.

Oh boy.

Elsie stopped dead in her tracks because she was the woman in that scenario. Somewhere along the way she'd fallen for him hard and deep. She fallen for his humor and kindness, and she'd fallen for *him*. Period.

Oh god, Elsie was in love and she was terrified.

She looked at her man on the miniscule stage that barely held a drummer, a guitarist, a bass player, and the lead singer. Then there was Rhett, on the edge, hyping up a kid who had to be no more than sixteen. Rhett's tone told Elsie that this was one of the musicians Rhett had mentored. Her belly fluttered with pride and, yes, love.

Elsie wrapped her arms around her center trying to hold back the emotion that was taking flight in her body, making her head light and her body buzz. She was in the beginnings of love, and it felt good.

It felt right.

"Of all the bars in all the world, you had to walk into this one," a familiar voice said. At her rat bastard of an ex's voice, Elsie closed her eyes for a moment, wishing she could disappear. Not only did she not possess that superpower, she could barely move because of the sheer amount of people.

She turned and rolled her eyes. Axel was dressed in shredded jeans, a vintage Slayer shirt—that she'd bought him for their last Christmas together—and hair that was effortlessly messy. He gave off enough rock-star energy to gain the attention of a group women around them—whose cleavage were winking his way.

Disappointedly, he looked good, like the divorce hadn't even affected him, while Elsie felt like she'd aged a decade. He'd always had this inexplicable factor about him that drew people to him. He looked famous even though he was just background noise in an overcrowded industry.

Portland wasn't that big of a city and he had family there too, so she knew they'd bump into each other eventually. She'd hoped it would have been after her company was up and running, after the magazine article had come out.

At that moment she would have settled for her plus-one to be there to hold her hand. She glanced around and saw that Rhett wasn't on stage and the young artist had started his set. She also noticed that Rhett's entire family was a few feet away watching the fireworks between them.

"You always were a cliché. I guess that's why you were never any good at writing," she said, then immediately regretted her words. Axel was the master at verbal annihilation and she'd just thrown the gauntlet.

"Funny thing there. I haven't ever been as creative as I have since our separation. So who's the problem now?"

Elsie swallowed the pain and disappointment, then decided Axel didn't have any say in her life anymore. She was over the pettiness, the arguing, and the pain. She'd moved on. Or so she'd thought, until she'd came nose to nose with the man who'd stolen eight years of her life.

Eight years of hopes and dreams gone. Eight years of planning for a family that never came. Eight years of wondering why she wasn't enough. Except this time, she knew she was enough. For the right man, she was enough and that was all that mattered.

"Where are they?" he asked.

"Where are what?" she said sweetly.

"Cut the crap, Els. Where are my lucky drumsticks? Just tell me they're safe."

Anger rose every second he stood there acting as if he belonged. Acting as if she were the unexpected addition to this super fun evening. "Safe like I didn't put them through the wood chipper?"

He blanched. "Please god, tell me you didn't."

She considered stringing him along a while longer, but she didn't want him to ruin her good mood. "They're safe and sound, in a box in storage." With the rest of the stuff she'd acquired in the divorce. She'd never wanted the drumsticks, but she'd taken them to piss off Axel. Which seemed childish now.

"Storage? They need to be kept in a dry environment." He pulled out his wallet. "Name your price. Anything."

She crossed her arms. "Fine. I want my house back."

He choked. "Are you crazy? I don't have that kind of money."

"I was your wife, remember? I know exactly how much money you have stashed in your hidey-holes."

"You can't seriously expect me to buy back the house."

She didn't really want the house. Maybe at one time, but not anymore. She was just fine with how things had worked out. And thinking back to her conversation with Rhett moments ago, she was happy with where things were headed.

"Why are you here?" she asked.

"I came to support local artists." She didn't mention she had a specific artist in mind.

A twinge of something bad pooled in her belly. "You aren't the support-someone-without-a-reason kind of guy." She narrowed her eyes. "What's your angle?"

Axel ran his hand over his face. And Elsie realized maybe he hadn't gotten away scot-free. Bloodshot eyes, thin stress marks bracketing his mouth and—upon closer inspection— a few new gray hairs. "I'm looking for a new gig."

"Which means you were dropped by your current gig?" she guessed. And, *bingo*, she was right. His expression said it all.

"Rhett's looking for a new drummer for his new album and tour. He and I are working out the details," he said, and Elsie wondered, if after everything Rhett had learned about her divorce, if Axel's statement had even an ounce of truth. And if it did, why didn't Rhett mention it. "Why are *you* here?" he asked.

She pushed her shoulders back. "I'm here to support Rhett." There. She'd said it out loud for everyone to hear. "And I've already missed enough, so shoo."

Axel was quiet for a moment, then he looked at Rhett's jacket, still wrapped around her and his lips curled into a smile. "So, you and him, huh? Not surprised."

"Why do you say that?"

"He always had a thing for you. That's why I was shocked when he hooked me up with my divorce attorney."

Her heart stopped dead in her chest. "I don't understand," she said, trying to take it all in, understand what he was saying. But the pounding of the bass and beating of her heart made it difficult to put it all together in a way that made sense. "He put you in contact with your attorney?"

The smile Axel gave had that spring of hope in her chest running dry. Rhett had to know the kind of firm Harry, Waxer, and Bush was, known of their vicious nature and reputation for demolishing the opposition. And she'd been demolished. Humiliated. Run down and then run over. But she'd made it back.

Yet, if this were true, she wasn't sure she'd survive this betrayal.

"Even did the introduction in person when he was in LA last. Isn't that right, buddy?"

Axel was talking to someone over her shoulder. She didn't need to turn to see that it was Rhett, she felt his energy move through her. Felt the separation forming when he didn't reach out to touch her shoulder in solidarity.

She slowly turned to face down the man who owned her heart and prayed that she hadn't been played, that she hadn't made a colossal mistake in judgment once again. There he stood, frozen behind the rope that separated the family from everyone else, leaving her feeling all alone.

"Els," he whispered, taking a step closer, but then stopping when she put up a shaking hand, begging him to keep his distance.

She'd talked about how brutal her divorce had been more than once and Rhett had never said a word.

Emotion clogged her throat, and she was certain she'd be sick.

"Els." This time there was an urgency to his voice, genuine concern for her. Which was okay because she was concerned for herself. For her future and for how she was going to make it through the rest of her life knowing that Rhett helped stick the stake right through her heart.

Suddenly he was in front of her, tilting her head up and that's when she realized that she hadn't held it together. In fact, she was falling to pieces every second she stood there.

She opened her mouth to ask him if it was true, if he'd really helped Axel slaughter her in court, but a silent sob erupted.

"Shit." Rhett pulled her into his arms. "I've got you."

She let him take the weight for a moment because it was too heavy to carry all by herself, but then she realized that she'd have a lifetime to carry it alone, so she'd better get used to it. She pulled away.

He'd befriended her, gained her trust, then sweet-talked her into sharing parts of her life she'd never shared with another soul. Pieces of her heart that she'd kept hidden from the world. And the whole time he'd known.

"I can't do this." Elsie turned on her heel and looked for the exit, which was impossible to find surrounded by five massive Eastons. That's when she became acutely aware that each and every Easton had heard the entire humiliating exchange. His brothers had formed a half circle around them, protecting her from prying eyes, but she'd rather have a stranger look at her than the way the Eastons were looking at her.

With pity.

She'd been the only one not in the know. Her heart gave one final beat in her chest for the man she'd fallen so foolishly in love with.

Clutching her chest, as if that would erase the ache, she looked Rhett in the eye, but the pain was so intense she doubled over. Even with her dad and Axel she'd never experienced anything so painful. It was like she'd been cut in two and the pieces of her heart couldn't find one another.

Chapter Twenty-one

Dating Tips from Elsie Dodd
*You will never have to chase
what wants to stay with you.*

"Let me explain," Rhett said, the words barely escaping his throat.

"I need to know if it's true," Elsie said, her voice so fragile and so full of hurt, the punch to Rhett's gut was so hard nausea roiled inside.

He opened his mouth to say it wasn't true, but he knew that would be a lie. He hadn't even though about that conversation with Axel since the day it happened, but it had happened. He wanted to say that he hadn't meant to hurt her, but nothing came out. His chest was too large for air to escape, let alone speak.

"It's a simple question. Did. You. Help. Axel. Torpedo me. In court?"

"It wasn't like that. He asked for legal advice. I was in the middle of my divorce, and I passed along my attorney's info."

Axel's gaze darted between Elsie and Rhett, and a smug smile slid across his face and Rhett wanted to punch him. A light of understanding flickered, and Axel laughed, loud enough to capture the attention of the people behind them.

Rhett's brothers were still forming a wall with their bodies, trying to give Elsie some privacy, but people were peeking over their heads and around their bodies.

"I guess you finally got the girl?"

Axel might as well have just high-fived him and asked to rate Elsie on the *How Good a Lay Is She?* scale.

"Shut up," Rhett said to Axel, who put up a hand in surrender but didn't abandon his front-seat view to the action.

Elsie was devastatingly horrified; he could see it on her face. This was exactly what she wanted to avoid—people knowing their business—and now it was on display for everyone with a cell phone to capture.

"You also passed along the GUIDEBOOK TO SCREWING OVER YOUR WIFE," she said as cold as Igloo Frost.

"You've got to believe me. It wasn't like that with me and Steph. The lawyers were more of arbitrators if anything."

"Well, good for you. My experience wasn't so peachy." Her eyes were filled with unspilled anguish. "After all our talks about how bad it was, how my divorce destroyed me, it never once popped into your mind to even mention you shared the same law firm?"

"Same attorney as well," Axel added.

"What part of *Shut the hell up* did you miss." Rhett took a step forward to punch the guy's lights out and Owen held him back.

"Not here," Owen said. "If you want to move this to my office, I'll hold the guy down for you. But you've got about a hundred cameras on you."

Elsie looked around the bar as if just remembering that there was a room full of people watching and recording the most humiliating moment of her life. "I forgot about this part."

He didn't need to ask which part, he knew. It was the spotlight, the lack of privacy, the fear that every fight or conversation wasn't sacred. It was the part of his world that he'd promised to protect her from and yet there they were, her heart served on a platter for the world to watch.

"Why didn't you tell me?"

"I didn't think there was anything to tell."

A collective gasp circling around him told him *that* was the wrong answer. But the tears swimming in her pretty eyes really hammered it home. The moment he'd given Axel support, he'd taken sides. Something he'd promised her that first night that he hadn't done.

"I never thought he'd go after you like that." Even to him it sounded like a hollow excuse.

"You knew Axel. You knew the lawyer. What did you think would happen?"

"I used them with my divorce, and it wasn't anything like what you went through."

"Because you're you!" she yelled. "Axel's not you. He's childish and selfish and mean. He's mean, Rhett. And you gave him the ammo to destroy me."

"Els." Once again he tried to hold her and she put out her hands.

"Don't touch me," she said, and he was stricken. "Do you have any idea what I went through? How I was questioned and probed and humiliated and taken advantage of just because I couldn't afford a cutthroat lawyer revered for going for the jugular."

"I didn't expect him to go at you so hard."

Her hand went to her throat in a defensive motion. "But you did expect him to go at me?"

Now that he thought about it, he knew he'd screwed up. He knew Axel, knew that he never liked to lose a fight and knew exactly how the guy would handle his wife walking out on their marriage. But instead of removing himself from the situation, Rhett had placed himself smack dab in the middle. No, it was worse, he'd placed himself solely on Axel's side. On the side that hurt Elsie. And he'd done it all without a second thought because he was still reeling from his own divorce and selfishly not thinking of anyone's problems but his own.

"Els, I am so sorry that I hurt you."

He took another step forward and she backed up until she bumped into Gage. Her eyes went around the circle, from the wives to his brothers, the entire Easton clan, who were there to support him. There was no one to support her and his family was reminding her of that fact. He knew she felt trapped.

He offered her his hand. "Why don't we go into Owen's office?"

She looked at his hands as if they were a deadly snake and he was certain she wouldn't take it, which she didn't, but she did move closer to him—then around him, pushing through the crowd that was pushing closer to get a picture of the woman Rhett Easton had made cry. Because she was crying. He could tell she hadn't figured it out yet, and when she did, she was going to be so mad, because she hated it when she cried. But there they were, streaming down her cheeks, a steady fall that had his gut twisting painfully.

She'd made it to the back corridor, near the employee's entrance, clearly aware that Rhett was right on her heels. She stopped. Her shoulders drawn, her gaze on her feet, it was as if her entire body had curled in on itself. And when she turned to face him, *god* when she turned, his heart broke into a million pieces.

"God, babe, don't cry." He ran his thumb down her cheek.

"Is Axel really your new drummer?" she whispered.

Rhett paused, seeing how everything would look to her in this moment and every wild, rash, from-the-hip decision he'd ever made came rushing back with a force that knocked the wind out of him. How he'd walk the line, procrastinate big decisions, even disappearing when things got hard. He was going to lose her and it was all his fault.

His heart gave an unsteady beat. "Hell, no! We hired someone else last week."

She worried her lower lips and gave the slightest nod of the head. "But he was a viable option?"

He thought back to Gage's question when he'd first brought up Axel as a possibility and suddenly he understood the gravity of his decision. Or non-decision as it were. Every show, every practice, every jam session in his home studio that Elsie had handcrafted, would include the asshole who broke her heart. Who cheated on her and used her kindness against her.

Here he'd been envisioning a future with her, and her ex would have been right in the middle of everything. He'd like to think he wouldn't have hired Axel, but if push had come to shove, and they hadn't been able to find an equally as talented alternative, what would Rhett have done? And what would he have told Elsie?

"No," he said confidently. "I wouldn't have hired Axel. I wouldn't have let him step foot in our house."

"Your house," she whispered. "It stopped being my house that day in your shower. I'll pack my things and be out by tomorrow morning."

"What about the shoot?"

"What about it?"

"You can't give that up because of this." Panic set in. He wasn't just losing her, she was already gone.

"What do you expect me to do? Hang up magazine photos of a house that I thought I'd spend the rest of my life in with the guy I thought I'd spend the rest of my life with? Be reminded every day that I once again bet on the wrong person? That I let my emotions cloud my good sense?"

"I can make this better."

"How? The way to make it better was to be up-front and honest with me. Even if you forgot about the lawyers, you should have told me you were considering hiring Axel for your tour so I could be prepared to run into him when I came to shows to support you." She choked on her emotion. "How stupid am I? I mean, you get to go off and live your dream while I get to stay behind and figure out how to revive mine. Again."

"I can fix this," he said. "I know I screwed up, but I can fix this. I promise, I just need you to believe me."

"I'm trying to, but it's really hard," she said. "I don't know what's the truth and what's you just being Rhett, the guy who would rather say nothing than hurt someone's feelings. Love takes trust, Rhett, and you broke my trust. You broke my heart." She'd stopped wiping at her tears and let them fall, each one more gut-wrenching than the last. "Then again, we're good at breaking rules. I shouldn't be surprised that you broke the last one."

She shot him a devastating look—a look he'd never forget—and then walked out the back door, slamming it behind her. He somehow made it to the exit right as she disappeared around the corner. In that moment he knew that whatever Axel had done was nothing compared to what Rhett had done. He'd gained her trust, then obliterated it. He'd completely devastated her world.

He dropped down on his haunches and pressed the heels of his hands to his eyes, knowing she was gone and never coming back.

A few seconds, a few minutes, hell a lifetime could have passed and Rhett hunched there replaying every step and decision that led him to the moment when he lost the woman he loved.

"You going to just let her go?" Gage asked quietly.

Rhett looked up to find his brothers standing behind him, their expressions as serious as the situation.

"I didn't let her go, she left." Left him standing there in the alley with his heart on the ground.

"Then go after her," Clay said, as if fixing this mess was as easy as that.

"And say what? That I screwed up and I'm sorry, but hey, I leave in a few days and I'll be gone, well, most of the next year."

Jesus, when he put it like that it was no wonder that she'd put a cap on their time together. Elsie was still finding her footing after a brutal divorce, that he'd had a hand in, and he was asking her to jump into his crazy world headfirst.

"You'd be surprised what you can do in a few days," Owen said, and Rhett shot him a look. "How far you can advance a relationship. Talk it out and find a solution."

"I don't think there's a solution to this."

Jesus, it was just hitting him. She'd actually walked away. He'd been afraid of this moment since that first kiss, but he never imagined that when she went, she'd take his freaking heart. And he never imagined that she'd walk away forever.

She'd warned him that it was hard to come back from friends with benefits, but he'd never doubted for a second that they'd pull through. Hell, until this moment he'd never doubted that he could talk her into more. Instead, he'd talked himself right out of a lifetime with love.

"There's always a solution," Gage said. "You have to be willing to fight for it."

"I don't want to hurt her anymore," he said.

"I don't think you could hurt her worse than she hurts now," Owen so helpfully pointed out.

"Thanks for that observation, asshole."

"All he means is that she's already taken the hit and when the shock of it wears off and you're not there, then you'll really lose her," Josh said.

"I've already lost her," he murmured to himself. "I just thought I'd have more time to convince her that this could work."

"You still have time," Gage said, resting a hand on his shoulder. "But it's what you do with that time that will determine just how deep you've stepped in it."

Oh, Rhett was in deep. So deeply in love with her he couldn't even think straight, which was why he was probably standing there like an idiot while his person was out there, hurting.

He hadn't planned on falling in love. Didn't have the time or inclination, yet it had happened anyway. But watching Elsie carve out her dream from nothing, tackle life with so much heart and determination, it made him realize something—he was missing the life part of living.

These last few weeks with her had been some of the best weeks of his life. And if he didn't figure his shit out, and quick, he was going to end up spending his life lonely and alone. He'd come home for peace and space, but what he'd really been craving was connection. And he'd never felt connected to another human being the way he was with Elsie.

He looked at his brothers and knew they were right. He needed to go after her. But before he could do that, he needed to have something to offer her besides empty promises and lonely nights.

He pulled his cell from his pocket and dialed her. It went to voice mail. "Els," he began, not surprised when his voice cracked with emotion, "I have a few things I need to do but don't give up. Just promise me you won't give up on us."

CHAPTER TWENTY-TWO

Dating Tips from Elsie Dodd
*Don't date your friends unless
you want to end up alone.*

Elsie needed to be better at following her own rules.

When she'd left Los Angeles in search of a new beginning, she hadn't expected to wake up on her grandma's couch with swollen eyes and a raw nose. Nor had she expected to suffer through the lowest moment of her life with a world-wide audience. She was actually trending.

The video of her heartbreak had gone viral even before she'd made it to Harriet's. She'd been deemed Rhett's Unknown Girlfriend. Just like after her divorce, her name had been erased—reduced to a headline. She was some unknown sap who'd fallen for a guy destined to break her heart.

Word of her non-relationship relationship had spread through her contacts like wildfire. Friends were blowing up her phone to get the latest gossip. Even Susan had called to see if the shoot was still a go. Elsie hadn't had the heart to tell her the deal was off because once she made the call it would all be real.

Then there were the calls from Rhett. Too many to count. They'd started the moment she'd left the bar and hadn't let up until last night. She hadn't listened to a single one, and when they stopped coming in, her heart ached even more. Because that meant it was really over.

Which was what the plan had always been, she reminded herself.

"You awake?" Faye asked, her voice rattling around Elsie's brain. She was hungover from crying.

"No," Elsie groaned, rolling over and smothering herself with the pillow.

Elsie felt her mother sit down next to her on the couch. "How did you sleep?"

"Fine." She hadn't slept at all. She'd spent the entire night sobbing into her pillow. She'd been such an emotional disaster that she'd hired a ride share to protect the other drivers at large. She hadn't even been able to stomach going to the house to collect some of her things, so she'd come straight to Harriet's looking for one of her grandmother's heal-all-the-hurt hugs, but Harriet was in Vegas living large. Which left Faye.

That had been two nights ago, and Elsie was still on the couch waiting for her grandmother to come home and make it all better.

In her mother's defense, Faye had given a valiant effort in trying to fill the void of Harriet's absence, but it wasn't the same. Faye had listened and nodded at the right moments and even held Elsie when the worst waves hit, but something had been missing.

"Well, when you're done with your pity party, I've got a fresh pot of coffee in the kitchen."

Elsie whipped the pillow off her face. "What do you mean pity party? I am a scorned woman."

"What's the saying? Oh right. Fool me once, shame on you. Fool me twice, shame on me. Fool me three times, shame on both of us."

Elsie bolted upright. "Are you kidding me? You barely know Rhett and you're taking his side?"

A fresh wave of hurt rolled through her at her mother's comment. After their moment on the porch, Elsie thought they'd moved their relationship forward. It shouldn't surprise her to be wrong twice in two days.

Faye's face softened. "Oh honey, why does there always have to be a side? Hurt doesn't choose sides and I imagine you're both hurting right now."

She didn't have to imagine what Rhett was feeling because she was feeling it all the way to her core. It was as if her chest had been carved out so that if she screamed it would echo through her body. She'd seen the same emptiness in Rhett's eyes when she walked away, the look of anguish and loss.

"He's a jerkface. He helped Axel railroad me and then didn't say a word. Not a single word," Elsie whispered. "We talked about the divorce, how awful it all was, and the whole time he'd been a part of the destruction of my life."

"He's also been a part of your healing."

"Is this something you read in one of your books? *Healing by Drive-by?*"

"It's something your grandmother told me when your father walked out and I wished I'd listened," Faye said, and Elsie was taken aback. Her mother never, *ever*, talked about Elsie's dad. "I was so caught up in the anger that I let it hold me back from healing."

"Are you saying you would have taken Dad back if he'd come around?"

"God no." Faye cringed. "The man was a cheat and a liar, but when he walked out, I let the anger consume me until I shut myself off from other opportunities. I spent years looking for red flags rather than possibilities. And it robbed me of experiences, not just with others, but with you."

Her mother's admission was unexpected and touching.

"I stopped looking for red flags, went for the experience," Elsie said. And she'd gone big. "And ended up burned."

"Stop assuming bad intent. Sometimes people make mistakes. That's part of life, it doesn't mean that their love for you is any less."

She snorted. She knew Rhett cared for her, a lot. But love? She was afraid that was a one-sided emotion. She'd know if he loved her. Right?

"But mistakes that cut soul-deep shouldn't be a part of love."

"Oh honey, love doesn't play by rules," she said. The word *love* jolted Elsie. "It's free-flowing and ever-changing, otherwise it would shrivel up and die."

Is that what she'd done? Boxed in the chance at something great with her rules? Rules that Rhett had gone along with—for her. Had she killed off any chance of more because she'd been scared? Or had her instincts been right that this would end in heartache.

"He broke my heart, Mom. Worse than Dad or Axel. It hurts worse than anything I've ever felt. It's like all the air was yanked from my lungs and I can't breathe."

"I know he did," Faye said. "And I'm betting that you broke his. And the only thing sadder than one broken heart is two."

And his heart was equally as damaged as hers. She knew it. The look of desperation to fix things quickly turned to desolation when she'd walked away.

"Oh my god," she said, pulling the blanket to her chest as if the motion would stop her heart from falling right out. "I walked away." Tears stung her eyes. "I walked away, Mom."

"Fear will do that."

"But *I* walked away. I gave up." Just like her dad had done. And Axel. And Stephanie. Rhett might have broken her heart, but she'd broken her promise that she was his. She'd left him standing there in the back alley of the bar by himself because things had become too real for her.

He might have made a stupid mistake, and that's what it was. A big, stupid, heart-wrenching mistake. But it hadn't been intentional. She, on the other hand, knowingly took off, reconfirming his biggest fear—that he wasn't enough to stick around for.

"He isn't the jerkface. I am." And she'd been too busy playing victim to see it. She'd been playing the victim card for long enough and it was not a good look—on anyone. Especially a woman who was supposed to be chasing her happy. And she'd found her happy; he was on his way to Los Angeles, probably wondering where he went wrong.

"We're all the jerkface at one time or another," Fay said in a very life coach tone. Then she did something very unexpected, very motherly. She cupped Elsie's cheek.

Elsie was so taken by the gesture she almost jerked back.

"We don't do this very well, do we?" her mom said sadly.

Elsie placed her hand over her mother's and gave a watery smile, "I think we're doing just fine."

CHAPTER TWENTY-THREE

Dating Tips from Elsie Dodd
*Be the kind of person they marry, not
the kind they only want to date.*

By the time Rhett pulled up to the Greenhill house, Littleshit was fast asleep in his carrier and Rhett was dead on his feet. He'd just returned from a trip to LA, which had been a turn and burn that lasted less than twenty-four hours. And every one of those hours were spent getting his shit together. If he was going to win Elsie back, it would take more than a few pretty words.

Pretty words, Rhett had learned, were for songs, not love—real love required action. Something he needed to do before he lost her for good. He was already nervous that he'd wasted too much time, but he needed to make sure he was doing this right.

He let himself into the house that had come to feel like a home to him. Only now it felt empty and hollow—kind of like his chest. All the lights were off and he didn't bother turning them on. Dumping his suitcase by the door, he carried Littleshit up the stairs and into the master. Not that he planned on sleeping there, it felt wrong being there without Elsie, but he needed a hot shower and a change of clothes.

It had been three days since he'd seen or heard from her. He hadn't been able to sleep or eat and his head was constantly pounding, because the night at the bar was on perma-play in his mind. He also hadn't been able to reach her, he didn't know where she'd gone to, or how she was doing—and the last part tore him in two.

Out of options, he headed back to the house to regroup before figuring out where her grandmother lived. Then he'd sit on her porch and beg until Elsie would agree to a conversation—a conversation that would show her how much she meant to him.

He flicked on the bedroom light and his heart stopped beating because there on the bed was Elsie, sitting cross-legged, looking like a beautiful lifeline he desperately needed. She was dressed in jeans and a pretty, green top, but he couldn't tear his gaze off her eyes, which were a warm, mossy green—and locked on his.

"Red," he said, and that was all he could get out before he ran out of air. "What are you doing here?"

"Returning your call," she said simply.

"Returning my call?" he repeated dumbly.

"Yes." She took a sip from a flute and that's when he saw the bottle of bubbly on the table. "I'm sorry it took so long but I had to figure some things out."

Besides setting the dog carrier down, he didn't move, couldn't. It was like his feet were glued to the floor with a powerful combination of fear and hope.

"What did you figure out?"

"That I was a jerkface," she said, and scooted to the end of the bed. "I shouldn't have left like that. I should have heard you out and taken a breath because then I'd realize what I was doing."

He took a step closer. "And what was that?"

"That I was breaking a promise about staying friends no matter what," she said, and Rhett's heart sank. Was friendship all she wanted? Hell, he would be lucky if she'd ever consider him a friend again after what he did.

She stood and took a step. His chest loosened a tiny bit because she was stepping toward him, not away. "I know I hurt you," she whispered. "And I am so sorry."

As if he couldn't breathe until she was near him, he closed the gap. "I'm the one who hurt you. I never should have even contemplated hiring Axel or given him my lawyers' information. You were right, I do know the kind of guy he's become but I was too wrapped up in my own drama to think things through." He wanted to reach out and touch her, but he still wasn't sure why she was there, and he didn't want to make the wrong move. "It was a shit move."

"It was." She gave a small, trembling laugh and that's when he realized she was as nervous as he was. And that gave him a glimmer of hope. He let out a breath and brushed the back of her hand with his. "But you didn't do it to hurt me," she went on. "You did it to help a friend, and I know that now."

"Axel isn't a friend. In fact, to me he isn't anyone except the prick who stole my girl."

"Your girl, huh?"

"Why are you here, Els?" He reached out to bring her closer, but she backed away, and it was like an arrow through the heart. She walked to the end table, where a bottle of champagne and a second flute sat. She filled the glass and he could see her hands were trembling.

"To celebrate, well, a lot of things. First, we never got to toast to you and your new house."

"I don't give a shit about the house."

She ignored this and stepped closer, handing him the flute. "Second, that you finished writing the songs for your album."

"I don't give a shit about that either. All I care about is us," he admitted, and it was as if a weight had been lifted. He was finally telling her what he should have told her that night at the bar. "I care about you and me, Red. And the chance to finish what we started ten years ago. I went along with your rules but it's not enough for me. And I realized something recently, I'm tired of giving up what I want, which is why I told Gage I needed more time here, with you."

"You did?"

He nodded. "I'm not recording the album in LA, I'm doing it here. I have a stunning, state-of-the-art music room and basement studio this amazing architect designed, why go anywhere else. As for my tour, it will be structured so that I work for two weeks and then get a solid week off to come home. Or one week on and one week off—whatever we decide on—and when I am home, I'll be home. No press, no appearances, just downtime."

"But your music is your life."

"*You* are my life and the thought of living it without you brings me to my knees. And this house is so goddamned empty without you in it. I'm not expecting you to go on the road with me," he added quickly. "I'd never make you give up your dream or career. I want to be in your life, whatever that looks like."

She swallowed hard and her eyes were wide and a little misty. "You'd do that for me?"

"I'd do it for us." He circled a hand around her waist. "Please tell me there's an us. Or at least the chance for me to prove to you that I'm worth being the other part of your us."

Her voice was soft as she reached up and cupped his cheek. "You don't have to prove anything to me, Rhett. You are so worthy of love, which brings me to our last toast." She lifted her glass. "I want to toast to love because I love you, Rhett. All of you. The musician, the man, my friend, my lover, and the best big spoon your girl could ask for."

"My girl?"

"I hope that's a forever title."

A rush of air left his lungs so fast it left his head spinning. He took both their glasses and set them on the table, then pulled her into him. "I love you so much I can't breathe when we're not together. Day one, I knew I loved you and that anything less than forever would never be enough." He tilted his head down until their foreheads were touching. "I love you, Elsie Dodd, and I can't imagine my world without you in it. I want to wake up every morning with you in my arms and fall asleep every night listening to you snore."

She gave his chest a playful nudge. "I don't snore."

He grinned. "Yeah, you do, but it's sweet. *You're sweet* and sexy and honest and the best person I've ever met. I want to be your last first date, Els." He felt the ring in his pocket. His plan had been to get down on one knee and do things right, but he didn't want to let her go. "Reach into my pocket."

She snorted. "Worst line ever." But she reached into his pocket, and he knew when she found it because her breath caught and she stilled. Then she pulled it out and her hand went to her mouth in surprise.

"Rhett," was all she said, and he couldn't tell by her expression if she thought it was a good thing or the worst idea ever.

He'd never been so nervous in his entire life.

"Marry me, Els." He brushed a kiss over her lips. "I know this might seemed rushed, but I've wanted to do this for nearly a decade. Marry me."

"Rhett," she whispered. "It's beautiful."

"I got it wrong ten years ago, so I want to make sure I get it right this time around." He dropped to a knee and asked, "Be my wife and I promise that I will put you first every day and love you the way you deserve to be loved. What do you say, Els?"

"Yes," she said, caressing his face and tugging him up to deliver a long, tender kiss that rocked his world. "All the yeses in the world wouldn't be enough. And two weeks a month isn't enough. I want that every morning thing you talked about. Which is why I'm sure we can sync our schedules to be together and still live out all our dreams."

Rhett picked her up and swung her around. He'd come home to find himself and instead he'd found what had been missing all along. Love. He might have been a little slow on the uptake when it came to getting it right, but he'd finally gotten his girl.

EPILOGUE

Dating Tips from Elsie Dodd
Don't wait for the net.
When it's right, just jump.

Six months later...

Elsie stood at the bow of the boat, the breeze picking up the vintage silk of her gown as she watched the sun melt into the river, turning the sky a swirl of pink and yellow. Behind her, the wedding reception, which was small and perfect and consisted of just family, was in full swing but she wanted to take a breath to appreciate this beautiful moment.

Twenty minutes ago, she'd become Elsie Dodd-Easton and her heart couldn't be fuller. Last week the magazine had released its new issue with her music room making the cover, and Rhett's album was complete—and amazing.

After several missteps, Elsie had finally stepped right into the perfect life and the perfect man. And he'd embraced her fully for exactly who she was.

Rhett walked up behind her and slid his arm around her as he leaned in and kissed her neck, before resting his chin on her shoulder. "Are you thinking of jumping? I wouldn't blame you. My family is a lot to take in all at once."

His family had been nothing but amazing. Even before today they'd welcomed her into their pack as one of their own. His brothers became her brothers, their partners her best friends, and his mother and her new husband, Eddie, her second parents. Then there was the relationship with her own family, which was becoming stronger every day.

"I love your family." She looked over her shoulder to meet his gaze, which was as blue as the water. "And I love you."

"Good thing because it's too late to back out. You already sealed the deal with a kiss."

She turned in his arms. "Maybe we should seal it again." And they did until they were both breathing heavy.

"Do you think anyone would notice if we disappeared below deck?" he asked against her lips.

Her knees wobbled at the thought. "I bet we could sneak away for a few minutes."

He leaned back, a testy look on his face that made her laugh. "A few minutes? Red, I need at least an hour to show off my best moves."

She snuggled closer. "I've seen your best moves and they take more than an hour."

His hands slid to her butt, his lips to her earlobe, where he gave a soft nip. "I like where you're going with this."

"Well, you'd better move fast because our moms are headed this way."

He waggled a brow. "There's still time to jump."

She looked into the eyes of the man she loved and said, "I'd go anywhere with you, Rhett Easton."

Because she knew that when she fell, he'd always be there to pick her up. And she him.

Continue *Summer Affair*

Turn the page to check out Abi and Owen's Clay's story, *Single Girl in the City*, a sexy, feel-good opposites attract, grumpy boss romantic comedy!

Chapter One

Happy Things:
~~Snickers bar~~
King-sized Snickers bar

Abilene Woods had barely secured her Good Samaritan hat and already she was having a crisis of faith.

It wasn't that Abi didn't know how to perform a random act of kindness. She was terrified that she'd do it wrong. After everything that had happened, after the two terrible tragedies she was partially responsible for, screwing this up wasn't an option. Which was why she'd been searching for signs ever since moving from Alabama back to Portland.

She wasn't sure what she'd imagined they'd look like. So when no shooting star lit the way and no kaleidoscope of monarch butterflies took flight, Abi did what any good former kindergarten teacher would do: she flipped the universe the big one, then crafted a NEED A GOOD DEED? sign-up sheet and posted it on the bulletin board at the tea shop where she worked.

Miracle of miracles, when she arrived at Sip Me that morning, she'd found not one, not two, but three posted wishes waiting to be granted—and not a one began with *For a good time call...*

So today, Abi was going to make a few lives a little easier. Not bad for her first day in the saddle.

Spring had finally arrived with a light drizzle and a gentle breeze, which carried the scent of dogwood blossom from the surrounding trees. Abi's first stop was at Food Hub and Grub, where she loaded her cart with all the wish-making essentials. She cruised the chip aisle, rescuing a bag of Cheetos, and rounded a display of pecans, which read WARM ROASTED NUTS, before turning down the self-care aisle where she found the last item on her list.

Palms sweaty, heart racing, she glanced right, then left, then up at the security camera overhead. Crossing her fingers that a security guard wasn't zeroed in on her aisle, she snatched the box and shoved it into the cart, sure to hide it beneath the HAPPY BIRTHDAY confetti.

She was reaching for another box and that's when she saw him. The one man she'd come to Portland to meet and had spent the past month avoiding.

Owen Easton. The biggest wrong she had to right. And the biggest flirt on the western seaboard. Dressed in faded jeans and a navy peacoat, he looked like an underwear model and an MMA champion collided, making him one hell of a sexy bad boy. And his smile—*oh lordy*—that smile, which was impossible to ignore, did things to her insides. Dangerous things that worried her.

He glanced her way, making direct eye contact.

Pretending she didn't see him, which only made his smile bigger, she crouched down low like a soldier crossing through enemy territory and dashed toward the cash register—the six birthday balloons floating overhead acting as a homing beacon that followed her every move.

She considered ditching the cart and running for the hills, but then she'd blow her first chance to make a real difference. A chance to help a stranger in need and, hopefully, bring some much-needed balance to her out-of-control world and prove that she was moving in the right direction so Karma would get off her back.

Telling herself to pull up those big-girl panties and there was nothing to be embarrassed about, she loaded up the conveyor belt. Tossing in a king-sized Snickers for strength, she kept her eyes glued to the person in front of her. When it was her turn, she waited impatiently for the cashier to scan each item. Then it happened, the moment she'd spent the past ten minutes obsessing over and stressing about. The cashier stopped when she got to the box of condoms and glanced up when she saw the second.

Abi flashed a bright smile. The cashier lifted a judgy brow, holding Abi hostage with a single look. The woman wore her silver hair in a twist, a Food Hub and Grub apron with PATRICE embroidered across the top, a magenta tracksuit that was bright enough to be seen from the Ozarks, and an expression that had Abi shifting in her shoes.

"You looking to get lucky?" Patrice asked.

Abi felt her face heat. "Excuse me?"

"The lottery's up to thirty million." She scanned the condoms. "You going to buy a lotto ticket?"

"No, ma'am. Just the items in my cart."

"You sure?"

Abi craned her neck, looking for *him*, relieved when he was nowhere in sight. "I'm sure."

"You got thirty million dollars?" Before Abi could answer, the clerk said, "Didn't think so. How many tickets?"

Abi shifted her weight from foot to foot. She had been short on patience her entire adult life, a sentiment she shared with her pint-sized students. Her need to be in constant motion stemmed from a childhood of waiting on everyone else and going nowhere fast. Today's impatience was more of a desperation born from an innate, life-or-death need to escape before Owen located her.

"I'll take one," she said, and then because she was Southern born and bred, she added a honey-sweet, "please."

This seemed to pacify Patrice. "What numbers, missy?"

"Whatever numbers the machine spits out will be fine, ma'am."

Patrice gasped, a horrified hand clutching her chest. "You can't live your life by chance. You've gotta take charge."

Something Abi was quickly learning. There were a lot of missed meant-to-bes in Abi's life. In fact, her life was apparently one big missed meant-to-be.

She rattled off her best friend's birthday, the day they met, and the number of words from the title of her favorite NSYNC song, which was the number three for "Bye, Bye, Bye"—but Patrice wasn't listening. She was too busy turning over the lip gloss tube, which Abi had bought as a special treat to herself for her upcoming do-gooder deeds.

The cashier read the color posted on the bottom. "Cream puff. My favorite pastry."

Abi sighed. Cream puff was also the name of Jenny's cat—a reminder so painful it made Abi want to cry, then devour the entire king-sized Snickers in one sitting.

"I hear you loud and clear, Jens," she whispered to her best friend, who Abi imagined was giving her two thumbs up from the big playground in the sky. "I hope you're happy because I love that color and it's the last one."

Patrice handed Abi the lip gloss and instead of bagging it, like she had the rest of her items, Abi held it out to the clerk. "It's for you. I think the shade would look great with your complexion," she said, doing her best Jenny impersonation.

This immediately brought on a wave of guilt because Jenny was the real deal, a from-the-heart, shirt-off-her-back kind of do-gooder, which was not Abby's first instinct, nor was it her second or third.

Patrice placed a hand over her mouth and her eyes went misty in a way that had Abi's heart growing just a tiny bit. "Oh my. Aren't you an angel?"

She didn't know about that, but the genuine appreciation in the older woman's expression ignited some feeling Abi had thought shattered in the accident.

"Champagne, lipstick, and condoms," a very sexy and unwelcomed voice said from behind. "You must be throwing one hell of a party."

Abi looked up and nearly swallowed her tongue whole. Because there he stood, her reason of reasons looking like sex on a stick. She'd caught glimpses of him over the past month, but always from a distance. A purposeful choice. Now she was close enough to smell his body wash and she realized just how big he was. Tall, broad shouldered, and I-bench-press-kegs-for-fun fit. And he was staring at her with amusement in those heart-stopping blue eyes.

Abi wished to disappear, but unfortunately whoever was granting wishes wasn't listening because how else could this moment come while she was dressed like a singing telegram?

It wasn't often that an amateur do-gooder got to face down her reason for do-gooding on her first day as a practicing Samaritan. By practicing, she meant stumbling, and Abi had stumbled right into the son of the man whose life she had inadvertently destroyed.

As she stood there, dressed in a red nose, clown shoes, and a unicorn headband while buying a giant box of condoms, a shot of guilt mixed with swelling panic caused the secret that she'd held for over a decade to stick in her throat.

People were defined by their choices and while Teen Abi had chosen to do something stupid, she hadn't been the only guilty party in the equation. Sadly, Owen hadn't chosen any of it, yet it was clear by what she'd surmised over the past several weeks that he was the one paying the price.

"Nice shoes," he commented.

"I'm doing a birthday party later."

He glanced at the condoms on the conveyor belt. "Those for the balloon animals?"

"Those are none of your business."

"Isn't that a shame?"

It was more than that. She was still riding the high from completing the first random act of kindness in Jenny's honor, but now she had to delete a point, bringing her back to square one. Because she was about to lie to a man who deserved the truth, the whole truth, and nothing but the truth.

"Do you have a habit of harassing strangers in grocery stores?"

His lip quirked. "Stranger, huh? We're playing that game? I see you at the tea shop all the time."

"No game. Just a fact."

Abi was terrible at secrets and even worse at lying, which was why she avoided it at all costs. But sometimes one did something that—even though it was the right thing to do— warranted secrecy.

For a self-proclaimed good girl, Abi had a lot to atone for. Which was why, after a decade of avoidance, she'd come back to Portland, the place she'd spent every summer while growing up, to right the first of very many wrongs. She was hoping to make up for her most recent wrong that had ended in a terrible tragedy. She'd learned the hard way that every decision had far-reaching consequences, like a single drop of rain on a still lake sending ripples in every direction.

Abi's ripples were powerful enough to tilt her world so far off axis that the only way to atone was to face her mistakes head-on. Even if it was in baby steps.

Recommitting herself to the task at hand, she tossed the condoms in her bag and glanced at the exit, then pulled out her credit card in preparation for a speedy escape.

"ID," Patrice asked loudly.

Distractedly, Abi glanced at the cashier. "What?"

"You belong to AARP?" she asked, and Abi shook her head. "Then if you want the booze, I have to scan your ID."

Aware of Owen peeking right over her shoulder, she stealthily took her ID from her wallet and held it out to Patrice, who studied it.

"Abilene Josephine Marie." She looked up. "And that's just your first name."

"I thought you only needed to scan it." Abi snatched it back.

"Abilene, huh?" Owen asked, the humor thick in his tone.

She ignored him. "I really need to go."

"Is the party leaving the station?"

"Yes, and before you ask, it's a private party."

He rested a casual hip against the counter and leaned in close. A breathe-too-deeply-and-you'll-brush-his-chest kind of close that made her sweat in uncomfortable places. "My favorite kind," he whispered.

Not touching that with a ten-foot pole, she paid for her things and, ignoring the Do Not Enter sign, the drizzle, and the amused chuckle behind her, she raced out of the store and headed toward her bike. Not a motorbike, not even a ten-speed.

Nope, the closest Abi came to transportation these days was Jenny's old lemon-yellow beach cruiser, with a kitty seat cover, and white basket on the handlebars.

She was almost in the clear when her phone buzzed. Her nerves said to keep moving but her guilt told her to check the text to make sure it wasn't an emergency. She glanced at the screen and sighed. It was her sister.

Dotti: IT'S AN EMERGENCY.

Everything in Dotti's world was an emergency. Abi shifted her bags to one hand, wincing when the weight of the wine bottles grazed the still-healing sore spot on her wrist from the accident, then quickly swiped off a return text.

Abi: Are we talking zombies or the Four Horsemen kind of emergency?

Dotti: Hank had to leave for work early and they've outnumbered me.

By *they*, Dotti meant her Irish twin toddlers, Lemon-Marie and Koi, who might just be the biggest emotional vampires this side of the Mississippi. Their objective was world domination, their weapon of choice, temper tantrums.

Abi: You ran emergency dispatch for a decade, surely you can handle your children. Which you planned and begged the universe for, BTW. Remember all the times you said, "All I want to be is a mom"? Well, guess what? You got your wish so suck it up.

Dotti: They found your stash of doughnuts. There's enough powdered sugar on the floor to make snow angels and mutiny is on the horizon.

Abi winced. She'd hidden her stash on the top shelf in the coat closet, shoved all the way to the back and stuffed in a Skechers box. Who knew two travel-sized tots could scale a coat rack? Regardless, it left her with two options: leave Dotti to fend for herself or be late for work. Reminding herself that her new lease on life was about doing the right thing, even when it was the hard thing, she texted:

Abi: Hide the permanent markers and finger paints. I'll be home as soon as I can.

Abi began to pocket her phone when she heard footsteps behind her. "You need help with those bags?"

"You need a bell," she mumbled, and she could have sworn he grinned. She glanced up and nearly rolled her eyes. He stood there easily balancing two bags on one arm, his bicep flexing her way.

Whatever bad juju she'd accumulated throughout her life was coming at her with a vengeance.

"Can I give you a ride?" he asked.

"I'm fine."

She unlocked her Huffy from the bike rack. Still pretending like he was nothing more than a figment of her ridiculously vivid imagination, she loaded up her bike, the balloons floating from her handlebars, the champagne bottles taking up the entire basket. No matter how many times she rearranged her items they didn't fit—the story of her life.

"Why do I have the feeling that's your mantra," he said as she stepped onto her bike. "Where are you going?"

Holding the lighter bag, Abi put one foot on the pedal. "The opposite direction of wherever you're going."

"Funny, your bike's pointed in the exact direction of my work and therefore your work, which happens to be next door to my bar."

She looked down at her clown shoes and lifted a brow. "Does it look like I'm headed into work?"

"Who knows, it could be dress-up day. You are wearing a tie and lace-up shoes." He reached out and tugged her oversized tie, then pinched her nose. It honked.

"Didn't your mama tell you it's rude to give someone a good honk?"

"So it was good for you too?"

She snorted. "I gotta go. I'm already late."

"Then let me give you a lift." There was no teasing or flirting in his tone, just deep concern. For her.

She'd had a lot of people expressing their concern after the crash. Heck, she was as concerned as they were. How was someone just supposed to pick up the pieces and move on? If Jenny were still alive, she'd tell Abi to put one foot in front of the other. And she'd do it with that bright, heal-the-world smile that Abi would forever miss in her life.

Not wanting to let Jenny down again, Abi started pedaling across the parking lot. Owen easily kept pace. Not surprising since she was moving at a snail's pace.

She looked over her shoulder and the bike wobbled. "Stay in your lane," she said. He slowed down so that he was directly behind her but didn't stop. "Now you're tailgating."

"I must say, I like your tail."

She stopped, put her feet on the concrete, and looked at him over her shoulder. He winked. She groaned. "What will it take for you to go on your way so I can go on mine?"

"Since we're both going the same way, you'd save me the worry of wondering if you made it to your final destination in one piece."

"I wouldn't want to *worry* you." Although secretly she loved the idea that she got to him. "You could be a serial killer."

"You're the one dressed like the guy from *It*."

Abi pulled a business card from her back pocket and handed it over. He read it and laughed out loud, throwing his head back and everything. *Such a handsome prick.* "CEO of Wishes by Abi." She pointed to the subtitle "Professional Good Samaritan."

"Yes, and right now I go by Winkie the Uni-Clown. Part unicorn, part clown. I do parties, weddings, and singing telegrams."

"You sing?"

"Today I do," she said, back to cycling slowly across the lot. Her big shoes were only partly to blame. Until last week, Abi hadn't been on a bike since she was twelve. But it was faster than walking and less deadly than other forms of transportation. "Move before I call the cops and tell them a strange man wanted to pinch my nose."

"So, you're still going with the not knowing each other game, Tea Girl?"

She came to a hard stop. "Fine. Darjeeling oolong, loose-leaf tea, six ounces of water, 180 degrees, with a splash of soy. We may have crossed paths professionally." He lifted a brow. "I didn't mean it like that."

"I don't know. The condoms, memorizing my order." He shoved his hands in his pockets and rocked back on his feet, clearly validated. "Is that barista for, 'What's your number?'"

"It's barista for, 'Your drink is lame.' If you ask me, the splash of soy is an amateur move."

As she attempted to leave, he reached for her handlebar, holding her in place. Or maybe it was his intense blue eyes that made her feet feel like she was pedaling through wet cement.

"Since we've ruled out serial killer and you know who I am, please let me give you a ride," he said. "I can put your bike in the back of my truck and drop you off anywhere."

"Anywhere?" she asked.

"Think of me as your own personal rideshare driver." She steadied her bike and he backed away slightly, but she could tell he didn't like it. "Come on, Abi, there's no sidewalk and this is a highway."

She was more than aware of that. Her heart had started thumping painfully in her chest the moment she locked eyes on the heavy traffic and endless line of headlights glowing in the mist. "Really, I'm—"

A bus blew past, the draft knocking her back a step. The smell of the exhaust and the sound of the gears downshifting took her breath away, until her lungs began to burn and her eyes began to water.

Shaken by the memory of the collision, she lost balance and went down to one knee, letting go of her bike in the process. It crashed against the ground, toppling the bottles of bubbly, the glass shattering on impact. The sound brought Abi right back to that day on the bus. Back to the nightmares she'd spent the past few months trying to get out of her head.

She gasped for air. Once, twice, but her lungs weren't cooperating. Neither was her head. She reminded herself that she was safe, that she was on steady ground, and that if she didn't get herself under control she would embarrass herself in front of the sexiest man alive. That was enough to break through the fear.

Too bad it was too late. She'd already lost her footing and she landed ass-backward in a puddle with teeth-jarring force.

Pain shot through her right leg, which had scraped against the bike's chain. Cold wetness seeped through her leggings and spilled into the shoes she'd rented from Costume Palooza and Pawn Shop. Her pride took a nosedive and the balloons bobbed above her like a buoy in the middle of the ocean.

"Shit," she said, experiencing her second collision in as many months. She looked up at the clouds and glared at whoever was beyond. "Shit, shit, shit!" If she hadn't been raised right, she would have said another four-letter word, but her grandma would come down from the heavens and stick a bar of soap in Abi's mouth. She did, however, smack her hands in the puddle like her niece in the middle of a tantrum. "How's that for calm and tranquil?"

When no one answered, she tried to roll over and groaned. Nothing was broken, but she was definitely bruised. She pushed herself to her knees and started to stand when a hand with a sexy tattoo running up the forearm gently wrapped around her elbow. An unexpected *snap* and *crackle* popped between them. She shrugged him off. "I'm fine."

"Give yourself a minute to make sure you're okay," her shadow said. "Where does it hurt?"

Everywhere. "Just a little rattled is all." He offered her his hand again and stubbornly she didn't want to take it, but she was too afraid she wouldn't be able to stand back up on her own. Common sense won out.

His big, masculine hand ran down her arm to take her hand. He was just trying to help her up, but at the simple contact, the air sparked. He looked at her for a long, heated moment, then his face went carefully blank.

"It looked like you went down pretty hard."

"I'm fine," she said again, this time with a bright smile. Her heart was racing, her head spinning, her hands tingling—and it had nothing to do with the fall. When he didn't believe her or move to release her hand, she assured him, "Really, I'm fine. But thank you for asking."

"The cast on your wrist suggests otherwise."

"It's a brace, not a cast." She unvelcroed and velcroed it as proof.

"Disappointing. I was going to ask if I could sign it. Write, 'You should see the other guy' or 'Stay cool, Tea Girl.' Or maybe leave my number."

She ignored this and began to right her bike when she noticed it. Her purse had toppled over, scattering the contents in every which direction— her notebook in the middle, displayed for the world to see. Even worse it was open to *his* page.

Not that it said *Owen*, Abi was too visual for that. But it had enough doodles and sketches, not to mention a swirly O and a drawing of his family's bar to paint a clear picture.

She bent down to grab it, but he was faster. In the end, they each held the notebook like a game of tug o' war, and she was on the losing end.

"You must be a fan of Stout. Funny, I've never seen you in there."

And with good reason. "I'm not really a bar kind of person."

"Then we have that in common."

She blinked. "But you own a bar."

"My family owns the bar, I only run it. Big difference."

Another mysterious clue to be filed away in her ever-growing O folder. "If you say so."

"I say so," he said, not letting go. "Seriously though, I just want to help."

She still held tight, studying him to access his current level of curiosity. "No questions or cute comments?"

"Not a one. Scout's honor." He held up a little two-finger salute and she let go. She even let him load up her bags and hold her bike.

She brushed her hands down her pants and then gave up. There was no point. She was soaked straight through to her bozo-bloomers.

Thanks." She mounted her bike, and a dull pain covered her entire backside. She came to a hard stop and maybe even winced a bit.

"Now, how about that ride?"

She looked at the busy street and then back to Owen. She'd finally found that kaleidoscope of monarchs she'd been searching for. Annoyingly, they were in her belly. And if that wasn't sign enough that this moment was Jenny-ordained, the sky opened and big droplets of rain hit her like ticks on a hound dog.

"Fine." She held up a halting finger. "But if it says twenty-five remember that's the limit, so we go twenty-five." Because limits were meant to keep people safe.

"It's actually safer to go with the flow of traffic."

"Isn't that a fun fact? Twenty-five or no deal."

With a smile, which she had to admit was sexy as all get out, he took her bike and led her to his truck. It was a classic. 1970s. Big cab, bigger tires, and cream with a brown stripe down the side. It was a giant truck for a giant of a man.

He opened the passenger door, and she froze. She looked at the cab and up at him, then, like her meditation app taught her, she closed her eyes and took in a deep breath.

"That is a battle for another day. Today it's about calm and tranquility."

She said it three more times until her heart was back to normal speed. She looked up to find him looking back.

There was a long pause and she braced for the onslaught of questions about her meltdown. He surprised her by not asking a single one, which was the nicest thing someone had done for her since Jenny offered to take her seat at the front of the bus with a couple of hellraisers who had put a fake spider on a fishing line and tugged it down the aisle, causing mass hysterics from the other students.

It ended up being the last good deed Jenny ever did.

Continue reading *Single Girl in the City*

Turn the page to check out my upcoming release, *Situationship*, which is a fresh and funny take on *How Stella Got her Groove back* meets *Virgin River*.

Chapter 1

If life gives you lemons, it's only fair that
a guy with vodka isn't far behind.
—Unknown

Teagan Bianchi was at the crossroads of Forgiveness and Letting Go when her GPS crapped out—a problem of living life on autopilot for too long. In the past she would have relied on her intuition. But intuition was one finicky prick.

"Are we there yet?" a tiny voice asked from the back seat. It was the fifth time since their last potty stop. One of thousands on their trip from Seattle to California.

Teagan always encouraged curiosity in her daughters, so it wasn't the question that bothered her. It was the feelings it evoked. It made her feel like a fraud. Even worse, a failure.

"What does your tablet say?" she asked Poppy, her elder daughter by seven minutes. After thirty-three weeks of sharing thirty-six centimeters, the twins had come out of the womb inseparable.

"Da blue dot is by da red dot," Poppy said, her Ts sounding more like Ds.

"What number does it show?" She glanced over her shoulder at her daughter, and all four years of her smiled back, filling Teagan with a sense of purpose. With the disillusionment of her marriage in the rearview mirror, she was moving away from her immediate past and toward a happier and simpler time.

"Five," she said, holding up the coordinating number of fingers. "One, two fwee. Four. Five."

"That's right. Good job," she said, and a bark of agreement came from the back seat as a wet nose nudged her shoulder.

Their horse-sized puppy, who'd broken free from his crate—with help from his two partners in crime—wedged his head between the two front seats.

"GD, back seat only."

Garbage Disposal barked excitedly at the mention of his name, then took a flying leap, and 120 pounds of dog landed on the passenger seat with a thud. Teagan leaned right, pressing herself against the window to avoid being smacked in the face by a wagging tire iron.

"You want me to pull over and put you in the cage?" she threatened but he panted happily and stuck his head out the open window so he could drool on the cars behind them. Part Portuguese water dog and part Great Dane, Garbage Disposal looked like a buffalo with two left feet fathered by Mr. Snuffleupagus. While he more than lived up to his name, he had a heart the size of his stomach.

Teagan pulled through the quaint downtown, noticing gas-lamped streets, brick sidewalks, and awninged storefronts, then turned down Lighthouse Way, where the landscape opened, revealing the crystal blue waters of the

Pacific Ocean. Coiling with intensity, the waves gathered speed before crashing against the cliffs ahead. On her left sat rolling hills dotted with cypress trees and rows of bright-colored Victorians. To her right was the road to fresh starts, childhood memories . . . and heartache.

It was the last part that had panic knotting in her chest and activating her internal countdown. She was *one, two, fwee, four minutes* away from the place she'd called home for most of her childhood—well, the happy parts anyway.

Pacific Cove was a sleepy beach town nestled between Monterey and Carmel. Settled by Episcopalians, it was a sea of steeples on a stunning horizon. It was later home to many military families during World War Two, thanks to its location close to three military bases: Army, Navy, and Coast Guard. Teagan's grandmother had been one of those Navy wives whose last missive from her husband had been a *Just in Case* letter with his wedding ring enclosed.

Grandma Rose had reinvented herself in this very town, and Teagan could too. Or at least that was the hope.

"Are we there yet?"

At a stop sign, Teagan turned back around to look at Poppy. "You just asked that question."

"Lily wants to know. You said we'd be there at *fwee-oh-oh.* And it's *four-oh-oh.*" Hushed negotiations ensued. "Lily say that four comes after fwee."

Teagan's ETA hadn't accounted for the wind drag of towing a twelve-foot trailer or the volume of potty breaks. "We're about four minutes out from Nonna's." Even though Nonna had passed and willed the beach cottage to Teagan, she always thought of it as Nonna Rose's house.

"We're about four minutes out from Nonna's." Word for word, Poppy repeated their ETA to Lily and then, doing their twin thing, her too-big-to-be-toddlers and too-small-to-be-schoolkids had a complete conversation without saying a word. "She's gotta go number one."

Better than number two. "Sweetie, can you hold it for just another few minutes?"

Lily, who was having a silent conversation with the tops of her shoes, shook her head, then gave a thumbs-down to her sister.

"She said no," Poppy translated, and Garbage Disposal barked in solidarity.

Teagan had known that last juice box was a bad idea. Almost as bad as adopting a rescue puppy three months before moving two states away. A clumsy, untrained, former outside dog who loved to be inside and eat Teagan's shoes, handbag, tampons—the list went on.

"Five minutes, that's all I'm asking for."

After an intense exchange of looks, Poppy said, "Fwee works but not four."

Teagan gunned it. She knew better than to tempt fate. Especially when Lily's Go Time was about as accurate as a nuclear countdown clock. T-minus fwee was Go Time—toilet optional.

She blew through the stop sign and took a hard right onto Seashell Circle. An ocean-soaked breeze filled the car—reducing the stench from Lily's bout of car sickness, which had kicked in her twin's sympathetic reflex.

Winding her way down the hill, she made the final turn into her old neighborhood and a sense of rightness, a sense of home, swept through her body. Because there it was, the purple and white Victorian where she'd spent the first half of her life making memories.

They'd arrived, intact, if not a little wrinkled around the edges, to begin their fresh start, leaving behind a history of pain and disappointment.

Complete with clapboard siding, massive stained-glass windows, and widow's walk, Nonna Rose's house—now Teagan's house—butted up to pristine beach, which was shared by the neighbors on Seashell Circle. At one time, this house had meant everything to her but as she pulled up to the empty drive, she was reminded that Nonna was gone, and Teagan's earlier excitement was painted with a coat of sorrow.

Another thing she intended to change.

With nine seconds to spare, Teagan pulled into the drive and pushed the button to open the side door. Her daughters freed themselves from their boosters and a flurry of arms and legs exploded out of the car. Garbage Disposal sailed through the window as if it was a fence and he was a thoroughbred at the Royal Cup.

Lily ran behind the big magnolia tree in the front yard, lifted her sundress, and squatted—a recently acquired skill. Adhering to the *where one goes, the other follows* philosophy, Poppy did the potty-squat even though she didn't have to go. Garbage Disposal barked and ran circles around them.

Teagan dropped her head against the steering wheel, accidently honking the horn and dislodging a cheesy poof from her hair. Yup, that pretty much summed up the past year.

She looked at the dog hair stuck to every surface, including but not limited to the passenger seat, the dash, and interior roof of the car. Then there were the grape juice stains on her armrest and clothes.

"Why couldn't you have packed lemonade?" That was the one chore she'd left for the morning: packing the kid's snack bags. Somehow in her exhaustion, she'd packed cheesy poofs and grape juice. It was almost as if karma was doing it on purpose.

She thunked her head to the wheel again, wondering about her next move.

"Careful, you might knock something loose." The voice startled her—in more ways than one.

She must be hearing things. Her sleep-free, peace-free, caffeine-free state was to blame. Surely when she looked up, no one would be standing outside the window smiling. The voice definitely had a smile to it. And brought a feeling of nostalgia that had her heart racing.

Don't stroke out.

Teagan closed her eyes for a moment to compose herself. Hard to do when she smelled like vomit and looked like roadkill.

With the bright smile of someone in control of their world, she looked up and—*yup*. She was definitely hallucinating. Because standing outside her window was a blast from her past, who did *not* look like roadkill. No, her unexpected visitor looked cool, calm, and incredibly handsome.

How was it she'd forgotten his family owned the vacation house next door to Nonna Rose? And how was it that the first time she'd seen him since her divorce she looked as if a convenience store bomb had gone off around her?

Colin West, in nothing but bare feet, wet jeans, and bare chest, still damp from washing his truck, looked like the sexy-dad-next-door.

He twirled his hand in the universal gesture for *roll down the window* and, even though her heart wasn't in it—it was lodged in her throat—she complied.

"Excuse that." Teagan looked at her daughters racing around the yard with their sundresses repurposed into superhero capes, leaving them naked. "I'm sorry, they're . . . it's been a day."

"Been there."

At the foreign voice, Garbage Disposal's head poked out from beneath a shrub. Covered in leaves, with one ear flopping topsy-turvy, he chewed on a garden hose—the neighbor's garden hose.

"Um, I think my dog . . ." *Oh boy.*

Garbage Disposal lurched. Hard and fast, galloping across the lawn in record time with all the grace of a flamingo in a snowbank. He was infamous for licking toes, knocking spillable things off tabletops with his tail, and knowing the precise latitude and longitude to give the ultimate doggie-high-fives to the crotch.

"Watch out, he's bigger than he looks. . . ."

With a single hand motion, Colin said, "Down," and Garbage Disposal lay down, resting his head on his big paws, looking up at Colin as if he were his new master.

"Good boy." He crouched down and gave the dog a good rub, which ended with Garbage Disposal rolling over on his back, proudly showing off his doggie bits.

"How did you do that?"

"Magic," he said, sitting back on his heels. That was it. No "Hello" or "Good to see you" or even "Why the hell are you here?" Just a single evocative word.

"Magic."

"He's still got some puppy left. How old is he?" he asked, his attention still on the dog.

"Oh, I have no idea. He isn't mine," she lied.

"Funny, he thinks you're his pack."

"Pack, smack. He looks all cute and innocent and, okay, he's kind of mine. The girls and I went to the shelter and he followed us home."

Colin chuckled.

"And before you tell me what a good dog he is, he's a dog training school flunk-out." Not that anyone could tell, since Garbage Disposal was giving a good-boy wagging of the tail as if he'd earned a gold star in obedience school, when in reality he'd flunked out three times. "Probably why he kept following us when we told him to stay."

"There aren't bad animals, only bad teachers." Colin looked up, his gaze tinged by amusement.

"Are you saying I'm the problem?"

At that exact moment, Poppy jumped up on the porch step. Hands raised to the heavens as if she were some Amazon warrior ready to wreak havoc on the mere mortals, she tied her dress around her neck and pumped a single hand in the air. Lily followed suit until there were two nearly naked tots chasing a dog around the magnolia tree.

"It *is* me," she admitted.

In a very Colin-like move, he rested his arms on the car door frame above her head, leaning in and getting up close and personal. It took everything she had not to stare at his chest, which—with his forearms on top of the door—was at direct gawking level. Looking at his face wasn't any better. He was near enough that she could ascertain he hadn't shaved recently and that his eyes were glimmering with amusement.

"Are you laughing at me?"

"Wouldn't think of it." He didn't bother to hide his grin. "First rule in long trips, superheroes aren't just for boys. Pack dress-up capes, coordinating flags, and plenty of tiaras or they'll get creative." He chuckled. "Just wait until they're teens."

"Is it worse than the terrible twos?" she asked.

"I thought they were older than that."

"They're four, but still going through the terrible twos. I'm afraid it's a permanent condition. You're a doctor. Tell me it gets easier."

"Vet," he clarified. "And I wish I could. Maddie hasn't been easy in seventeen years."

Right about now, Teagan would give anything to go back and be a bright-eyed, naive, and trusting teenager again.

When had everything become so difficult?

"Maddison's a teenager?"

"Unfortunately," he said. "In fact, you just missed her stomping off and slamming the door because I looked at her wrong."

"How did we get so old?"

His eyes slowly slid down her body. "You don't look a day older than you did that summer before sophomore year, when I first saw you."

She smiled with the same mischievous smile she'd worn when she snuck out her bedroom window and met him at the cove. It had been her first time sneaking out, her first time skinny-dipping—oh, she'd had a lot of firsts that night. She could tell by the smile on his face, his thoughts weren't far from hers.

"Just be grateful yours don't talk back yet."

"Only one talks." It hadn't always been that way. Lily had always been the quieter of the two, more cerebral, but after her dad moved out, Lily stopped talking. To anyone who wasn't her twin.

"Even better."

"Oh, Poppy talks enough for everyone in the family. In fact, there wasn't a silent moment on the entire trip from Seattle."

He looked at the small trailer behind her. "Movers coming tomorrow?"

"Nope. This is it." She swallowed because *this was it*. This was the moment every recent divorcée dreaded. The *where's your other half* question.

Surprisingly, he didn't say a word about Frank's absence, but his gaze did shift to the empty passenger seat, and she thought she'd be sick.

Her ex. Her lying, selfish, bonehead of an ex, who'd cost her family nearly everything. The writing was still wet on the dotted line of the divorce papers, but they'd separated a year ago, when things took a turn for the worse.

She knew all too well how confusing it could be for kids when their parents reenacted *The War of the Roses* on a regular basis. By the time Teagan's parents divorced, things had become so bitter, she'd promised herself if she ever had kids, she would never put them through that, so she'd stayed in her marriage as long as she could.

She'd tried so hard to make it work. Frank wasn't a bad man; in fact he was an incredibly sweet man and a good father. But he lived with his head in the clouds and his money on a poker table.

For a long time, she'd obsessed over what she could have changed. Done differently.

"You okay, Bianchi?" His voice was quiet, and she knew he'd figured it out. He only used her nickname when he was razzing her or concerned for her. This time it was a little of both.

She waved a dismissive hand. "Oh, just tired from the drive." Her pants were going to burst into flames for that lie. But the last thing she wanted to do was talk about her last ex with her first ex.

He studied her and then thankfully let it go without any further questions. "If you need help unloading the trailer, I'm right next door." She was tempted to take him up on the offer. She was exhausted, her back was killing her from the long drive, and she still had to empty the boxes in the

U-Haul trailer, which was due back tomorrow before ten. But his voice held a cool distant tone.

Maybe the past wasn't buried in the past. Not that she blamed him.

"I've got it," she said, even though she totally didn't have it.

"If you change your mind." He jabbed a thumb over his shoulder.

"Noted."

His face went carefully blank, and he stepped back from the car. "I forgot. You're good at notes."

Well played but *ouch.*

"If you change your mind, let me know. Oh, and for the record, lemonade is overrated, unless it has something stronger in it."

Continue reading Situationship

ABOUT THE AUTHOR

Marina Adair is a *New York Times* and #1 National best-selling author whose fun, flirty contemporary romcoms have sold over a million copies. In addition to the Easton series, she is the author of the When in Rome series, the Heroes of St. Helena series, the Sugar, Georgia series, and the St. Helena Vineyard series, which was the inspiration behind the original Hallmark Channel Vineyard movies: *Autumn in the Vineyard, Summer in the Vineyard,* and *Valentines in the Vineyard.* Raised in the San Francisco Bay Area, she holds an MFA from San Jose University and currently lives in Northern California with her husband, daughter, and two neurotic cats. Please visit her online at MarinaAdair.com and sign up for her newsletter at www.MarinaAdair.com/newsletter.

Sign Me Up!

Made in the USA
Monee, IL
02 July 2022